To Graham,

The Twenty Murders

Drew Augustine

You inspired me to write this, and gave me the courage to publish it.

With warm wishes,

Drew x

Copyright © 2024 by Drew Augustine

All rights reserved.

The characters and events portrayed in this book are fictitious. Any similarity to real persons, living or dead, is coincidental and not intended by the author.

No part of this book may be reproduced in any form without written permission of the copyright owner except for the use of quotations in a book review.

'The further a society drifts from the truth, the more it will hate those that speak it.'

——— **George Orwell**

Warning

This story contains descriptions of sexual assault and violence which may be distressing to some audiences but are essential to the plot. Reader discretion is advised.

It also contains truths. Unspeakable truths.

Prologue

It wasn't the life-changing event at the art class that killed Betty. It was what happened afterwards.

Betty Wilson sat in the community hall putting the finishing touches to a watercolour painting of a Victorian house. Once complete, it would be a gift for her friend and ex-neighbour Audrey. She hoped it would remind Audrey of her former family home now that she'd moved into a care home, a soulless place that smelled of disinfectant and urine. Betty disliked visiting, but it seemed to cheer up her friend who still seemed to recognise her.

She'd been planning to visit her later but Betty felt nauseous. Perhaps she'd picked up a bug from the grandchildren at the weekend or it was the microwave meal for one she'd eaten the previous evening. Since losing her husband Derek three years ago, she rarely had the heart to cook from scratch just for herself. Whatever it was, she'd a splitting headache and a queasy stomach. Betty glanced at her watch, relieved the art class was almost over.

Douglas, the group's tutor, minced by and complimented her work. This was praise indeed. In his late fifties, Douglas was as camp as a field full of pink tents, and a highly accomplished portrait artist. She'd never understood why he'd agreed to teach a group of elderly women who were mainly here for a chat and to keep warm. She supposed the money came in handy. Plus, he had a sweet tooth.

Douglas pointed at a small corner of her canvas and said, "This is coming along very nicely, however, you might want to make a little adjustment to the shading here."

Betty squinted at the blurry shape, realising her vision on one side was slightly fuzzy, as if she had a migraine coming on. That would explain her dickie tummy. She thanked Douglas and daubed some paint on the area he'd indicated. When the colours swirled, she put down her brush. It would have to wait until next time when she felt better.

Douglas glanced at the large wall clock in the hall, clapped his hands and announced, "Ooh, look at the time ladies, I believe it's cake o'clock."

Betty packed up her easel and paints. She fished around in her handbag and found painkillers for her headache which was getting steadily worse. She scooped up the packet along with her Tupperware box of cupcakes which she'd baked in honour of Anne's birthday. Anne, who'd been a member of the group for many years, had just turned 82. Or was it 83? Betty couldn't quite remember in her muddled state. In any case, coffee and cake was the highlight of the class; the painting was incidental.

As Betty tottered towards the kitchenette to join the others, a sudden wave of weakness rippled down the left side of her body. Her knees buckled and the room pitched, and that was the last she remembered until she woke hours later.

***

Beeping. Whispered voices. Squeak of footsteps on vinyl. Smell of cleaning fluid.

Betty's eyes fluttered open and she blinked at her unfamiliar surroundings. Encased in crisp white sheets, she lay motionless staring up at the stained ceiling tiles. Her vision was clouded and shadows danced at the edges. A soft light from a pulsing monitor cast a pale glow over the cubicle which was enclosed by a thin blue curtain. She had no memory of how she'd got here.

Her mouth felt as though it was full of cotton wool and she swallowed painfully. She tried to turn her head only to find she couldn't. Her limbs were stubbornly unresponsive. Fear gripped her heart as she attempted to call out, but she only managed a faint moan.

Panic set in.

Tears welled up and she fought them back, refusing to accept the nightmare she found herself trapped in.

Footsteps approached and a nurse appeared by her bedside. The woman was in her mid-30s and her nametag revealed she was called Irina. Smiling compassionately, she spoke in a soft Eastern European accent. "Betty, you're safe. You're in hospital. Can you hear me?"

A feeble grunt escaped Betty's lips.

"You've had a stroke so you may feel some paralysis and numbness. This is normal though and we're here to help you."

Betty's tears fell steadily, and her breath came in short bursts.

Squeezing Betty's hand gently, Irina said, "I know you're scared but I promise we'll take good care of you. Your daughter was here but she's just left. It's late now and she'll be back in the morning."

Betty's daughter lived miles away and she realised she must have been unconscious for some time. Irina checked Betty's vitals and the readouts on the various monitors, recording the results on a clipboard which she hung at the end of the bed. She helped her sip a little water from a cup.

"The doctor will be along to see you in the morning and I'll be checking on you regularly. Try to get some sleep." And then, with a smile, Irina was gone.

Left alone with her thoughts, more tears fell. How long would the paralysis last? Was it permanent? Would she be able to return home and live independently or would she be a burden on her family? Unable to move, unable to speak, the outcome seemed bleak. Part of her prayed for the blackness to claim her, yet the fear of never waking again was worse.

The ward was quiet, the only sound the gentle snoring of a nearby patient and rain tapping against the windows. Betty drifted in and out of consciousness for what seemed like hours; she couldn't tell. Sometimes Irina was there, sometimes not.

She woke to the sound of a distant buzzer and muffled far-off voices. It was still dark but the rain had abated. The patient in the next bed stirred and she heard shuffling sounds from behind the curtain. The blue fabric parted and a face appeared. The features were wrong, grotesque.

The figure closed the curtains and approached the bed. Betty tried blinking the face into focus but all she could see was the twisted grin.

Dear God, is it the stroke or the drugs inducing this nightmare?

But the shape was real. It clapped a meaty hand over Betty's mouth stifling any sound and clambered on top of her. Peering down with black, malevolent eyes, it hoisted her hospital gown up above her waist.

Betty's screams were audible only in her head.

Chapter 1

Strathmurray, Scotland, 5 years later

Constable Morven MacLeod had arrested plenty of wee jakies during her nineteen years on the force, and she'd always done it by the book. Until now.

Maybe it was 'compassion fatigue'. Apparently, that was a thing. She'd learned about it in a recent health and wellbeing training session. The police were keen on soft skills these days in an attempt to clean up their image after a series of scandals including the rape and murder of a woman by a serving Met officer. Even in a town like Strathmurray, they were feeling the ripple effects of the numerous public inquiries. Morven guessed it was easier to conduct surveys on tackling violence against women and girls and deliver fluffy seminars on discrimination than it was to actually root out unfit officers.

Shivering with cold, she stood at the base of the oak and gazed up at the thief that she and her partner had cornered. He was perched on a thick branch high in the canopy. A scrawny youth dressed in a dark hoodie and tracksuit bottoms, he had the gaunt complexion of a regular drug user. It didn't surprise her; most of her regulars on the estate where she was a Community Officer were either users or dealers. But this guy's face was new so maybe he ran with another gang and crossed county lines for richer pickings. He'd regret that when she got him down … if she got him down; he'd been up there for almost an hour.

Morven exhaled a long breath which misted in the freezing December air. After a long shift, she was tired, hungry and in no mood for this. And she had painful period cramps. She and Rob had begun the evening dealing with an alcohol-fuelled domestic, a brawl outside a pub, and anti-social behaviour from a gang of teenagers who ought to have been home in bed. The latter were easy to handle; after confiscating their spray paint, vapes and a weapon, she'd sent them on their way with a tongue-lashing. A few of the kids were from troubled families — some she encountered on a weekly basis — and she didn't see the point in adding a criminal record to their issues.

She'd learned about the teenage brain on a mental health awareness course, and how it didn't fully mature until around 23–25 years of age. This fact had stuck in her own brain since it meant another ten years of dealing with her son's adolescent challenges.

And now, to top it all, she and Rob were attending yet another break-in. There'd been a spate of these 'slip-ins', so called because the opportunist checked for unlocked doors and windows and slipped inside. These had been going on for months and, despite almost fifty incidents, CID hadn't bothered their backsides to do anything about them. Instead, they seemed content to sit back while elderly residents were robbed as they slept. It was only a matter of time until someone died since, in each case, the burglar placed kitchen knives at the foot of the stairs, presumably to stab any curious homeowners.

Morven rubbed her frozen hands together and stamped her feet on the ground. "C'mon," she shouted up, "we both know how this will end. Get your arse down here now and save us all the grief."

"Fuck off!" He punctuated his reply with a large gob of saliva which she narrowly dodged.

Sighing, she stepped out of the spit zone and into the unwavering beam of a security LED floodlight. There was no moss in the crisp manicured lawn beneath her feet and no weeds poking their heads up in the tidy flowerbeds. At the bottom of the garden, a wheelbarrow lent against a freshly painted potting shed next to a compost heap. Morven wished her scruffy postage stamp of a yard looked like this.

Her teeth began to chitter. It was far too bloody cold for this nonsense. Pulling the collar of her jacket against the chill, she glanced towards the back of the house.

The internal lights illuminated a long bank of sliding doors leading into a modern kitchen where the great hulking figure of Rob comforted the elderly homeowner. The young constable was over six foot tall and built like an ox, and Morven hoped his bearing would reassure the woman after she'd been woken by the intruder.

The burglar threw his shoe at Morven striking her hard on the side of the head.

She yelped in pain and shouted, "What the hell are you playing at?"

Rubbing her temple, she was regretting leaving her hat in the car, not that it was much protection against footwear. Every muscle in her body felt like it was stiffening up from the cold. Deciding she'd had enough, Morven glared up at the youth and cursed. No way was she hanging around getting frostbite until the dog handler deigned to show up with his land shark. The support team were also busy on another job and it could be hours before they arrived. She suspected they were all at a staff Christmas party. In any case, it was almost 3 am and she needed to be home promptly for Ollie. Although her son was almost sixteen, he had a big day ahead and she couldn't let him down; there was enough tension in the house as it was.

She needed this eejit down. And soon.

Rob appeared at her side. "Tarzan still up there?" he asked, peering into the branches.

"Aye." Then, indicating the homeowner observing from the upstairs window, Morven asked "How is she? She must have got the fright of her life."

"Bit shaken. She's 81 and on her own. It's lucky she didn't have heart failure. Her daughter's on her way to fetch her."

When the woman vanished, they turned their attention back to the tree-dweller. He'd stretched himself along the length of the branch with his back to the trunk.

Rob muttered, "He's looking a wee bit too comfy up there."

"Aye, but not for long." When her partner looked at her askance, Morven said, "Wait here a minute."

Morven marched down the garden path to the gate at the bottom where the youth had entered. She and Rob had watched his movements from the shadows of the lockup garages opposite. The stake-out had been her idea and Rob, being the soft, easy-going lump he was, was happy to go along with it. Each nightshift, whenever there was a lull, they parked up and kept watch since the slip-ins always happened in the wee small hours. Plus it was a chance for her to work on Rob's self-esteem, something her capable partner was sadly lacking. This was their third week of surveillance and Morven hoped they'd finally struck gold.

She unlocked the boot of the police car and retrieved the weapon she'd seized earlier from one of the kids. She had one last use for it before it was surrendered for destruction.

When she returned to where Rob paced at the base of the tree, he gawped at what she held. His look of surprise then turned to one of amusement. Her new partner was shaping up to be a good officer; he just needed to work on his assertiveness. And Morven was about to give him a practical demonstration, although there'd be nothing fluffy about this lesson.

"What the fuck?" came the shout from the branches above. "You cannae dae that!"

Ignoring him, Morven checked the upstairs windows to make sure the woman wasn't watching. The last thing she needed was a witness. Thanking her lucky stars Police Scotland had yet to roll out body cameras, she loaded the catapult with a small pebble and aimed it at the jakey. Squealing, the lad sprung into a crouch and attempted to wriggle behind the trunk.

"You have two choices," she called. "Either you come down by yourself or I shoot you down. Which is it?"

Less cocksure now, he yelled, "No fuckin' way. I have rights. Human rights!"

Yep, compassion fatigue's definitely a thing.

Morven let go the elastic.

Ten minutes later, she watched as Rob manhandled the handcuffed jakey up the garden towards the police car. His name was Haydon Murphy and he'd taken a surprising number of stones to his buttocks to persuade him down. Rob bundled him into the back of the vehicle and shut the door while Morven returned the catapult to the boot. Rob joined her at the rear of the vehicle.

"Is it back to the station?" he asked.

She shook her head. "If CID suspect we've caught the 'Strathmurray Slip-in', they'll be all over it like a rash. No way I'm letting those lazy bastards take credit for our collar."

"*Your* collar," said Rob. "It was your idea for the stakeout, and you're the one that got him down."

"*Our* collar."

Glancing at their passenger, Rob dropped his voice to a low whisper. "D'you really think he's the one responsible for all the break-ins?"

"Almost certainly. Same MO in every case. But we need him to 'fess up before we take him back to the station."

Rob frowned. "And how are we going to get him to do that?"

Placing her hands on her slender hips, Morven looked up at Rob and grinned. "Well, that's where a strapping great partner like you comes in handy." He frowned and she said, "You know how we've talked about being more confident and assured, well now's your chance to put what you've learned into action." When Rob's brow furrowed deeper, she added, "He just needs a little persuasion."

Rob glanced at the catapult. "When you say persuasion?"

"Tempting as it is, we're not going to shoot him again." Then, chuckling, she looked Rob up and down, "but I'm sure a big strong guy like yourself will think of a way."

"You mean...?" Rob looked horrified.

"I want him threatened, not harmed," said Morven, "but he's hardly going to be intimidated by a 9-stone weakling like me, is he?"

Rob grinned.

***

Taylor's Grill had been parked in a layby near the Strathmurray roundabout for as long as Morven could remember. A food van serving hot rolls and sandwiches around-the-clock to local factory workers, she and her colleagues had been frequenting the place since she was a probationer, and she reckoned the grease on the hotplates was unchanged in all those years.

Old Taylor had retired a few years back, but his son Junior was his spitting image; short, bald and plump with a sheen of oil, much like that on the sausages he was flipping on the grill. The smell was intoxicating and Morven's stomach growled in anticipation. Watching Taylor Junior, she wondered when he slept as he always seemed to be here.

"Busy night?" asked Junior, piling sausage, bacon and egg onto three rolls. He glanced over to where the pool car was parked.

Like his father, Junior was a rich source of information to Morven and her colleagues. His customers came from all walks of life and not much happened in this town that he didn't know about. The local coppers were amongst his best customers and this meant the Kennedy Gang left Junior alone. His van had never been vandalised and the Taylors didn't pay protection money. However, Morven suspected Junior fed the Kennedys just as much information as he did bacon rolls.

"Aye, fairly quiet," said Morven.

"Who's your friend? I don't recognise him". He hitched his chin at the car where Rob sat in the front with Haydon in the rear.

"Just a wee stray we picked up," she said. "We're going to feed him and return him to his owner."

Junior chuckled. Morven only told him things when she wanted something in return. It was mutually beneficial, and he appeared to respect that.

He handed her the rolls wrapped in white paper bags and winked, "Reckon a lot of people will sleep easier tonight once he's in the pound."

Morven thanked Junior and returned to the car with the food and three builder's brews. She passed them to Rob through the passenger window and jumped into the driver seat. She and Rob exchanged a wry look. They let the aroma of fried food drift through the car, and Rob took a mouthful of his roll and moaned out his pleasure.

"Right," said Morven, turning to meet Haydon's ravenous gaze. The lad looked like he hadn't eaten for a week and his eyes were fixated on the roll in Rob's hand. "After we've all had a bite to eat, we're going for a wee drive so you can point out every single house you've broken into over the last few months."

Haydon tore his gaze from the food and gaped at her as if she was mad. "I told you already, I havnae broken into anywhere, I was just oot for a wee walk tonight and lost my way."

Morven glared at him. "Aye right, next you'll be pissing down my back and telling me it's raining. So where do we begin our tour?"

Haydon spat out, "No way, I know ma rights. Why the hell would I incriminate myself?"

Rob twisted his enormous frame around to face Haydon and gave him a menacing stare. The lad blanched.

Leaning forward, Rob snarled, "Because if you don't ... I'm going to FUCK YOU!"

Chapter 2

Several hours later, Morven and Rob stood at the charge bar in the station with Haydon. They'd radioed ahead to let Danny Galbraith, the custody sergeant, know they were bringing him in. During the booking-in process, Galbraith raised an eyebrow as Morven rhymed off all the burglaries on Haydon's charge sheet. The list was long.

On their tour of the Strathmurray housing estate, the lad had confessed to forty-eight in total, almost all of them on Morven's patch. When he refused to reveal the name of the fence to whom he'd sold the goods, Rob had waved a foil pack containing a condom, and all colour had drained from Haydon's face. It'd taken every ounce of Morven's self-control not to laugh, but the tactic worked and they'd a name; one Morven knew all too well.

She glanced at the clock, knowing it wouldn't take long for news of their arrest to spread around the station. How long until CID came sniffing around for scraps?

After they'd photographed and fingerprinted Haydon, Danny led him away to the cells. As Morven watched them go, she looked at Rob and finally let out the laugh she'd been holding in.

Bracing her hands on her thighs, she wheezed, "Oh my God, I thought I was gonnae shite a blue light."

Rob joined in with her laughter.

"I'd no idea what you were going to do" she said, "but I wasn't expecting ... THAT."

Rob sniggered, "Just as well he didn't spot the expiry date on the johnny, it's been in my wallet for ages."

Morven attempted to appear stern. "Listen, I know I asked you to intimidate him but you can't threaten rape. Ever. If Haydon makes a complaint, you'll be in deep shit."

"Sorry," said Rob, looking suitably chastised.

"Don't apologise, just don't do it again."

They made their way to the Community Office two floors above. A pitiful Christmas tree stood forlornly in one corner of the open-plan area, and someone had strung fairy lights across the bank of windows. The area was quiet except for a couple of officers huddled around a screen. Morven waved a greeting and then slumped into her chair by the window with a heavy sigh. It was still dark outside as she began completing the Crime Report Form on her computer.

Because of the number of offences, the CRF took time, and she was still typing when the alarm on her phone sounded. Cursing, she looked at the clock and then at the unfinished report, aware she hadn't even started on the Summation. She was needed at home but there was no way she could leave this task unfinished.

Ollie will never forgive me.

Bracing herself, she phoned her friend Natalie who slept over at Morven's home when she was on nightshift. Although her son was old enough to get himself up and dressed, Morven preferred someone to be there. Despite the early hour, Natalie answered on the second ring.

Without a word of greeting, Natalie said, "You're not going to make it, are you?"

"I'm really sorry, something's happened and I can't get away."

"Something always happens Morven. For crying out loud, it's his first day at a new school. He's anxious as hell, especially after what happened at the last place."

The memory was all too fresh and Morven put her head in her hands and cursed silently. "I'll explain later but please apologise to him." Then she plucked up the courage to ask, "I don't suppose you could drop him?"

"He wants you there, not me." A pause and then Natalie exhaled loudly. "Oh fine, whatever."

She could hear her friend's judgement but Natalie was right – Ollie wanted his mother there. "Wish him luck from me," she said.

But the line had gone dead.

Morven blew out a hard breath and sent her son an apologetic WhatsApp message to wish him luck. She stared at the message but the two grey delivery arrows stubbornly refused to turn blue. She tried calling him but he didn't pick up.

Rob craned his neck round his monitor and offered her a coffee.

"Thanks," she said, "but you get off home. I'll finish up here."

He grinned. "No way, not after last night, I'm still buzzing. Anyway, I want to help with the paperwork."

She suggested he check over the CRF and while Rob did that, Morven made a start on the Summation which would be read by the shiny arses upstairs. Knowing Haydon's arrest would have a dramatic effect on the clear-up rate, she wanted to ensure their names appeared on this report, especially Rob's. It would do her partner good when it came to his appraisal.

For herself, she cared less; her career had been in the doldrums since 'Blackford Gate' as she'd come to think of it. It had happened sixteen years ago when she was a young constable and it had almost ended her career and a colleague's life. It was the reason she'd transferred to Community; that and having a baby. Juggling a full-time job in the police and childcare wasn't easy at the best of times but after her marriage had ended, it was almost impossible.

As she settled to her task, the door swung open and in strode Detective Sergeant Dave Newton looking like he owned the place.

The devil himself.

Morven suppressed a groan — she and Dave had a long and troubled history. Dave, Morven and her ex-husband had all trained at the police academy together and after graduating she and Dave had worked in the same department. That was until 'Blackford Gate', the visible reminder of which flared across Dave's throat like a terrible, ragged smile.

Dave strutted towards her, and she pulled her gaze from his livid scar to the tailored navy suit and silk tie he wore. Gold cufflinks flashed from starched white cuffs, and his leather brogues gleamed. She reckoned his outfit probably cost more than her monthly salary, and she wondered if detectives got a clothing allowance. The fabric of his shirt strained against the bulky musculature beneath, and she caught a whiff of expensive aftershave. She was reminded of a peacock.

Morven rearranged her face into a smile as he approached her desk.

Didn't take you long, did it Dave?

He held out a takeaway cup and paper bag emblazoned with the logo of a local coffee shop which he placed on her desk. Dave perched on the corner and flashed her a smile.

Morven gazed at the offerings. "What have I done to deserve this pleasure?"

As if I didn't know.

Sweeping back thick blonde hair from his forehead, he said, "Considering you just caught the Strathmurray Slip-in, it was the very least I could do."

You probably expensed the coffee.

She peeked in the paper bag and then tilted her head at Rob. "It was a joint effort. Where's Rob's?"

Dave ignored the remark and kept his piercing blue eyes on hers. "That was quite a stroke of luck."

"There was no luck involved, it was only a matter of waiting for the wee shite to show up."

Like you should've done.

Dave raised an eyebrow. "But that's hardly the job of neighbourhood watch."

Morven's anger flared. "Well, perhaps if you'd been doing yours, we wouldn't have needed to."

She glowered at him for what seemed like an age until finally, Dave raised his palms in surrender. "Listen, I didn't come here to argue, I just wanted to congratulate you."

"In that case, *we* thank you." She looked at him as if to say, 'so what else do you want?'.

Dave cleared his throat and fixed her with a steely gaze. "I'd like to help with the Summation."

And there it was, as clear as day.

In a voice dripping with sarcasm, she said, "That is *so* kind of you Dave, but I'm almost done."

He put out his hand for the document and with a hint of desperation said, "Really, it's no trouble."

Morven took a sip of coffee and smacked her lips together. "If I wasn't just a community officer, I'd suspect you were trying to add your name to it."

Dave's jaw tightened. "Listen Morv, you know how it works round here. You furry suits aren't expected to investigate but we are. It makes absolutely no difference if your name's on the Summation."

Morven bit out, "It makes all the bloody difference, and you know it. Rob in particular deserves the credit, his review's coming up."

Continuing to pretend the young constable didn't exist, Dave said. "And I'm up for promotion soon." He stared at her. Hard.

Rob stopped typing and a heavy silence descended as Morven and Dave glared at one another. Long moments passed. Morven's eyes flicked to the wound at Dave's neck and she'd a sudden flashback to that terrible night. She could recollect it only as a set of jerky scenes, spliced carelessly together, like a grainy film.

With a shudder, she snatched up the form and shoved it at Dave. "You're a real arsehole."

"I love you too Morv," he replied with a sardonic grin.

"And make sure Rob's mentioned."

Dave gave a gruff nod and left with the document. She cursed silently as she watched him go, aware of her colleague's incredulous gaze.

When he was gone, Rob said, "Why did you do that?"

Shaking her head, she muttered, "Trust me, it's a long story."

Before Rob could question her further, in walked the gaffer, Chief Inspector Frank Beamish. He was munching on a bacon roll and grease had dripped onto his tie. Early-fifties and carrying too many pounds, the buttons on his shirt strained against his belly. 'Beamer' as he was known, headed up their department and Morven had worked for him for longer than she cared to remember.

Beamer was out of breath from climbing the stairs and he waddled towards them smiling.

"I've just heard," he puffed, "the Strathmurray Slip-in. That's a fantastic result. Well done, both of you."

They thanked him in unison and chatted about the arrest.

Beamer gave Morven a quizzical look and asked, "Are you okay? I thought you'd be dancing a merry jig."

Yawning, she said, "I'm fine, it's just been a long shift."

"Pop into my office before you head home," he said, before shuffling away.

Morven folded her arms and sighed. She could guess what this was about, and the answer would still be no. She was fond of Beamer, he was a good boss, but he was a persistent bugger. She knew he meant well, and she was flattered that he thought so highly of her but, right now, all she wanted was to crawl into bed and sleep for a week.

She switched off her computer, said goodbye to Rob and knocked on the gaffer's door. He beckoned her in, and she sat opposite him. She slid the CRF document towards him.

Beamer lent his elbows on the desk and steepled his fingers. "Have you thought any more about the secondment?"

She shook her head. "CID's not for me. I'm happy as a beat cop."

Beamer shook his head. "You're a good officer but you're wasted here." Pointing to the CRF, he added, "And this proves it."

"The hours wouldn't suit me."

Beamer looked sceptical. "What age is Ollie now? 15?" When she nodded, he said, "Old enough to fend for himself."

"He still needs me."

Beamer nodded. "Kids always need their parents but isn't it time you thought about your own career? Do you really want to be chasing thieves up trees for the rest of your days?"

"I like it here. I like working for you."

Beamer gave an avuncular smile and gazed wistfully out the window. "I like it here too and I've a good team but the service is changing so fast I barely recognise it. In any case I'll be retiring in a few months." He glanced back at her, his eyebrows raised. "And Lord only knows who they'll bring in to replace me."

Morven stared at him; there was something in his tone. "You know, don't you?" she said. When Beamer said nothing, she persisted. "Who is it? Who's your replacement?"

He said in a low voice. "It's not definite, but it's looking like Cavendish."

Morven's hand shot to her mouth and she groaned. She'd heard rumours about Cavendish.

After joining on the graduate scheme, Bethany Cavendish had risen through the ranks at an astronomical pace, helped by the fact her father played golf with the Chief Constable. Every station had its muppet, and Cavendish was theirs. To contain the problem, she was shuffled from one department to another, leaving a royal mess in her wake. Now it seemed that it was Community's turn to practise damage limitation.

Beamer produced an application form from his drawer and pushed it towards her. "Think about it." Morven noticed it was already part-filled in with his recommendation.

"Thanks, I have thought about it, but I'm afraid the answer's still no." She slid the form back.

Beamer gave a heavy sigh. "For Pete's Sake Morven, if you won't do it for yourself, then do it for me. Call it a retirement present." He proffered the document again.

Snatching it up, she huffed. "Why can't you just settle for a carriage clock like everyone else?"

Chapter 3

As Morven made her way out of the station, she almost collided with Danny Galbraith on the stairs. Late forties and well-built, the custody sergeant had been injured in the line of duty several years back and had since been given a desk job. Morven liked Danny and he'd been kind to her over the years. He was one of the few uniforms who showed her genuine respect.

"Upstairs will be well chuffed," he said with a smile. "How did you get Murphy to talk?"

"Rob can be very persuasive."

Danny laughed. "I bet he can. He's a dark horse that one."

"How's the wee shite settling in?" asked Morven. "Crying for his mammy?"

"All tucked up in his PJs and sleeping like a baby," said Danny. "Anyway, I'm glad I caught you, I'm after a wee favour."

Feeling weary to her bones, Morven suppressed a groan. "Aye, what's that?"

"Would you mind swinging by the Strathmurray library on your way home?"

"You got overdue books?"

Danny explained the manager's wife had called him to report that her husband hadn't returned home last night and wasn't answering his phone. She'd asked if they'd take a look since she didn't drive.

"Really?" exclaimed Morven. "Are we now expected to check the whereabouts of every errant husband?"

Danny looked contrite. "I wouldn't normally ask but she's a friend of my missus, and I'm not off-shift for another couple of hours. She says it's very out of character for her husband and she's worried something has happened to him".

Morven puffed out a breath. "You've checked the hospitals, ANPR —"

"— aye, all the usual and nothing's flagged up."

She tried not to let her exhaustion show. "Okay, but only because it's you."

With a grateful smile, Danny said, "The bloke's name is Mike Carrigan."

***

The sun was only starting to hint at the horizon when Morven parked her old Volvo in the Strathmurray Public Library carpark beside another vehicle.

She knew the library well and, when Ollie was little, she'd often brought him here for children's story hour. She called the station to report her position and check the registration number of the parked car. The dispatcher confirmed it belonged to a Michael Carrigan. Morven sighed as all thoughts of finding Mike alive and well in his mistresses' bed vanished. Perhaps he'd fallen asleep at his desk?

Taking a heavy Maglite torch from the car, she approached the glass-fronted building and tried the door only to find it locked. Peering into the darkness beyond, she spotted a reading light on at a desk but otherwise there were no signs of life. She knocked and called out, but this went unanswered. Morven circled the outside of the library, examining the windows and doors as she went, and she checked around the back for signs of a break in. There were none, and no CCTV cameras.

At the rear, she spotted an open window high up on the back wall. It was too much of a stretch to reach so she rolled one of the council dumpster bins beneath it and clambered on top and peered in. The sight that met her sent a shiver down her spine.

The lifeless body of a middle-aged man lay sprawled on the tiled floor below. He was dressed in shirt and trousers and lay on his back, eyes staring blankly at the ceiling. There was a dark pool of blood around his head. His skin was chalk-white, and his lips were tinged with blue, indicating he'd been dead for some time.

Poor bugger.

Morven called it in. While waiting for uniform and the keyholder to arrive, she sat in the car until she spotted the approach of blue lights flashing silently in the distance.

She greeted the officers and they spoke for a few minutes until one of the library staff, a woman in her sixties, appeared with a bunch of keys. She was visibly upset and, while two uniforms entered the building, Morven chatted to her. Her name was Janet and she told Morven that she'd worked at the library for over thirty years.

Janet glanced at the building and sobbed, "Is it Mike?"

Morven explained they were unable to give details at this stage, and this prompted a fresh bout of tears. Thin and frail, the woman looked as though the slightest gust of wind might blow her over.

When the two officers reappeared, Morven asked Janet to wait in her car while she spoke to them. Uniform confirmed the man was dead.

"Did you find keys inside?" asked Morven.

The older officer shook his head. "No, which begs the question 'Who locked up?'" He glanced back at the building. "It looks like an accident but we'll have to treat it as a suspicious death."

Morven cursed, knowing CID were now involved which meant a further wait. She found Janet and explained to her what was happening. As she comforted Janet, she spotted another car approach. To Morven's dismay, the first detective to arrive at the scene was Dave Newton.

Of all the arseholes to send!

Dave greeted her bluntly. "What the hell are you doing here? Thought you'd finished for the day."

She explained about Danny's request.

Dave said, "Shall we take a look?"

Surprised at the invitation, she said wearily, "You really want neighbourhood watch tagging along?"

"You're here, and since you keep sticking your beak in where it doesn't belong, you might as well." Without waiting for a reply, he spun on his heel and strode towards the library.

Cursing beneath her breath, Morven trotted after him through the entrance and into the cavernous room beyond. The morning sun cast long shadows across the bookcases, lending an eerie atmosphere to the place.

She followed Dave to the rear where the door to the gents' toilets was ajar. He put on latex gloves and pushed it open to reveal the body. Morven wrinkled her nose at the smell of bleach tinged with something else. Something unpleasant.

Dave crouched beside the body, careful not to disturb the area around it. Shaking his head, he said, "He's been dead awhile." He rose and pointed to a smudge on one of the sinks. "Looks like he might have banged his head."

While Dave phoned in an update, Morven studied the dead man's face, noting the rictal smile and clenched fists. It was as if he'd been fighting death. A paperback book lay beside him, its pages soaked in blood. Other than the head injury, there were no other obvious signs of trauma, but something about the scene felt off.

Spotting the look on her face, Dave asked, "What's wrong?"

"I've dealt with a few accidentals over the years," she said, "but I've never seen an expression like that on a body."

Dave shook his head, "I'm not seeing anything that suggests foul play. The poor sod probably slipped and cracked open his skull."

Morven wrinkled her nose. "While he was reading in the loo?"

The sound of footsteps drew their attention.

Dave said, "That'll be the doctor. He'll soon confirm I'm right."

But it was a woman who appeared and not the police surgeon. She gave them a curt nod and introduced herself as Dr Tanya Hellberg, a forensic pathologist. In her late forties with a long mane of auburn hair tied into a high pony tail, Hellberg was dressed in an androgynous trouser suit with sensible shoes protected by plastic shoe covers. She'd a no-nonsense attitude to her work and Morven knew of her reputation for chewing out officers for interfering with a crime scene.

Hellberg cast an emotionless and methodical eye over the bathroom.

Dave asked where the usual dour medical examiner was.

Eying him, she replied with a terse, "Busy on another job."

Hellberg was clearly a match for Dave and Morven liked her immediately.

Kneeling, the doctor pulled on latex gloves and examined the body. "Aye, he's dead alright," she said wryly. "There will need to be a postmortem, but if I'd to hazard a guess, I'd say he's been here about seven or eight hours."

"And if you'd to guess at the cause?" asked Dave.

She fixed him with a cool stare. "You'll need to wait for the PM, and it won't be any time soon, there's a backlog."

"Of course," said Dave. "But humour me with your best guess. Are we dealing with a suspicious death?"

Hellberg scowled at him. "Don't quote me but it looks natural, probably the result of an accident."

Dave shot Morven a smug 'I told you so', look and thanked the doctor.

They left Hellberg to her work and returned to the main part of the library. While Dave checked in with the constable stationed at the entrance, Morven perused the paperwork on what she presumed was Mike's desk. The reading light was still on and strewn across the surface were printed reports and spreadsheets. A copy of the local rag lay open at an article about a protest that had recently taken place outside of the library. The photograph showed a line of people holding placards that read 'Protect our children' and 'Wake up! This is child abuse.'

As she began to read the story, Dave reappeared. She pointed to the newspaper but Dave just shrugged and asked where the keyholder was. Morven led him out to meet Janet. The woman looked frozen so, after clearing it with the IDENT team who were processing the scene, Dave invited her to sit inside the library where it was warm.

Janet sat, sparrow-like, on the edge of a chair and sobbed. Morven fetched her a glass of water and they waited until she had worked through her shock.

Dave perched next to her and asked if she felt able to answer a few questions. His manner was gentler than Morven expected. Janet wiped her eyes with the back of her hand and nodded.

Dave produced a packet of tissues from his jacket pocket and offered her one. "When did you last see your colleague?"

She told them she'd finished her shift at four the previous afternoon. She explained that Mike was the manager and he often worked late. Morven jotted down the details in her pocketbook.

"And did he seem himself?" asked Dave.

She confirmed he'd behaved as normal.

"Anything out of the ordinary happen recently?"

When Janet shook her head, Morven stopped herself from asking the question burning in her mind. But, if Dave was right and this was an accidental death, what would be the point in upsetting the woman further with questions about the protest. Dave thanked Janet and offered to have an officer drive her home.

After Janet left, Morven yawned and checked the time, afraid that if she sat for any longer, she'd fall asleep. "Can I go? I haven't slept in days."

"Not until I say so," said Dave, "and I'll need a statement from you." He stared down at her, "And, in future, leave the investigations to us."

She shot him a look of undisguised loathing.

Chapter 4

Too wired to sleep, Morven lay in bed, wide-eyed and staring at the ugly stain on her bedroom ceiling. The gutters needing cleaning, a job her ex-husband used to do each autumn. Now Mark would be doing those chores in another woman's house, for his new family.

But it wasn't Mark and his long-ago affair that troubled her — she'd cried enough tears over her ex — it was her neglect of their son Ollie. It should have been her, not Natalie, dropping him at his new school today and offering him words of support. Guilt licked at her conscience, as it often did.

Mark had left when Ollie was a baby and, although he saw his son occasionally, Morven considered herself a single parent. As a father and husband, Mark was unreliable, showing up with gifts when he felt like it, only to vanish again. He took no part in Ollie's day-to-day life and showed little interest in the boy beyond what was expected. Mark hadn't been around when Ollie had had a rough patch at his previous school, and it had been down to Morven to pick up the pieces.

The child maintenance Mark paid was the minimum and barely enough to feed and clothe the boy. Morven had had little choice but to return to work. For almost a decade, she'd muddled by part-time — the only way she could juggle family with work — and she relied heavily on her friend Natalie. Without her, Morven wouldn't have coped. However, in terms of forging a career, it had been a disaster, and she could only watch as Dave and the others had shot up through the ranks. Morven believed the gender pay gap was due in part to women bearing the burden of child rearing.

Recently, she'd begun to think the gaffer was right and now that Ollie was in secondary school, it was time to think about her own career. But then her son had some trouble and had left in the middle of the school year. However, that wasn't the only reason she'd discounted a secondment to CID. If she was being honest with herself, she simply didn't feel up to the job. Collaring petty thieves and antisocial teenagers was one thing; investigating serious crime was quite another.

In any case, the last thing she wanted was to work alongside Dave Newton and his ilk, and this morning's events only underlined that. Her cheeks burned at how he'd used his position as leverage to get his name on the Summation. Thinking about the fiery scar on his neck, she pushed aside the memory of how he'd gotten it — no way she'd get a wink of sleep if she went down that rabbit hole — but maybe she did owe it to him. The thought vexed her.

Finally, exhaustion won and Morven drifted into a fitful sleep haunted by images of knife-wielding men and gaping neck wounds.

The buzzing of her phone woke her.

***

Weary having slept little, Morven weaved her car through the busy traffic towards St Agatha's High School. Winter had asserted itself and, although it was dry and sunny, there was a chill in the air.

The head of house who'd called her, a Mrs MacFadden, declined to say what'd happened until Morven got there, only that Ollie was fine. A familiar feeling of dread crept over Morven as she parked near the entrance to the school. Surely the same thing hadn't happened again, and on his first day. Perhaps it was true that bullies could sense weakness in others, and her years spent holding the thin blue line had only reinforced this belief.

Ollie had always been an intelligent and gentle soul who enjoyed art and drama. That and being slightly overweight meant he'd been picked on relentlessly at his previous school. He didn't fit in, didn't conform, and the bullying had gone on for years, culminating in a vicious attack that left him with two fractured ribs, a broken nose and a chipped tooth. But with no witnesses, the school had refused to exclude the perpetrator, and Ollie had been too afraid to return.

In a matter of months, her son had gone from being a happy outgoing boy to one who refused to leave the house. All interest in painting and acting vanished, and he retreated into an online world. Morven was concerned about the time he spent in his bedroom gaming and on social media, but she feared that without this tentative connection to the outside world, he might retreat from society entirely. It was only after help from a social worker that her son had agreed to attend this new school.

Inside the school gates, Morven parked in an allocated visitor space. She entered the spacious foyer which was bedecked in rainbow flags and approached the expansive horseshoe-shaped reception desk. A modern school, it had been built in the early noughties under a PFI scheme which Morven reckoned the taxpayer would still be footing the bill for well into the next century.

The receptionist, a middle-aged woman with a thin mouth, glanced up in annoyance at the squeak of shoes on the gleaming flooring. Morven could hear raised voices coming from one of the offices in the far corner. It sounded like arguing.

With a heavy sigh, the receptionist rose and trudged towards Morven. "May I help you?" she said in a manner that suggested she'd rather not.

"I'm here to see Mrs MacFadden. I'm Morven MacLeod, Ollie's mother."

The woman indicated the sitting area. "Wait there and I'll let her know that you're here."

Morven took a seat on a brushed chrome chair, wondering if it was possible to design a more uncomfortable item of furniture. The shrill voices grew louder but she couldn't make out what was being said. The receptionist glanced anxiously at the office door and then at Morven, before returning her eyes to the computer.

The headteacher's door burst open and an irate woman stormed out tugging a teenage girl by the upper arm. The girl was crying. Morven recognised the woman who had an older child at the same drama club as Ollie. She couldn't remember the boy's name, only the mother's: Kerry something.

Mrs Semple, the headteacher, rushed after the woman, visibly rattled. "Mrs Connelly," she said, "my hands are tied."

Kerry spun around to face her. "It's Dr Connelly, and it's your job to protect children," she said. She pulled the girl again, saying, "C'mon Erin, let's get you home where you'll be safe." She emphasised 'safe'.

Kerry marched out with the girl in tow while the headteacher looked on despairingly. After swapping a glance with the receptionist, the head retreated to her office and closed the door.

Before Morven could ponder on what this was about, a woman in a checked pinafore dress emerged from the adjacent office. In her thirties, she was tall and slender with short blonde hair. With a warm smile that was reflected in her eyes, she introduced herself as Alice MacFadden. Morven followed her into her office, a small room with an institutional grey carpet and white walls. Ollie was sitting at the desk holding a handkerchief to his nose. His shirt was stained with blood and his blazer sleeve was torn.

"Good God, what happened?" exclaimed Morven, crouching beside him.

"I'm fine." Ollie's voice was muffled.

"You don't look fine. Who did this?" She threw a questioning look at the teacher.

"There was a misunderstanding and Ollie got hurt. The other boy has been dealt with."

Morven stood, wishing she was still in her uniform. "What do you mean 'a misunderstanding'? What happened exactly? And I want to know the name of the boy who did this to my son."

Ollie rose. "Don't start Mum, I don't want a scene. It really was a misunderstanding." Scowling, he grabbed his school bag and darted out the office.

Morven called after him to wait before turning her attention back to Alice. The teacher closed the door and invited Morven to sit. She then explained that Ollie had gotten into a fight with another senior boy after he'd accidentally strayed into the girls' toilets.

"It's his first day," said Alice, "it was an easy mistake to make."

"He's been assaulted," said Morven, "that's an offence. I want to know the name of the boy who hit him and what age he is." When Alice said nothing, she added, "Well, are you going to tell me or not?"

"I'm sorry, but I'm not at liberty to. All I can say is the boy has been disciplined and his parents informed."

Morven exhaled. "He's been beaten up on his first day. How's that supposed to reassure me he's in a safe environment?" She realised she sounded like Kerry and briefly wondered if the two incidents were connected.

"Ollie and I have had a long talk and he doesn't want this taken further."

Realising if this were true, there was no point in her pursuing it further. Morven shook her head and stalked from the office, conscious of the receptionist's curdling glare.

Ollie said nothing in the car, despite Morven's prompting. Back home, he darted straight upstairs into his bedroom and slammed the door. She sat in the kitchen for a few minutes with her head in her hands wondering what this episode would do to Ollie's self-confidence and whether he'd ever agree to return to this school.

She considered knocking on his door but knew he needed space. Whenever upset, Ollie required time to calm down, and he'd been like that since he was a small child. She'd have to wait, frustrating as it was.

She busied herself with the laundry and then, when tiredness washed over her in a wave, she made tea and stretched out on the sofa. She flicked on the television which was tuned to Ollie's favourite nature channel. She stared blankly at the screen as a pack of hyenas stalked a zebra and its foal. When they moved in for the kill, Morven turned it off. She drifted off to sleep only to be woken twenty minutes later by her phone vibrating. It was Rob telling her the gaffer was in hospital.

Beamer had had a heart attack.

***

Kerry Connelly drove home with her daughter Erin bawling her eyes out in the passenger seat. There was nothing she could say to console her. Spotting the golden arches, she pulled into the local McDonald's car park in the hope that a burger and a strawberry milkshake would stem her tears. Looking at Erin, she was not so sure.

School had called earlier to inform her that there had been an incident involving both her son and her daughter. She'd panicked but the teacher assured her that both were fine but Erin needed collecting, and her son Michael had been sent to the 'reflection room'. Kerry had been at work and had to quickly organise cover for her lectures and tutorials for that day.

She parked in a quiet corner of the parking lot and turned to Erin. "Want to tell me what happened because I'm still not clear?"

Erin shook her head and wept some more. Kerry fetched them takeaway and returned to the car, and they sat in silence and ate their burgers. With Erin it was always a waiting game and Kerry knew that, with patience, she'd eventually open up. Finally, Erin broke the silence.

"I started my period."

Kerry leaned over and hugged her daughter. "Honey, that's wonderful news. Why are you upset?"

Erin's words came out staccato through her sobs. "I was in Chemistry and I knew it had started. I asked to be excused but Mr Watson wouldn't let me use the toilets. They keep them locked during lessons so you have to wait for the break."

Kerry fumed but said nothing, afraid if she interrupted Erin now, she'd clam up again.

"By the time the lunchtime bell went, I'd blood on my skirt." She cried again, "it was so embarrassing."

Erin explained how she'd tied her jacket around her waist and run down to the girls' loos on the ground floor which she knew would be open. She'd gone into a stall and cleaned herself up as best she could and changed into her PE kit. Then Erin went silent and Kerry could see the effort she was putting in to continue.

"When I came out," she sniffed, "my hands were covered in blood. I needed to wash them but there was this lad in the toilets, hanging about at the sinks ... and I just ..." Erin burst into floods of tears.

Kerry's blood turned to ice. "What was he doing in the girls' toilets?"

Erin looked at her through wet lashes. "They let boys use the girls' toilets if they want to."

"WHAT? Since when?" Kerry had read about this happening at other schools, but not at her children's.

"Since as long as I've been there. Most of the boys don't but there are some ... you know ... that say they're girls and they can use the Ladies."

"Aren't there separate toilets they could use? Why do they have to use the girls' facilities?"

Erin shrugged.

Kerry battled to remain calm. "So, you'd to deal with having your first period in front of a male ... inside a female toilet?"

Erin nodded and cried some more. "I can't go back," she wailed, "I'd die of embarrassment."

Kerry placed a hand on her daughter's arm. "Oh honey, I am so sorry. That should never have happened to you or to any other girl. I'll have a word with school to make sure it never happens again."

Erin pushed her away. "No, you'll only make it worse. I don't want you getting involved."

Kerry gawped at her. "But I have to. You should never have been put in that situation."

"If you do," wailed Erin, "I'll never tell you anything ever again."

Kerry felt like she'd been slapped. After a long pause in which Erin continued to cry, she steered the conversation onto how her son had gotten involved. "So how did Michael get into trouble?"

Erin explained that her older brother had spotted her coming out of the toilets. He could see she was upset and then when he saw Ollie emerge, he flipped and gave him a pounding. The fight drew a crowd and the teachers got involved. She, Michael and Ollie were then taken to the Head's office.

"Please don't say anything to school," said Erin.

"But what if it happens again?"

Erin shook her head. "It won't. I'm not going to school when I'm on my period. I can't use the bathrooms during lessons and I don't want to explain it to a teacher, especially a man. And even if they do let me use the toilets, there are boys in them." She began to cry again.

Kerry drew in slow steady breaths and in a controlled tone said, "Let's go home. We'll talk about this more later."

She pulled into the traffic knowing there was no way that she could let this go. Dealing with school was now number one on Kerry's priority list.

***

"There is absolutely no excuse for assault!" yelled Kerry at her son.

They were standing in the kitchen, Michael leaning against the back of the counter for support, and Kerry furiously chopping vegetables at the island. Kerry had swept her long dark hair back into a loose ponytail. Her son still had his football kit on and his knees were caked with mud. She noticed his knuckles were swollen and bruised. She'd hoped to talk calmly about his exclusion from school while Erin was upstairs in the bath, but the discussion had escalated into a full-blown argument.

Michael clenched his jaw and stood up to his full six-foot height. "Fuck that, what the hell did you think I was going to do?"

Kerry put the knife down on the chopping board and looked up at him. "Firstly, do not use that language and secondly, the boy hadn't done anything."

"What was I supposed to think? I'm standing with my mates and my wee sister comes running out the girls' loos bawling her eyes out, followed by a guy."

"You shouldn't have hit him. It's the school's fault for allowing him in there."

"He's lucky I didn't break his jaw. I will next time if I catch him anywhere near her."

Kerry sighed. Part of her was grateful Michael was protective of his sister, but she couldn't condone violence.

"You're lucky the police aren't involved or you'd end up with a criminal record."

That message appeared to hit its mark. Michael exhaled loudly and flopped into a chair. After a pause, he said, "It's not right though, he shouldn't be allowed in the girls' bogs."

She asked him how long the policy had been in place in school and he reckoned about a year or so after a couple of trans girls — or, as Michael described them, 'sissy boys' — had joined in first year.

Michael sidled up to her and helped with the chopping. "It wasn't a big deal when they were eleven and twelve-year-olds, but that lad is much older. No way he should've been in the same toilet as my sister."

At least they were agreed on that, thought Kerry. But she also knew that being outraged about it in her own kitchen wasn't enough to stop it from happening again. To Erin or any other girl.

After putting the casserole into the Aga, Kerry slipped into her running gear and left the house. She checked the time on her Fitbit estimating that she'd about an hour to spare. Jogging helped her think. And think she would ... because something had to be done.

Chapter 5

Early next morning, Morven received a text asking her to attend a meeting at 10 o'clock although she was not on shift. She woke Ollie but he refused to go to school and she hadn't the strength to fight with him about it. Having endured a fitful sleep after the news about Beamer, Morven felt bone weary.

At the station, she joined the rest of the team in the briefing area. The atmosphere was subdued as they awaited news about the gaffer. The last anyone had heard was that he was in the Intensive Care Unit. Morven didn't know if he was still alive or if he'd ever return to work and the thought saddened her. Beamer was one of the good 'uns.

Chief Superintendent Bob Lawless entered, his face grim. An ominous silence descended, broken only by a muttered curse from one of the constables when Chief Inspector Cavendish appeared in Bob's wake.

Without preamble, Bob thanked everyone for coming and said, "As you know, Chief Inspector Beamish suffered a heart attack yesterday and is in ICU."

Morven held her breath.

"But it looks like the tough old goat will pull through, and all the signs are hopeful."

There was a collective sigh of relief and muted applause.

Bob continued, "It'll be a while before Beamer's well enough to return to work, so I'm pleased to say Chief Inspector Cavendish has agreed to step in while he recuperates."

Tall, thin and aloof, a pale-faced Cavendish cast cool grey eyes over her new team. Her platinum hair was pulled back in a ponytail so tight she would have to loosen it to blink.

Bob continued. "Before the Chief Inspector introduces herself, I wanted to let you know we're having a whip round for Beamer which Constable Patel is organising." He indicated Usha Patel, one of the young WPCs.

Lawless took a step back and offered Cavendish the floor. Morven had spotted her around the station, but she'd never had any dealings with her. She'd often supposed the rumours about Cavendish to be untrue, and likely fuelled by jealousy and resentment because a young woman had been promoted. Surely, she couldn't be that bad? Morven decided to give her the benefit of the doubt.

Cavendish cleared her throat and in a thin, reedy voice said, "I'm sure you'll join me in wishing Chief Inspector Beamish a speedy recovery. However, when he does return, I'd like him to find the department in excellent shape. To that end, I'm introducing the new Police Scotland policy on diversity, equality, and inclusion."

The room stirred with murmurs. Gary Gillespie, one of the veterans, rolled his eyes and grumbled, "Probably another initiative to show we're doing something without actually doing anything."

Cavendish shot him a steely glare but continued, unfazed. "You might be sceptical, and frankly, you have every right to be. But let me be clear — this isn't just a checkbox exercise. We're committed to real change, and this policy is the first step."

Despite the dubious expressions, Cavendish pressed on. "Some of you might think it's just a way to curry favour with the public. Well, I won't deny public image is a factor, but the core of this policy is about fostering a workplace where everyone feels valued and respected."

Gillespie said, "How do we know this isn't just another PR stunt?"

Cavendish gave him a tight smile. "Actions speak louder than words. We're implementing tangible changes such as unbiased hiring practices and mandatory diversity training for everyone."

"Deep joy," muttered Gillespie. Cavendish glared at him.

"Change is difficult, I get that," she snapped. "But it's also necessary. We're not expecting everyone to embrace this with open arms immediately, but we do expect your cooperation. We want everyone to feel that they belong and have equal opportunities."

She paused and surveyed the room for reactions. When no one spoke, she added, "So, whether you're on board or not, get ready because change is coming."

Lawless reiterated his support for the initiative with a face that suggested he knew it would go down like a turd in a gin and tonic. After he and Cavendish wound up the meeting, Morven and her colleagues returned to their seats in silence.

As she pondered the possible implications of this initiative for the team, Morven was a lot less sure about giving Cavendish the benefit of the doubt.

***

The day after collecting her daughter from school, Kerry once again sat in the headteacher's office at St Agatha's, this time at her behest. The head, Mrs Semple, had drafted in reinforcements in the form of Michael's head of house, Miss Rawlings, and the assistant head Mr Nicholson. Kerry sat in a low chair across the desk from them, convinced the seating arrangement was designed to intimidate her.

You'll have to try harder than that.

With a false smile, Mrs Semple said, "How is Erin feeling today? I understand she's not in school."

Erin had refused to go to school that morning and was unaware her mother was having this meeting. Michael was also none the wiser, and Kerry felt a twinge of guilt at not being transparent with her children. She pushed it aside; this issue was too important.

"Erin's well enough to be in school, but she feels unable to because of the toilet situation."

Semple raised an eyebrow. "What situation is that?"

"As you're aware, Erin started her period yesterday during a lesson."

Mr Nicholson's ears turned red and he suddenly appeared to find his shoes interesting.

Kerry said, "But I understand pupils are not allowed to visit the toilet during class."

Semple interrupted, "We've had to restrict access to break times because of antisocial behaviour."

Kerry said, "Erin was too embarrassed to ask to be excused. And then when she did go, there was a male present in the toilet. Have you any idea how humiliating and degrading that was for her?"

Miss Rawlings said, "What happened was regrettable but it doesn't excuse Michael's response. We won't tolerate pupils assaulting other students."

Kerry's voice increased in anger. "Michael was protecting his sister."

Semple countered. "Michael's actions mean he'll be excluded from school for a week."

"Well, that's just wonderful," said Kerry folding her arms over her chest, "so, both my children will have their education disrupted because you're letting boys use the girls' toilets."

Nicholson, who wore a rainbow lanyard around his neck, waded in. "St Agatha's prides itself on being a welcoming and inclusive school for all students. And since the pupil in question identifies as a girl, we have to affirm and respect their wishes."

Kerry gawped at him. "What about respecting my daughter's need for privacy, dignity and safety? Did anyone bother to ask the girls how they feel about this policy?"

"The Equality Law," said Nicholson, "states gender identity is a protected characteristic."

Kerry shot back, "It also states biological sex is a protected characteristic and, as such, schools in Scotland are required to provide separate toilets for boys and girls... and this relates to biological sex, not gender." She knew she was correct; she'd spent the previous evening researching the subject.

When Nicholson had no answer, Semple said, "Our hands are tied. The local authority has issued guidance that trans pupils are to be afforded the same rights as the gender they identify with."

"Then the local authority is breaking the law. You can only change your gender through a legal process when you're over the age of 18."

"But in the meantime," said Nicholson, "we must respect their identity."

Kerry's voice rose higher. "You have a safeguarding duty. Just because a boy identifies as a girl doesn't make him one."

Semple raised her hands in surrender. "I don't wish to argue. The fact is we've been instructed to let them use the girls' toilets."

"Why can't he access another? Don't you have unisex facilities?"

"Yes, but that would discriminate against them."

"So, it's okay to put the girls in danger because of the wishes of a small group of males?"

"They identify as girls, and there is no danger," said Semple.

Kerry fished in her handbag and slapped a copy of a newspaper article on the desk. It was headed *SCHOOL SEX ATTACKS - Girls sexually assaulted in gender-neutral toilets as teen boy arrested*. She narrowed her eyes at Semple. "Really, because this is just one of numerous incidents I discovered."

Semple said, "Erin didn't report an assault. Has she said anything to you?"

"No, but that's not the point," fumed Kerry, "are you seriously telling me she has to be raped before you will protect girls?"

"Like I said, we're simply following the guidance," said Semple.

Kerry had had enough. "The guidance is wrong and is misinterpreting the Equality Act. I couldn't care less that a boy identifies as a girl, it doesn't make him one, and it does not give him the right to use spaces reserved for females."

Semple made a tsk-ing sound. "I'm afraid if you're going to make transphobic remarks, I will have no choice but to end this meeting."

Kerry rose. "Humans can't change sex so how can stating a basic scientific fact be transphobic?" She opened the door and then turned to face them, "Your policy is not only wrong, it's dangerous, and you haven't heard the last of this."

***

It was Friday afternoon and Morven and her son sat across from one another in a corner booth at the local pizza parlour. The bruise on the left side of Ollie's face had faded from blue to a swirl of pale purple and yellow, but his hair was long enough to conceal it when left loose.

They'd hardly spoken since she'd collected him from school, and he hadn't returned to St Agatha's. She hadn't pushed him, afraid that if she did, he'd refuse to go back at all. Once again, Ollie had retreated to his bedroom, only emerging for food, and all her attempts to have a conversation with him had been rebuffed. However, the lure of a stuffed-crust meat feast from Luigi's had done the trick and he'd even showered.

Ollie finished chewing and wiped his face on a white napkin, leaving a flesh-coloured smudge. Had he applied some of her foundation to cover the bruise? Morven said nothing.

Their waitress brought dessert and they shared a chocolate ice-cream sundae. It reminded Morven of other meals they'd once shared after she'd collected him from drama club which always finished with a sweet treat. She missed those carefree days when her son would gabble away to her unselfconsciously, and she wondered if they'd ever return.

Natalie's theory was that children were like caterpillars and, during their teenage years, they'd vanish into a chrysalis only to later emerge as beautiful butterflies. Looking at the miserable moody pupa sitting across from her, Morven hoped Natalie was right.

She waited until Ollie had finished eating before asking tentatively, "D'you want to talk about what happened the other day?"

Ollie shook his head. She said nothing, hoping he'd fill the silence. He didn't.

"Okay, I understand you don't want to talk about it, but is there anything I can do to help?"

"Nope."

After a long pause, she said in a low voice, "I'm just worried about you, especially after last time…"

Ollie leapt to his feet and snapped, "Just leave it. Why do you always have to interfere?" He grabbed his jacket and marched out the restaurant.

She called after him but he ignored her. People stared and she ignored them. After settling the bill, she left a cash tip and returned to the car. Ollie was nowhere to be seen and he didn't answer his phone.

Close to tears, Morven sat for several minutes with her head on the steering wheel.

***

Kerry sat in her office in Lothian University's Social Sciences Department. It was a cramped space with a narrow window overlooking the rear carpark, but at least she had a room to herself. A desk piled high with papers jutted against one wall leaving just enough room to swivel on the chair and avoid hitting the overstuffed bookcases.

A modern university, Lothian had begun life as an ambitious polytechnic. After merging with another college, it had mushroomed into a sprawling institution with several campuses dotted all over the region.

Kerry felt grateful to be part of academia again. After obtaining her PhD in Mathematics from Glasgow University, Kerry had worked as a lecturer at various institutions until taking a career break when Michael was born. While her children were young, she'd hardly worked and had only recently returned to part-time employment with the job offer from Lothian.

Kerry enjoyed her new role lecturing on data collection and statistics and supervising the work of the postgraduate students. The subject matter was fascinating since it dealt with human behaviour in all of its social and cultural aspects.

She also taught basic stats to undergraduates in sociology, psychology, political science, and economics.

There was a knock on the door. Kerry glanced at the time as she wasn't expecting anyone and her tutorial wasn't for another hour. "Come in," she called.

William, one of the PhD students, entered carrying his laptop and looking flustered. William had majored in criminology and was undertaking a research project into sexual cyber-crimes in Scotland. Kerry had been helping him review and interpret official sources of data as well as advising on a questionnaire to gather information from a sample of women and girls.

Kerry greeted him and moved some documents off the spare chair so that William could sit.

William bit his fingernails which were covered in chipped black varnish. Mid-twenties, he rocked the 'emo' look with jet black hair and thick eyeliner. He was also smart as a whip.

He spoke with a strong Glaswegian accent. "I've just hud a meeting wi' Professor Owen and he says ah huv tae redesign ma survey."

Kerry suppressed a groan. Owen was a member of the faculty's leadership team and, in Kerry's opinion, an arrogant prick. The professor had an impressive pedigree, having held positions in redbrick universities, and he'd published a swathe of academic papers. However, despite possessing a beautiful mind, Owen had appalling social skills and Kerry reckoned this was the reason he'd ended up at an upstart university like Lothian.

She inquired about Owen's objections and William explained that he disapproved of the wording in his survey. William opened his laptop and pointed to the question 'What is your sex?' for which there were two options: Male or Female.

Although she already knew the answer, Kerry asked, "What exactly is Professor Owen's issue?"

William wrung his hands. "He says ah shouldnae record data on sex, only on self-identified gender."

Kerry sighed. "I'm afraid the professor is wrong about this, especially with regard to your research."

William looked at her anxiously. "I don't know what tae do ... no offence but he's a professor."

There are a lot of clever fools in academia.

"Leave it with me, I'll have a word with him and sort it out."

William gave a shaky laugh. "Ah was hoping you'd say that."

As she watched William depart, Kerry had a sinking feeling in her gut. This was not a conversation she looked forward to.

Chapter 6

Over the course of the following week, Chief Inspector Cavendish scheduled meetings with each member of her new team and Morven was among the first for 'the chat'. The reminder popped up on her screen as she was catching up on paperwork towards the end of a long shift.

Morven sat opposite her new boss in what had once been Beamer's office. Cavendish wore a pale grey skirt suit with her hair tied back so tight it gave her face a sharp feline likeness. In comparison, Morven felt plain and mousey in her uniform.

The gaffer's desk had been cleared of all personal effects, and the walls stripped of his commendations. A cardboard box sat in the corner piled high with certificates and Beamish family pictures. In their place was a photograph of Cavendish in full uniform with the Chief Constable and, on the desk, a row of scrabble letters in a wooden holder that spelled *The Gaffer*.

"I believe congratulations are in order," purred Cavendish. She spoke with a posh Scots accent, honed at the private school in Edinburgh where her mother still taught. "I understand you were instrumental in the capture of the Strathmurray Slip-in'.

Instrumental? I caught the fucker!

Morven fought the urge to correct her, knowing it would be unwise to get off on the wrong foot. "Rob and I played a part, yes."

Cavendish pawed at the contents of the buff-coloured folder on her desk and observed Morven like a cat eying its prey. She retrieved a document and showed it to Morven.

Oh crap!

"Unfortunately Mr Murphy has made a formal complaint," said Cavendish. "He alleges you shot him with a catapult and your partner threatened to sexually assault him."

Morven battled to keep her expression neutral. "Mr Murphy clearly has a vivid imagination."

Cavendish returned the document to the folder. "There will need to be an internal investigation." She scrutinised Morven once again. "In any case, aren't we getting a little old to be chasing after burglars?"

Morven felt her cheeks burn and she spluttered, "Not at all, and I passed the fitness test with flying colours."

I'm thirty-nine, not a hundred and nine!

Cavendish gave a smile that failed to reach her eyes. "Still, it's the sort of thing best left to the youngsters, don't you think?"

Morven said nothing, wondering where Cavendish was going with this.

"I believe the team needs to play to its strengths," said Cavendish, "and I intend to make the changes necessary to ensure we are more efficient." She rose, stood in front of the glass overlooking the office, and surveyed her new territory. "We have to embrace modern ways of working." She looked at Morven. "Don't you agree?"

"Yes of course ma'am."

Cavendish closed the venetian blinds and returned to sit behind the desk. "For starters, I don't want my senior officers injuring themselves when they could be more effective at a computer."

"I'm all for modern policing," said Morven, "but Rob and I wouldn't have caught Murphy if I'd been sat at a desk."

Cavendish made a tsking noise. "Rob would be the one doing the running, not you. Really, I'm disappointed. I thought you'd be all for it. Dave Newton tells me you're a ... hmm, let's just say ... very inquisitive officer." She emphasised 'inquisitive'.

I bet he did. What else has that snake been telling you?

After Dave's divorce, there'd been rumours that he and Cavendish were in a relationship. The pair deserved one another.

Cavendish continued. "If you were to apply your knowledge and experience to digital police work, imagine what a wonderful asset you'd be to the team."

The subtext was clear — she wasn't currently a wonderful asset. Morven suspected Cavendish wanted Beamer's old guard replaced by a younger team loyal to her.

"But I enjoy being a Community Officer, I don't want to be desk-bound."

Cavendish grinned like a Cheshire cat. "I'm afraid I've already made my decision, especially in light of the complaint made against you." She opened a drawer and produced a thick copy of the Home Office Large Major Enquiry System (HOLMES) training manual which landed on the desk with a thud. "You'll begin your new role next month. I suggest you make a start on this prior to the training course."

Stunned, Morven picked up the guide, as heavy as a doorstop.

Cavendish said, "Thank you Constable MacLeod, that'll be all."

***

Kerry approached Professor Owen's office with trepidation. Although she'd had few dealings with him, she was aware of his fierce reputation and legendary ability to reduce staff and students to tears. She took a deep breath, knocked and entered.

Owen was sat at his computer. A wiry individual in his mid-fifties with wild grey hair and a counterculture t-shirt, Owen epitomised the dotty professor.

He glanced up as she entered and then returned his attention to the computer. Without looking at her, he huffed, "Sit down, I'll be with you shortly."

Then he made her wait. And wait.

Finally, he wheeled away from his desk, folded his arms across his chest and stared at her. "What can I do for you Dr Connelly?"

Kerry took a steadying breath and said, "I believe you raised concerns with one of my research students about his methodology." When he returned a blank look, she added, "William Smith."

"Ah yes, what is it you want to discuss?"

"Well William's research hinges on him being able to determine specific characteristics about victims of sexual cyber-assault and perpetrators of these crimes, and to do this he needs to know their sex."

"No, he must request self-reported gender rather than so-called 'biological sex'." He wrinkled his nose in disgust.

Kerry forced a breath of deep frustration through her lips. "With respect professor, only a tiny number of females commit sexual crimes so, if William were to include males who identify as women, it'll skew the results and render his data worthless." She braced herself for Owen's ire. He did not disappoint.

He sat up and puffed out his chest. "Self-determination is considered politically appropriate and reflects more meaningful psychological responses. In any case, the concept of biological sex is nothing other than a social construct."

Keep calm.

This was worse than Kerry had anticipated. She gathered her thoughts and replied in a cool voice, "Regardless of whether you believe biological sex is a social construct or not, it's important to know the sex registered at birth of both the victims and perpetrators."

Owen pursed his lips. "Sex is *assigned* at birth, haven't you done the Diversity, Equality and Inclusion training?"

"Of course, professor which is why I know that sex is a protected characteristic that institutions such as ourselves can collect data about."

His face clouded. "Gender identity is also a protected characteristic which is the reason William's survey question must be reworded as 'What is your gender identity?'" He sent her a challenging glare.

Kerry was prepared for this having done her own research. "But if a perpetrator's gender identity is female but they're actually male, then the stats will show an increase in sex offending by women which will be wrong."

Owen's voice was low and dangerous. "If a respondent *identifies* as a female, then she's female."

Don't lose it.

In a moderate tone she said, "I beg to differ professor. People can identify however they like but it does not change their sex."

Owen slapped his palm onto the desk making Kerry jump. "Trans women are women. In all instances!"

Kerry gawped at him in disbelief. "Really? No exceptions?"

"Yes Dr Connelly, in *all instances*." He shot her a look that dared her to say otherwise.

She knew she should walk away at this point but she couldn't, despite the warning voice in her head. What he was saying was so illogical it had to be challenged. She held up her index finger and began her gambit. "If that's true, then please answer me one question."

Owen glared at her and she continued.

"Suppose for a moment that you and your partner were unable to have children." When he looked as though he was about to explode, she raised a hand, "Please hear me out." Before he could object, she said, "So you decide to use a surrogate to have a baby. You have a close friend who's a transwoman. Would you ask them to be your surrogate?"

Owen's mouth fell open and he made a spluttering sound. But Kerry wasn't finished.

"So, not in all instances then?" She emphasised 'all instances'.

Check mate.

When Owen still had no words, she rose saying, "As scientists, we need to ask the right questions that enable us to answer serious research topics, rather than concerning ourselves with what's politically palatable. The question William is asking must therefore stand."

Owen leapt to his feet and shouted, "I find your bigoted views offensive, and I will not tolerate them in this department. I suggest you reflect on your decision and advise your student accordingly ... for your sake and his."

He then sat down and swivelled his chair to face his computer, signalling that the meeting was over. Stunned by his response and the veiled threat, she retreated to her office and closed the door.

Kerry contemplated her next move.

***

Feeling like she'd been poleaxed, Morven slunk into a toilet cubicle and let loose the tears that had been building. So, this was her thanks for nineteen years of loyal service: put out to pasture behind a desk.

Outside, the laughter of younger colleagues washing their hands reminded her of Cavendish's humiliating remarks. She waited until they'd left before venturing from the stall. She examined herself in the mirror. Sure, she had a few laughter lines and the odd grey hair amongst the blonde ones, but she wasn't old. Was she? She remembered her mother telling her how invisible she felt as she aged. Was this the beginning of her own disappearance? The realisation her youth was behind her was made worse by the fact she had no social life. And as for a love life ... Morven couldn't remember the last time she'd been with a man, and the thought of that part of her life being over filled her with sadness.

She splashed water on her face and finger-combed her hair, making a mental note to get her roots done at the hairdresser. She returned to her desk holding the manual. Rob looked up and asked if everything was alright.

"Not really," she muttered, conscious of Cavendish watching from her office.

Morven opened the HOLMES guide and scanned the table of contents. After a few moments, a message popped up on her screen from Rob:

> Canteen in 5?

She sent him a thumbs up emoji.

Rob grabbed his jacket and left and she followed a few minutes later. Cavendish's blinds were now closed and Morven wondered who was next for 'the chat'.

She found Rob at a table in the far corner of the staff canteen with two mugs of coffee. She gave him a grateful smile and slid into the chair opposite. He asked what Cavendish had said to her. When Morven told him, Rob swore.

"She can't do that," he protested.

"She just did, and I doubt I'm the only one on her hit list."

He shook his head and asked what she was going to do.

She shrugged. "What can I do? I'll have to try and ride it out until Beamer returns or they muppet shuffle Cavendish elsewhere."

Before either could say anymore, Dave Newton appeared dressed in a sharp navy suit. He was carrying a manila folder, and he made a beeline towards Morven. She wondered if her day could get any worse.

"Can I have a word?" said Dave. He glanced at Rob adding, "in private."

Rob took the hint, and with a last swig of coffee, left. Dave slid into the seat he'd vacated and observed her. "What's up with your face?"

This lit the blue touch paper and Morven's anger flared. Leaning over the table, she hissed, "Really? First, you take the credit for Murphy's arrest and then you've the bloody audacity to ask me what's up when you fine well know that your girlfriend has just demoted me to back-office duties."

Startled, Dave said, "Whoa, what are you on about?"

She rose, snarling, "So thanks Dave, thanks a lot."

He got to his feet. "Morv, wait...."

She stalked off before he could finish.

***

Morven stood at the kitchen stove stirring a pan of boiling pasta. Although her anger at Cavendish's treatment had faded to hurt and humiliation, the memory of it still occupied her mind.

The home phone rang again and she ignored it, along with the flashing messages on the answering machine. Work had her mobile number so whatever it was could wait.

Macaroni cheese was one of Ollie's favourites but she seldom had time to prepare it, and when she did it was usually with a packet of powdered sauce. Tonight she'd gone to extra effort and prepared it from scratch. After combining the ingredients, she spooned the mixture into an ovenproof dish and sprinkled freshly grated cheese on top. She carried the dish to the oven and with her other hand opened the door. The handle came off, and the ashet fell to the floor and smashed on the tiles. Morven swore.

The noise drew Ollie from his room, the first she'd seen of him since arriving home, and he helped clean up the mess. He wore a crumpled t-shirt and joggies that looked like they'd been slept in, and his hair was greasy. She caught a pungent whiff which reminded her of charity shops. She needed to have a word with him about his personal hygiene, but now was not the time.

"Sorry love. I'll fetch us fish and chips if you fancy."

"No, I'm alright," he muttered.

"You need to eat something. How about cheese on toast?"

"I'm no hungry."

Morven rolled the remains of their dinner into newspaper and placed it in the bin. "So, how was your day?" she asked.

"Have you spoken to Dad? He's been trying to get hold of you."

"Err, no, what does he want?" *Mark always wants something.*

Ollie straightened up and looked her in the eye. "I've decided to go and live with him."

His words hit her like a punch to the gut. Morven leant against the kitchen counter for support and tried to fight down her panic. "Ollie, what in heaven's name has brought this on?"

"Huh, you really want to know?" He shot her a contemptuous glare.

"Is it school because if it is, we'll find you another."

"This has NOTHING to do with school." He pointed at her. "It's YOU. All you care about is WORK."

She attempted to keep her composure. "I'd no idea you felt like that."

"Well maybe if you were actually home once in while you might. It's like you don't care."

Her eyes filled with tears and she blinked them back. "Ollie, that's unfair, of course I care."

His frustration grew until it bubbled over. "At least I'll get a home-cooked meal at Dad's."

Her anger ignited and she shot back, "The food might not be up to much but who do you think puts it on the table?" Her voice rose higher and higher. "Your father? No, I have to work just to make ends meet."

"I'm moving out at the weekend." He stormed off upstairs.

She ran to the foot of the staircase and shouted after him, "You can't. We've a custody agreement, and I'm responsible for you."

Ollie stopped mid-flight and turned, his expression a mixture of fury and desperation. "Go to court for all I care, but I'm not staying here any longer."

"You really think his BITCH of a wife wants YOU there?" She regretted her words as soon as they were out.

Her son's look of disappointment stung more than anything he could have said. Ollie retreated to his room and slammed the door.

Morven slid to the floor, hugged her knees to her chest and wept.

Chapter 7

"What are you going to do?" asked Sam.

Kerry and Sam were sat in a corner of the staff room drinking bitter-tasting coffee. A clinical psychologist, Samantha lectured part-time at Lothian and she and Kerry had struck up a friendship. They'd kids of a similar age and Sam was one of few senior women in the department.

Kerry blew out a breath. "I've advised William to leave the question as it is. He needs data on sex, not gender identity, and if he changes it to placate Owen, the results will be wrong if his sample includes even a small number of males." When Sam said nothing. Kerry asked, "You think I'm wrong?"

Sam glanced around the empty room and whispered, "I think you're right; I'm just worried about the consequences for you personally."

Kerry shrugged. "What's the worst that can happen? Owen will throw a hissy fit and report me, but if it goes to a panel, they'll soon see I'm right."

"I wouldn't be so sure," said Sam. "You might be in for a rough ride."

Kerry raised an eyebrow. "You think?"

"I know." She leant over and in a low voice said, "A couple of years ago, I'd a part-time PhD student who wanted to study people who decide to reverse gender reassignment. She's a therapist who specialises in transgender patients and in her clinical practice she was seeing a lot of detransitioners. She'd even secured funding for the research."

"What happened?"? asked Kerry.

"The Ethics Committee rejected it. They said it was politically incorrect and if there was criticism of her research it would reflect badly on the university."

Kerry gaped at her. "But that's outrageous."

Sam nodded, "I know, especially as there's hardly any data on detransitioning." She glanced around again and in a low register said, "So, my advice is to tread carefully. You know how toxic this issue is and what's happened to other gender-critical academics."

Kerry had read the stories and followed the trials and employment tribunals. "But these were in places like Brighton, the gay capital of Britain."

"What about Edinburgh Uni?" said Sam, "It's everywhere. People are afraid in case they lose their jobs ... or worse."

Kerry exhaled loudly. "Do you remember the name of your student, the one who wanted to study detransitioning?"

Sam's brow furrowed. "Kuzi something, I'll send you her details." She glanced around furtively and whispered, "Have you heard of *Real Women Scotland*?" When Kerry shook her head, she said, "It's a free-speech group for women. We don't have any political affiliations; we just talk about issues that affect women. You might be interested in joining."

Kerry asked for the details and Sam said she'd send a message via Signal because it was safer. Before Kerry could quiz her further, a couple of staff members entered, at which point Sam announced she ought to get home.

Kerry had never seen her colleague look so afraid.

***

Next morning, Morven examined her face in the bathroom mirror. Her eyes were red and puffy from crying and ringed by dark sleep bruises. She'd spent the night coiled on the sofa, in a blur of despair, replaying Ollie's hurtful words over and over in her head. Only when the cold light of dawn stole through the thin curtains did she drag herself into the shower.

A headache thumped behind her temples, and she couldn't face breakfast. She swallowed two painkillers with a glass of water and battled to retain them in her churning stomach. Unfocused, she drove to the station through heavy traffic as rain hammered on the windscreen.

She pulled into the carpark at the rear of the station. She sat for a while fighting back tears and trying to muster the courage to face the working day. She no longer cared if she was late.

There was a loud thump on the passenger seat window and she leapt. Dave Newton, his raincoat held over his head, tried the doorhandle. Finding it locked, he yelled at her to let him in. Although tempted to drive off at speed, she opened the door. Cursing at the weather, Dave jumped in sending droplets of water flying.

Before she could ask him just what the hell he was playing at, he turned to her and said, "Listen, I know you're pissed off and you've every right to be, but I'd no idea what Beth had planned."

Morven didn't believe him; he surely must've known the effect it would have on her career.

"Anyway," said Dave, "that's not why I'm here." From under his coat, he produced a rain-splattered folder and opened it.

He handed her a photograph of a corpse lying on a stainless-steel gurney, adding, "If it's any consolation, you were right."

***

Half an hour later and Morven sat at a corner table in the canteen flicking through the file Dave had given her. It contained details about the death of Michael Carrigan, the librarian. Morven scanned the information but kept going back to the photograph from the postmortem.

Dave approached holding mugs of steaming coffee. Grim-faced, he handed her one and slid into the seat opposite.

Morven took a sip and regarded him over the rim. "So, he was murdered."

It wasn't a question; there was no doubt after what the pathologist had found lodged in his gullet. She glanced at the picture again, "What does it mean?"

Dave shrugged. "Haven't a scooby but Dougie's launched a full murder investigation."

The forensic pathologist's examination of Mike's body revealed that he'd died as the result of a blow to the back of his skull from a blunt instrument, and not from hitting his head on the sink. During the postmortem, Dr Hellberg had also discovered a folded piece of paper rammed deep inside Mike's oesophagus. It was a printed flyer for an event that had taken place at the library.

Scrawled across the flyer in bright red pen was the number '20'.

***

Kuziwakwashe Freeman's office was located above a dry cleaner on a busy street lined with shops and takeaways. Squeezed between an estate agent and an insurance broker was an entrance bearing a shiny plaque with a list of businesses. Kerry took the stairs to an opaque glazed door on the 1st floor and entered a small reception area. The inner door beyond was open and a woman's voice invited her to enter.

Dr Freeman got up from her chair and with a warm smile extended her hand, "You must be Dr Connelly," she said in a soft lilting voice, "I'm Kuzi." She was in her mid-thirties with ebony skin, almond-shaped eyes and black braided hair tied in a ponytail. Kerry warmed to her immediately.

Kuzi made coffee and they exchanged small talk about academia. They sat opposite one another and Kuzi asked how she could help. Kerry explained about her PhD student's project and how this had hit an ideological wall which concerned her as a scientist. She inquired about Kuzi's own attempts at carrying out similar research and Kuzi relayed her experience at Lothian University, and her worries about what she was seeing in her clinic.

During their discussion, Kerry had the feeling Kuzi was trying to determine whether she could trust her or not.

Kerry said, "I've two kids, a boy and a girl, so I'm interested in this as an academic and as a parent."

The psychologist appeared to drop her guard. "In the last few years, I've seen more and more young adults wanting to reverse their decision to change gender. Some have taken puberty blockers and cross-sex hormones for several years which have caused irreversible changes in their body. I've natal females — in other words, biological women — with deep voices, facial hair and male-pattern baldness, and I've a patient who developed osteoporosis at sixteen after taking testosterone."

Putting her hands to her mouth, Kerry exclaimed, "Sixteen?"

Kuzi nodded, "There are recorded cases in even younger children. And neither them nor their parents understood the side-effects of taking drugs which were never licensed to be used in this way. They were told it would just put a pause on puberty."

Kerry said, "So these kids have been experimented on?"

"Yes, and I'm only seeing the tip of the iceberg. The Tavistock 'treated' — she made air quotes with her fingers — thousands of these kids. Even though the Gender Clinic has been shut down, clinicians are continuing to prescribe these drugs."

"Why is the practice being allowed to continue?"

Kuzi shook her head, "There are still many psychologists who believe gender dysphoria should be treated with drugs and surgery."

Kerry asked if she'd any patients who'd had operations and Kuzi confirmed she had a couple of females on her books who'd undergone 'top surgery' to remove their breasts. She also had a male who'd had his penis formed into a 'neo vagina'.

"Trouble is," said Kuzi, "the lad was so young when he began taking puberty blockers, that not enough penile tissue developed with which to form a cavity, so the surgeon used intestines instead. The operation was a failure and he's had all sorts of problems."

Kerry shook her head in disbelief although she didn't doubt the psychologist's words. She wondered what had happened to the medical principle 'first, do no harm'.

"Yet this is still going on," said Kuzi. "But what really concerns me is if gender identity is included in a new law to ban conversion therapy. If that happens, it'll be illegal for parents, teachers and therapists to talk to children about gender identity without affirming their new 'trans' status."

"By 'affirming', I take it you mean that you won't be able to question it at all?"

Kuzi nodded. "Or explore what else might be causing the problem. As a therapist I'll be forced to validate the delusion, and this goes against every ethical principle I live and work by. And it's dangerous because if I go along with the idea they're born in the wrong body, I might cause future psychological problems."

They chatted about the increasing number of girls that were presenting in her clinic, and Kerry asked her what she believed was the main cause of gender dysphoria.

"Every case is different," said Kuzi, "but many of my patients have suffered anxiety, abuse, trauma, or have autism or ADHD." She paused and then added, "about 30% of the kids treated by the Tavistock were neurodiverse, and many were in the care system."

She then looked at Kerry as if trying to decide whether to say more before adding, "Many of these kids are same sex attracted and, if simply left alone, they'll eventually come to terms with their sexuality. That's why it's so important to carry out psychological assessment over a long period and offer therapeutic intervention where necessary."

Kerry blew out a breath at the enormity of what she'd just heard.

Kuzi continued. "There was a dark joke at the Tavistock that, at the rate they were treating kids, there would be no gay ones left."

Dark indeed.

"Why wasn't this stopped sooner?"

Kuzi shrugged. "There are some very powerful and well-funded lobby groups and pharmaceutical companies behind this. The Mermaids charity had considerable influence at the Tavistock." She chuckled, "You probably think I'm some sort of conspiracy theorist now."

"No, no I don't. I'm just shocked about what's been going on, and for how long."

"In time, it'll probably be the biggest medical class action law suit we've ever seen. It's akin to the lobotomy scandal of the last century."

That gave them both pause for thought.

"Meanwhile," said Kuzi, "we're crying out for research into the long-term effects of these treatments and surgeries, and to find out why so many people are detransitioning. That's why I submitted my proposal to Lothian."

Kerry smiled. "Which is the reason I wanted to talk to you."

***

With Dave's news still swirling like a maelstrom in her head, Morven made her way to the Community Office. She passed Cavendish's door; the blinds were closed which wasn't a good sign. Rob was already at his desk and they exchanged a greeting.

Indicating Beamer's office, Morven whispered, "Who's she with now?"

"Gary Gillespie," said Rob.

Morven gave a low groan. Gillespie was an excellent cop. He knew his patch like the back of his hand and nothing went down there without him knowing about it. Information like that was their lifeblood and losing Gillespie would hamper their ability to do their job. After Cavendish had finished her purge, they'd be lucky to catch a cold, never mind a criminal.

Morven cast her eye over the department. She'd worked here for almost fourteen years and knew every face. She'd been at these people's weddings, their kids' christenings, and more funerals than she cared to remember. The thought of all this disappearing because of the ambition and stupidity of one over-promoted and inexperienced idiot filled her with despondency. She thought about Beamer who'd given his life to policing, although it had almost cost him his.

For years, Morven had resisted change. She enjoyed her job but that rug had been pulled from under her feet leaving her flailing. Her reason for not seeking advancement in other departments had also vanished now that Ollie would no longer be living at home. She'd decided not to contest his decision to stay with his father since she feared he would only rail against it. Instead, she hoped that after a few weeks at Mark's, Ollie would return home with his tail between his legs. In the meantime, it'd be hard because without her son, she'd have nothing to go home to. The job was all she had, and that realisation filled her with despair.

With a heavy sigh, Morven opened her desk drawer and retrieved the application form that Beamer had given her. The CID placement would only be for six months and, with luck, this would be sufficient time for Cavendish to screw up and move on. But could she put up with Dave Newton for that long?

Cursing beneath her breath, Morven began to fill out the form.

Chapter 8

Morven picked her way over the icy pavements towards the café where she and Ollie's father had arranged to meet to discuss the new living arrangements for their son. Since his announcement, she and Ollie had hardly spoken and he'd kept to his room. Any interactions between them were strained.

A group of carol singers stood outside singing their own rendition of *Silent Night* called *Stereotypes*, the lyrics of which made Morven chuckle. They were collecting for the local women's refuge and she dropped some coins into their collection box.

Inside the coffee shop, she spotted Mark sitting in the far corner alone. She'd refused to meet his wife, Brittney; the situation was bad enough without her being involved. Morven didn't want Ollie in the same town as that woman, never mind in the same house. She blamed Brittney for the breakdown of her marriage and she struggled not to let her bitterness show.

Mark gave a hesitant wave and she sat opposite him. He slid a coffee cup towards her. "Err, got you a latte," he said. "Do you still drink coffee?"

Mark looked haggard. His once glossy black hair was flecked with grey and he had bags beneath his eyes. Maybe the new baby was keeping him awake at night. She hoped so.

Morven took a sip of the coffee. It was cold and left a bitter taste. Without preamble, she said, "Did you know he was planning this?"

"Of course not. I only found out when you did."

Mark explained that Ollie had just pitched up on his doorstep to ask if he could move in.

"And I suppose you said yes," said Morven.

He sighed. "What could I say? He's my son too."

"You could've told him he belongs with his mother."

Mark raised his palms in surrender. "Listen, I don't want to argue. This is where we're at, so can we just sort something out that works for us all?"

She knew he was right and that rankled. "I just want what's best for Ollie," she conceded. "What's Brittney saying to it? I can't imagine she'll be over the moon at having a moody teenager as well as three young 'uns to deal with."

His face told her she'd hit a nerve. "We'll cope."

Morven ordered more coffees and they spent the next hour making arrangements around their son. They agreed Ollie would spend every other weekend with Morven, shift work permitting, and half of the holidays. Mark had contacted a school in the neighbouring town where he worked and arranged for Ollie to continue his studies there. This news came as a welcome relief to Morven who'd feared he'd drop out altogether. She and Mark also sorted out the financial side which seemed to please her ex-husband, and she wondered if money was tight.

"He's a good kid but he's going through a really tough time," she said. She told Mark about the recent assault Ollie had suffered at school.

Mark looked pensive. "I'm glad you told me because I couldn't get anything out of him, just that he'd been in a fight."

After everything was settled, Mark inquired about her work and she explained about her upcoming secondment.

"CID?" he said, "wow that's really exciting."

Was that envy she detected? Mark had left the police after Ollie was born and now worked as a management consultant. Compared to that, CID probably did sound exciting. Mark arranged to collect Ollie the following day and they parted on good terms.

After, she drove home dreading the moment she'd have to wave goodbye to her son. She held onto the thought that, after a few weeks with Mark, Brittney and three screaming weans, Ollie would soon be back home where he belonged.

***

Kerry sat in her cramped office at the university and rubbed her temples as a migraine threatened behind her eyes. The chipped formica surface of her desk was obscured beneath layers of papers, magazines and handwritten notes which spilled over the edges and onto the floor below. Towering stacks of books, some leaning precariously, dominated every inch of space not occupied by her laptop. All this chaos was the result of several weeks of research into transgenderism following her spat with Professor Owen.

Taking a methodical approach, Kerry had begun by scrutinising the philosophy underpinning gender identity and the trans rights movement. She read up on queer theory which questioned assumptions about what's 'normal' and the binary nature of sex. She waded through lofty academic papers arguing that biological sex is nothing but an artificial category designed to exclude some groups and prop up others. She perused texts by radical feminists who argued that there are no natural differences between males and females. Next, she'd analysed gender identity theory which promulgated the idea that it is an inner psychological sense of being male or female that makes you a man or a woman, rather than your chromosomes.

Little wonder she had a headache. What Kerry had discovered shocked her, not just as a mother, but also as an academic. Sure, she had been on 'planet baby' while her kids were young, but she'd kept up to date with current affairs, and she'd always considered herself to be a progressive, so how had she missed the spread of this ideology? The incoherent sophistry of these theories lacked the logic and beauty of mathematics and Kerry found herself yearning for the harmony of numbers.

Needing a change of scenery, Kerry scooped up the textbook she'd been reading and made her way to the staffroom. Lunchtime was not for another hour and the space was mercifully quiet. After swallowing down a couple of painkillers, she brewed a mug of tea and flopped down on a squishy sofa. Beside her on the coffee table was the university's latest Diversity, Equality and Inclusion (DEI) policy booklet. Kerry flicked through it, wrinkled her nose at the references to 'non men', and returned to her textbook. However, the author's twisted logic and double-speak jargon made her head throb.

As the staffroom began to fill up, Kerry finished the dregs of her tea. A voice said, "Enjoying the book?" With dismay, she looked up to see Dr Edwina Taylor approaching.

Edwina was a short squat woman in her forties with curly brown hair who dressed as though she scavenged clothes from the charity shop sale rail. A senior lecturer on the postgraduate social work course, Edwina headed up the university's DEI department. She also wore a shiny 'they/them' pronoun badge.

Kerry didn't feel like engaging in conversation or revealing what she really thought of the book so she gave a non-committal reply. Edwina, however, appeared determined to chat and settled her ample bottom down on the chair opposite.

Peering through her thick-lensed glasses, Edwina said, "Do you agree biological sex is an outdated category?"

Kerry paused before responding. No way did she want to open this can of worms here of all places but the idea that the material world was nothing other than a shimmering illusion was too preposterous to let slide.

"As a statistician," said Kerry, choosing her words carefully, "I'm astounded at how devoid of empirical evidence these arguments are."

Edwina looked startled and pointed at the book Kerry held. "It's been proven that sex is not binary and is instead a continuum." Her tone attracted attention from others in the room and the normal hubbub ceased.

"No, science proves sex is binary," said Kerry, "and it's the presence or absence of a Y chromosome that makes you male or female. The existence of a tiny fraction of people with disorders of sexual development does not disprove that fact."

There were audible gasps and Edwina reacted as if Kerry had just decreed that the Earth was flat. The room fell silent as though everyone was holding their breath, and Kerry felt a flush creep up her neck.

Edwina sat up straight and said shrilly, "Surely it's your inner feeling of being male or female that makes you a man or a woman, rather than your chromosomes?"

During her research, Kerry had reflected on her own gender identity, recalling that she'd been a tomboy in her youth, eschewing all things feminine. However, by every standard of logic, she was patently female, and not least because her reproductive system had produced two beautiful children.

Kerry shook her head. "If such a thing as gender identity exists, you're conflating it with sex. They're two different things."

The head of DEI glared at Kerry as if she'd made a racist remark. "Goodness me," gasped Edwina, "I didn't expect to hear such views in this staffroom."

Vexed now, Kerry said, "Oh come off it Edwina, you don't honestly believe men can become women, and vice versa? People can dress and identify however they want, but they can't change sex."

Edwina sat up and puffed out her large chest making her pronoun badge bounce. Utterly convinced of her own rectitude, she said, "I believe gender identity is far more important."

"Most of the time sex doesn't matter," retorted Kerry, "but sometimes it's all that matters. Surely you can see the problem with putting rapists in female prisons or allowing males to compete against female athletes?"

"I'm truly shocked," said Edwina, glancing around at their colleagues for support.

The hostility in the room was almost visible, and Kerry wondered when academia had stopped being a place that fostered free speech. She was reminded of articles she'd read about academics being dismissed for stating that biological sex is real. In one case, a professor had been hounded out of her job by masked trans activists (branded the 'Black Pampers') who had set off flares during protests calling for her to be sacked.

"What's shocking," said Kerry, addressing the wider audience, "is how this ideology has crept unchallenged into every institution, including ours, to the extent people are too afraid to state the facts."

Undeterred by the sea of truculent faces, Kerry continued, this time directing her comments at Edwina, "What's also shocking is the erasure of the word 'woman' from policies which are supposed to be about inclusion." Kerry picked up the DEI booklet. "I'm not a 'cis-woman'. I'm a woman, an adult human female."

To the sound of loud exhalations, Kerry scooped up her things and beat a hasty retreat.

As she fled back to the relative safety of her office, she pondered on how society been duped into believing that self-determined gender was more important than, or even replaced, biological sex? How had institutions and mainstream media been so thoroughly captured by this ideology, and how had language, female-only spaces, and women's sports been appropriated? But, most importantly of all, how had children and vulnerable people been experimented on, mutilated, and sterilised in the name of medicine?

Kerry realised she had 'peaked'.

***

Morven entered the all-too-familiar police station with a sense of trepidation.

After submitting her application to CID, she'd been accepted on a 6-month secondment, and things had moved rapidly. Rob had organised farewell drinks in the local pub and the team had gone for curry afterwards. All except Cavendish. It was bittersweet saying goodbye to her colleagues in Community, especially Rob. Beamer had signed her card and was back home recuperating, and she made a mental note to visit him soon. Christmas and New Year had passed in a blur of despair without Ollie being home for some of the festivities.

It felt strange climbing the extra flight of stairs to the Criminal Investigation Department. Even stranger to be in plain clothes after years spent in uniform. She'd spent hours shopping for something to wear which would be practical yet smart. There was no clothing allowance and, in the end, she'd settled on trouser suits in muted colours like the navy one she currently wore with a white blouse and flat shoes. Natalie had described her attire as the 'lesbian starter kit'. And she should know.

Outside the door to CID, Morven took a deep breath. She felt like a fraud as she swiped her card, half expecting to be told she didn't belong here. Inside, the space looked similar to the floor below: a large open-plan area with desks separated by low baffle boards. Glass-fronted offices lined one wall and there was a dedicated briefing area. It was busier than she'd expected with a dozen staff already at their desks.

She glanced around nervously looking for the office of the Chief DI, Dougie Campbell. She spotted him in the corner but his door was closed and he was on the phone. He saw her, waved and flashed his fingers to indicate he'd be five minutes. Feeling conspicuously like the new girl, Morven went in search of coffee.

"Lost your way?" said a voice she recognised.

Dave Newton leant against the counter in the small kitchenette, a mug in his hand and a smirk on his face. He was dressed immaculately in a dark grey suit and his hair looked as though it had been styled for the runway. Morven readied herself for a barrage of sarcastic remarks and Dave didn't disappoint.

"Shouldn't you be downstairs in neighbourhood watch?" he said, looking her up and down. "And what's with the suit?"

Hands on hips, she replied, "You know fine well why I'm here."

"Guess we need someone to make the tea," he chuckled.

"Stop being an arsehole and get out of my way."

Still chuffing, Dave opened a cabinet and took out a mug. "Our standards must be slipping."

When Morven didn't react to his goading, he made her a cappuccino using the fancy coffee machine and handed it to her. She muttered her thanks and with a cheeky smile he was gone. She examined the mug. Printed on the side was 'Tea Lady'.

Pig!

Back in the main office, Dougie was winding up his phone call and he beckoned her inside. She closed the door and sat opposite him.

Early fifties with a sturdy stature, deep-set blue eyes, and cropped salt-and-pepper hair, the Chief DI had a commanding presence.

He stretched a hand over the desk and with a warm smile said, "Welcome to CID Morven. We're really happy to have you onboard."

"Thank you, sir."

"Call me Dougie, we're pretty informal up here."

Dougie rifled through the snowdrift of papers covering his desk and found her application. "I'm afraid you catch us at a very busy time so you'll be thrown in at the deep end."

"Not a problem sir ... err, Dougie."

"But you're an experienced officer and Beamer speaks very highly of you, so I reckon you'll cope just fine." He scanned the document, adding, "Oh and well done on your arrest of the Strathmurray Slip-in. Dave said you did a brilliant job catching Murphy."

Surprised, she asked, "Dave Newton?"

"Aye. With the cuts in budget," continued Dougie, "the brass in their wisdom have decided that burglaries are no longer a priority." He looked up and smiled, "But thank goodness we've officers like yourself prepared to go above and beyond what's expected."

Morven had assumed robberies weren't sexy enough for CID, and she felt a twinge of guilt for having accused them of laziness.

As if he could read her mind, he said, "It's not like in the movies. Most of our work isn't very glamorous. It mainly involves sitting at a desk trawling through statements, call data, social media and financials."

She nodded in understanding. "It'll make a nice change." Then hesitantly, she said, "You're aware I'm under investigation for the complaint Murphy made against me?"

"Let's cross that bridge when we come to it. In any case, these things take time."

She interpreted that as 'You'll be back in Community before I have to deal with it.'

Dougie leant back in his seat and folded his arms across his chest. "So, I understand you and Dave have worked together before."

The question surfaced like a stain and Morven waited for what she was sure was coming next.

But to her surprise, Dougie didn't go there. Instead, he said, "Now that Dave's up for promotion, I'd like him to take on more responsibility before DI Arnold retires. I thought perhaps you could partner with him, learn the ropes so to speak." Morven stifled a gasp but Dougie didn't appear to notice. "Plus, you're already familiar with the case he's working on – the murder of the librarian."

She returned a dazed nod.

"How does that sound?" He scrutinised her face.

"Err ... fine, yes that's fine," she lied. It was anything but fine.

"Good, in that case I'll introduce you to the team and Dave will bring you up to speed. Any questions?"

What the hell have I let myself in for?

When Morven said nothing, Dougie trotted off to fetch Dave. With a groan, she slumped back in the chair, unable to believe that she'd have Dave Newton as her new partner. If she'd known this would be the case, she would never have applied for the job. And, if Dougie thought this was a good idea, with their history, he was sadly mistaken. They couldn't stand one another.

Morven had a bad feeling about this. A very bad feeling.

Chapter 9

Dougie returned to his office with Dave at his heels.

Dave flashed her a cheeky grin, stuck out his hand and said, "It's a pleasure to see you again Morv."

Dougie looked pleased. "Excellent, I'm glad that's sorted. I'll leave you two to get reacquainted." Turning to Morven, he said, "We'll have a chat later once you've settled in."

After they left Dougie's office, Morven trailed Dave to the briefing area.

She whispered, "Did you know about this?"

"About what?"

"Me and you ... partners?"

Dave turned and wagged a finger at her. "Let's get one thing straight from the start. You and I are NOT partners." He pointed at her. "You work for me. Is that understood?"

She exhaled loudly. "Perfectly."

He raised an eyebrow and waited.

Between clenched teeth, she forced herself to say, "sir."

He rewarded her with a smug grin. "I'm glad we understand each other."

Tosser!

At the back of the briefing area was a portable whiteboard featuring a 'murder wall', the centre of which featured a large photograph of Michael Carrigan. Seeing his face reminded Morven of the reason she was here and she focused on that and not her anger. With the aid of the board, Dave explained what he and the team had discovered since the postmortem on Mike.

After further examination, no fingerprints or forensic evidence had been discovered at the scene or on the body, and the lab reports showed no trace of anything suspicious. The murder weapon used to bludgeon Mike had not been found, and nor had his keys to the library.

Dave had interviewed Mike's wife, family and colleagues and all were in the clear. CID's new digital analyst had begun digging into Mike's background but he'd yet to turn up anything untoward. So far, Mike appeared to have been a happily married man with no vices or skeletons in the cupboard.

Pointing to the flyer that had been found in Mike's gullet, Dave said, "We're concentrating all our efforts on this. A few weeks before Mike died, there was a protest outside the library about the guest speaker at children's story hour."

The flyer depicted a drag queen who wore a Snow White costume, a purple wig and thick, theatrical makeup; a perfect parody of womanhood. When this entertainer had been invited to read to the children, it had prompted a wave of protests from parents, women's groups and religious organisations. Dave handed Morven a copy of a newspaper article similar to the one she'd spotted on Mike's desk. In one picture, a pastor held aloft a sign that read 'No God-given rights for sodomites' and in another a woman waved a banner that stated, 'Stop sexualising our children'.

Although Morven also questioned the wisdom of inviting a drag queen to entertain kids, she kept her opinion to herself.

Dave explained that on the day of the protest the police had been called and, for safety, the event had been cancelled.

He said, "We've been unable to get a hold of the mysterious drag artist who goes by the name Iona Dick — his real name's Barry Mills by the way — but I've talked to his agent. Says Barry's buggered off on holiday and isn't responding to his calls. Our tech guy hasn't been able to trace him either so we'll have to wait until he surfaces."

"Did Mike arrange the event?" asked Morven.

Dave nodded. "Very good, detective. It was organised through Barry's agent." He pointed to the protesters, "Which means we may be looking at one of these activists."

Morven wouldn't have termed them activists but again didn't share her thoughts. She'd pick her battles with Dave.

He said, "We're trying to identify all the people involved in the protest and eliminate them from our enquiries." He turned to look at her, "and that's where you can help. But first I need to introduce you to Ross, our tech guy."

Dave led her to a desk where a man in his thirties pored over a collage of photographs from the protest.

Dave said, "Ross, I'd like you to meet Morven who's joined the team today."

Ross looked up and gave her a smile that would snap knicker elastic at fifty paces. Tall with rugged good looks, Ross Forsyth looked like he could grace the cover of GQ magazine. She noted the absence of a wedding ring and any family photographs on his desk.

"Morven will be helping you on the Cardigan case."

"You mean the Carrigan case?" corrected Morven, wondering if she'd misheard.

Dave gave a contrite look. "The bloke was so squeaky clean, we call it the Cardigan case ... err ... just not outside these four walls."

She gave him a disapproving look, and asked Ross how she could help.

Dave butted in. "Before you get started Morv, be a sweetheart and fetch us a coffee."

It was only day one and already she wanted to throat punch Dave Newton. But, before she could protest, they were interrupted by Dougie who rushed from his office with a phone plastered to his ear.

"Dave," he called, "there's been another murder."

***

Kerry sat in front of the Faculty Head's desk and fidgeted. She'd been summoned to his office for what his PA described as a 'brief chat'. She wondered if the meeting concerned the research proposal she'd submitted to the Ethics Committee, in which case she expected it to be more like a dressing down from the headmaster.

Professor McLaughlan was in his late fifties and wore a well-cut grey suit which Kerry considered more befitting of the Business Studies department. The walls of his office were covered in certificates, awards and photographs of him in a ceremonial gown and mortar board.

An eminently regarded sociologist, McLaughlan's appointment had been instrumental in promoting Lothian's position in the university league tables. However, other than a fleeting introduction when she'd started, Kerry had had little interaction with him. Until now.

McLaughlan steepled his hands and regarded her. He spoke in a plummy accent and said, "As a member of Stonewall's Diversity Champion scheme, we must always respect self-identified gender status. I believe Professor Owen has explained this to you."

Kerry unclenched her jaw and aimed for a neutral tone. "I understand and, when dealing with students, I always respect their pronouns. However, when it comes to scientific research, it's important to record facts, not beliefs."

McLaughlan's brow furrowed. "Professor Owen's concerned about the potential backlash and I admit he has a point. Given the bigger picture, I don't see the harm in rewording the question so William can continue his study and we can prevent reprisals."

Ah so this is about William's survey, not my own research.

"With respect Professor, Stonewall would have us believe that being a woman has nothing to do with biology and everything to do with a subjective inner sense. However, I believe sex and gender identity are different things and being male or female is a biological fact that cannot be changed."

McLaughlan made a dismissive gesture with his hand. "You're entitled to your beliefs but that isn't the problem. The issue is when these beliefs prejudice research."

Kerry shot back. "Which is exactly my point. The belief in gender identity — and it's a belief, not a fact — is impacting academic research. If we break data down by gender identity and not biological sex, the result may distort our understanding of social and medical phenomena."

He glared at her in disbelief. "I can't think of a single example where it would make any difference."

"Well, I can think of multiple examples, including William's study of sexual cybercrime."

From her bag, Kerry retrieved a bundle of documents pertaining to her research and placed them in front of her. She flicked through the papers to find a table of statistics which she passed to McLaughlin saying, "Recording gender identity alone could have a significant impact on the accuracy and reliability of crime statistics."

She pointed to Scottish government data showing the offending patterns between the sexes. "98% of sexual offences are committed by males. If William includes even a small number of men who identify as women, this will skew the female criminal statistics. That's why his research must record biological sex."

McLaughlin frowned. "Surely, transwomen are a special case?"

"What, like priests, scout leaders and gymnastic coaches? They exhibit the same male offending pattern."

He pursed his lips and thought for a moment. "There will always be edge cases such as this but we have to balance these with what's politically expedient."

Kerry resisted the urge to point out this was hardly an edge case since much research was needed to expressly examine women and girls as a specific social category and sex class. McLaughlin and Owen ought to know this so why were they being so obtuse? It simply didn't make sense.

He said, "I have the university's reputation to consider and it's already a struggle to attract funding without us also courting bad publicity. We can't risk being smeared as transphobes."

In a measured pitch, Kerry replied, "Both Lothian and William's reputations will suffer if we produce deeply flawed research. Are you prepared to risk that just to appease Stonewall?"

McLaughlan gazed at her for several long moments. "I think it might be best if another member of the faculty took over the supervision of William's project and you find something else to interest you."

His words stung as if he'd slapped her across the face. And this was before he knew about her proposal.

With a tight smile, he rose and slid the document back towards her signalling an end to the meeting. "In any case, to be successful in academia, you'll want to carry out your own research and obtain grants for this."

McLaughlan's words sounded more like a threat than helpful advice.

***

Dave wove the Audi through heavy traffic to Strathmurray Medical Centre, a modern brick-built surgery tacked onto the back of a high street pharmacy. Morven knew it well although it wasn't the place she and Ollie were registered with.

Dave flashed his badge at the uniform stationed at the entrance and parked between a team car and the forensics van. It was gusty but the rain had eased to a drizzle and Morven pulled the collar of her thin jacket against the cold as they made their way inside.

The area had already been sealed and a length of police tape fluttered across the railings either side of the doorway. Morven and Dave checked in with the officer responsible for the crime scene who issued them forensic suits to put on. Inside, they filed past the empty reception and into the gloomy waiting area. Chairs lined the perimeter of the rectangular space, off of which were doors to the consulting rooms. In one corner was a television mounted high on the wall above a children's table littered with wooden toys. The room was empty except for a woman in a cleaning smock who sat weeping. Morven recognised the uniformed officer comforting her; it was her old partner.

Rob made towards her, and Morven thought it strange to meet him in her new capacity.

"You the first responder?" asked Dave.

Rob acknowledged with a glum nod.

"What you got for us?"

Rob explained that the cleaner had pitched up as usual that morning and discovered the body of one of the GPs. He pointed to the examination room in the far corner. "It's Alastair McNab, he's in there. Forensics are just finishing up."

"Any signs of a break-in?" said Dave.

"None and the cleaner found the place locked." Rob hesitated and then added, "It looks like he's been injected with something."

"Leave the investigations to us son," said Dave. "And keep the cleaner here, we'll need a statement from her."

Dave strode in the direction of McNab's room, and Morven and Rob exchanged a look that expressed exactly what they each thought of him.

"He's your partner?" whispered Rob, incredulous. When she nodded, he said, "It's not too late to change your mind."

As she followed Dave, she muttered, "Believe me, I'm considering it."

The scene that greeted her sent shivers down her spine. A man of indeterminate age sat slumped over a desk with a syringe sticking out of the left side of his neck. His eyes were wide open, frozen in terror.

Two Scene of Crime Officers in white overalls with hoods were packing up their cases. One of the SOCOs recognised Dave and said, "It's all yours. Pathologist is on her way."

Crouching, Morven peered at the syringe which was fully depressed. Whatever it had contained was in McNab's body, straight into the main artery in his neck. There was surprisingly little blood.

The other SOCO said, "You might want to look at what's on his desk."

Next to McNab's right hand, which the SOCOs had bagged, was a blank prescription pad. Scrawled in large numbers across it in red pen was the number '20'. Dave and Morven exchanged a look; they both knew what this meant.

Morven had a poke around the room which was otherwise tidy and showed no signs of a struggle. Dave prodded the mouse with his pen and the computer whirred to life. On-screen appeared a record for whom they presumed was McNab's last patient, a man called Gavin Templeton. Morven jotted down his details.

Dave said to her, "We'll need McNab's patient list and his diary for yesterday."

The forensic pathologist appeared and cast a dispassionate eye over the scene. Dr Hellberg wore white overalls with a hood that concealed her thick auburn hair. Without formalities, she got straight to work.

Crouching to get a better view of the syringe, she remarked, "Straight into the carotid by the looks of things." She produced a thermometer and took McNab's temperature.

After a few minutes of watching her, Dave said, "You know what I'm going to ask, Doc."

She stood to face him, hands on hips. "And you know what I'm going to reply, detective."

"Just a rough guestimate," he said flashing Hellberg a smile that appeared to have no effect.

"It's difficult to estimate the time of death," said Hellberg. "There are so many variables to contend with." She glanced around the room and then checked a weather app on her phone. "But given that he's inside and he's quite slender, and then factoring in overnight temperatures, I'd estimate he's been dead for about ten to twelve hours."

"So, sometime yesterday evening, from say six o'clock?" ventured Dave.

She nodded, "But you'll need to wait for the PM." She glanced at her watch and added, "We've cleared the backlog so I can schedule it in for eleven this morning."

They thanked Hellberg and left her to it while they went to speak to the cleaner. Her name was Louise and she'd worked at the surgery for almost five years. Mid-forties, pretty, with short blonde hair, she was clearly in shock. Dave asked a WPC to make her hot sweet tea. Morven bit her tongue; she'd have asked Rob.

Once Louise had stopped shaking, Dave sat beside her and inquired if she was up to answering questions. Louise nodded; her face was streaked with lines of black mascara. He handed her a tissue and Morven was surprised by Dave's gentle consideration which seemed at odds with the way he treated his female colleagues.

Louise recounted how she'd arrived at 6:30 am as normal and used her swipe card to gain entry. After vacuuming the foyer and waiting area, she'd made a start on the examination rooms. She discovered the body about an hour into her shift and called the police.

Dave asked if she ever spoke to the medical staff and she said it was rare for their paths to cross, although sometimes the practice manager arrived as she was leaving.

"So, you've never talked to Dr McNab?" asked Dave.

She shook her head. "I've seen him around when I've come to the office on occasion but we've never spoken."

Dave thanked her and asked her to wait until she'd given a formal statement.

Another staff member arrived and they ushered her into one of the small offices. A petite blonde in her forties, her name was Steph and she was the practice manager. She took the news of McNab's death badly, explaining the GP was married with two young children.

Steph said tearfully, "His wife and kids are on holiday with her family at CenterParcs."

Morven didn't relish being the one to inform the widow.

They quizzed Steph about McNab's schedule the previous day, and she recalled he'd done house calls in the morning, including one to a local women's refuge, and then held a surgery for patients in the afternoon. When she'd left around 6pm, his door was still closed and she'd assumed he was working late, which wasn't unusual.

They were interrupted by Dougie's arrival. The Chief DI gave them a nod, the lines between his eyebrows deeply furrowed. Morven and Dave left Steph in the hands of a uniform and followed the gaffer out to the car park. They huddled around Dave's car, pulling their jackets against the cold wind.

Dougie said, "I've just taken a look and spoken to the pathologist." He shoved his hands deep into his trouser pockets and in a low voice said, "It seems we have a situation on our hands."

"No doubt about it," said Dave.

Dougie said, "Finish up here and then head back to the station. I'll assemble the team." He then turned to Morven. "As first days go, this is about as bad as it gets."

Morven could not disagree.

Chapter 10

The atmosphere in the CID offices felt different to earlier, and Morven couldn't believe only a few hours had passed. Her annoyance at Dave's attitude towards her seemed unimportant now, and this was hammered home by the photograph of Dr McNab now pinned to the board next to Mike's.

Dougie had wasted no time in assembling another squad to handle McNab's murder. It was headed up by a bear of a man called Bill Arnold, a grizzled senior detective in his early fifties.

She counted at least twenty officers, with only a few she recognised including the cyber analyst Ross who'd pin-up looks no female would forget. With insufficient seating in the briefing area, staff stood or leant against walls and radiators. Dougie paced at the front and began the meeting.

"You'll have heard by now," he said, "that we've another murder." He pointed to McNab's picture. "This time, a general practitioner called Alistair McNab. Although the method appears to be different, the killer's left the same sign." He indicated a photograph of the prescription pad which had been enlarged to clearly show the number twenty.

There were mutterings of disquiet and Dougie waited for the room to settle. He shook his head as if he couldn't quite believe what he was saying. "We need to know what connects these two victims. Were they friends? Was Carrigan a patient? Is there a family or work connection? Were they in Scouts together or at the same sports club?" He jabbed a finger at the photographs. "Something or someone connects them."

He let that sink in for a few moments before continuing. "Before I hand you over to Dave for an update, for those of you new to the team, I'd like to introduce you to Ross."

He pointed Mr Handsome out and everyone turned, and Ross raised a hand.

"Ross is our HOLMES expert and absolutely everything — and I mean everything, no matter how trivial it might seem — must go through him." He cast a stern look over his officers and added, "Needless to say, all leave is cancelled and overtime is available."

Dougie then yielded the floor to Dave who introduced the new faces to the rest of the team, including Morven. He then assigned each a specific task which he jotted on the white board. He announced they'd reconvene later after McNab's postmortem.

Morven had just enough time to visit the loo and grab another hot drink before Dave said it was time to head to the mortuary.

The coffee curdled in her stomach at the prospect.

***

While Dave spoke to the receptionist at the mortuary, Morven joined the huddle of other ashen-faced detectives in the foyer. The mood was sombre and no one spoke. She'd seen a dead body before — a visit to the morgue was part of the training — but she'd never witnessed a postmortem.

Dave appeared at her side clutching a packet of mints. He offered her a sweet and when she shook her head, he said, "Take one, it helps."

Morven didn't have long to wait to find out what he meant. A mortuary assistant ushered them into an anteroom where they were issued with Wellington boots and gowns, before entering the main theatre or, as Dave called it, the 'cutting room'.

The smell hit her immediately: a pungent mixture of formalin and disinfectant mingled with bodily fluids. She sucked harder on the mint, grateful Dave had cajoled her into eating one. She hoped it would last.

McNab's body lay face up on a stainless-steel gurney, naked save for a white linen cloth draped over the groin. Morven wondered why they bothered with dignity in a place like this. She'd watched enough episodes of *Silent Witness* to know what happened next. The syringe had been removed from McNab's neck and neatly bagged as evidence.

Dr Hellberg bustled in wearing white wellies and scrubs. She greeted them brusquely and got straight to work. First, she carried out a visual examination of the exterior, aided by two mortuary assistants who helped turn the cadaver, noting her findings in a voice recorder. She checked every surface and crevice, even between the toes and buttocks. Other than the wound on the neck, there were no signs of trauma.

Morven watched with a mixture of fascination and revulsion as Hellberg then made a Y-shaped incision from both shoulders, joining at the sternum, and continuing down to the pubic bone. She then moved aside the skin and underlying tissues, and opened the front of the rib cage to expose the cavity.

As Hellberg inspected each organ, Morven felt the acid rise in her throat. Dave flicked a look at her and pressed another mint into her palm. She popped it in her mouth with a grateful nod.

The pathologist looked at her audience and explained that she was examining each organ to determine whether it was healthy or not.

With a wry smile, she said, "I know it's blindingly obvious it's murder but we need to rule out natural causes."

She spoke with enthusiasm as she removed, prodded and weighed each lump of human offal. Hellberg paid close attention to the heart before opening the deceased's throat. She detached the large strap muscle that ran from the base of the neck to the ear, and pushed it aside to reveal the tissues beneath.

She beckoned them forward. "Come," she said, pointing to a gory mass within McNab's neck. "This is what we call the Holy Trinity; the carotid artery, the jugular vein, and the vagus nerve."

They took it in turns to peer in. Morven felt the bile rise in her own neck and swallowed it down. Hellberg caught her expression and asked if she was going to be sick. Heads turned and Morven felt the colour rising in her cheeks. She shook her head.

Don't hurl. Whatever you do, don't hurl.

Hellberg continued, "Whoever did this knew exactly where to strike. The needle pierced the vagus nerve and this stopped his heart." She cast an eye over her audience and focused on Dave. "There's scientific dispute about the exact mechanism, but death would have been almost instantaneous, regardless of whether there was anything in the syringe or not."

Dave asked, "Any idea what the injection contained?"

"We won't know until we get the tox report but my guess is that the needle killed him before anything entered his bloodstream."

Hellberg appeared pensive for a few moments before musing aloud. "But if I was going to murder someone, this would be a belt and braces approach: stick him with a needle and if that didn't work, the drugs would."

She almost looked impressed and Morven reminded herself never to get on the wrong side of the pathologist.

Hellberg pursed her lips. "Your killer may have some knowledge of anatomy. I've students who'd struggle to locate the neurovascular bundle so precisely. And whoever did this would not have needed much strength, not if they were accurate."

Dave said, "Can you be any more specific about the time of death?"

"Early evening, from approximately six o'clock until eight, I'd say."

"Anything else?" He almost sounded desperate.

She removed her gloves saying she'd expedite the tox report and have it sent over. Dave thanked her and the group shuffled back to the anteroom to the soft rustle of the assistants cleaning up.

After disrobing, Morven went to the toilet and threw up the contents of her stomach. She drank from the cold-water tap, swilling the water around in her mouth, but couldn't banish the taste nor the smell of the morgue.

Dave stood alone in the foyer, hands shoved into the pockets of his trousers. "I thought you'd have a tougher constitution than that, Morv?"

"My name's Morven, and I don't think I'll ever get used to that."

She swept past him and he laughed. Bloody laughed!

***

They drove in silence back towards the station, Dave weaving the car confidently through the lunchtime traffic. Morven watched passersby go about their daily business unaware they'd a murderer in their midst.

Dave pulled up outside a sandwich shop. "Want anything?" he asked, the corner of his mouth twitching.

"Not unless you want me to ruin your upholstery."

Chuckling, he left her and bounded into the café. He returned with a bacon roll and a cardboard tray with two takeaway cups. The smell made her want to puke.

He handed her a drink. "Got you a tea, you'll feel better with something in your stomach."

"How can you eat," she said, "after seeing that?"

"You get used to it."

Morven doubted it. Sipping her tea, she watched him surreptitiously as he drove. She couldn't figure Dave out. One minute he made her feel like a silly wee schoolgirl, the next he was being considerate. Not knowing whether she'd get 'good Dave' or 'bad Dave' frustrated the hell out of her. She wondered what sort of partner he was to Cavendish, unable to imagine an ice maiden like her putting up with him.

Back at the station, Morven noticed their numbers had swelled and extra desks had been brought in. Dave went in search of Dougie and Morven took the opportunity to brush her teeth and splash water on her face in the toilet. She then joined the rest of the team in the briefing area. The roller blinds had been pulled down over each external facing window. She perched beside Ross, the tech guy. He smiled and asked how her first day was going, and the look she gave him made him chuckle. His warm brown eyes sparkled with mirth and she caught a faint whiff of his aftershave.

Dougie appeared with Dave in tow and called the team to order. Pacing in front of the 'murder wall' Dougie pointed to the photographs.

In a solemn tone, he said, "Serial homicide is the unlawful killing of two or more victims in separate events. It is an intentional, premeditated act, not something carried out on impulse or in response to a provocation or threat." He cast a grim eye over his officers. "It's extremely rare but unfortunately there's little doubt that this is exactly what we're dealing with."

He paused to let his words sink in before warning his officers that he expected the press to be all over this like a rash. From now on, he explained, all communications had to go through him and the Press Liaison Officer. Later, they would release a statement with basic information confirming time, date and locus, and nothing else.

Dougie pointed to the windows. "The blinds must remain closed at all times. We've already had a drone hovering outside the building."

He also reminded them of the need to use the confidential bins to dispose of paperwork as this would be incinerated, since journalists were not above raking through dustbins for scraps. He then handed over to Dave for an update on the investigation into Mike's death.

Dave explained that although no murder weapon had been found, the pathologist thought a hammer had likely been used. There was little forensic evidence from the scene or on the body, and nothing on the leaflet. And, since several hundred flyers had been printed and distributed, they were unlikely to be able to trace where it had come from.

Dave flicked on the wall-mounted television screen to display video footage from the recent protest. "Given the leaflet rammed down Mike's throat, we're focusing our attention on the demonstration outside the library. Drag-queen story hour was one of a series of events that Mike scheduled to attract visitors, but it's the only one that drew criticism."

He paused the video and zoomed in on the pastor and a couple of women holding placards. "We've been able to identify a number of people and most are local parents. There are also a few seasoned activists amongst them, some of whom have shown up on our systems. We've eliminated most of them."

He pointed to a picture of Iona Dick and said, "We've been unable to locate Barry Mills. According to his agent, he's gone on his annual pilgrimage to Brighton, but we'll interview him as soon as he resurfaces. In the meantime, I've asked his agent to contact Barry since he's not returning our calls."

Dave explained that Janet, one of the library staff, had suffered a mild stroke shortly after Mike's death but was now well enough to be interviewed. Bill Arnold then introduced his new squad and summarised the findings from the postmortem on Dr McNab, stressing the pathologist's suspicion that the killer may have some knowledge of anatomy.

Ross asked, "So, are we looking for someone in the medical profession, or who's had training?"

Morven suspected Ross was already formulating searches with which to interrogate HOLMES.

"Possibly," said Dougie, "which immediately points a finger of suspicion at McNab's colleagues." He turned to a couple of detectives and said, "We need to know their movements and also which patients were in that building yesterday."

"And if they've a library card," muttered Bill Arnold. Even Dougie smiled.

One of the women — Morven couldn't remember her name — reported that there was no CCTV footage from around the surgery or carpark. The cameras had stopped working the day before, but they'd recovered footage from the High Street which they were sifting through. She said it'd take a few hours.

Dave said, "The failure of the CCTV is suspicious so we need to know who had access."

One of Bill's team offered to look into it.

Dougie paced and said, "Currently, the only link we have between these murders is the message the killer left. We need to find a connection between Mike

Carrigan and Dr McNab." He pointed to the exhibits on the wall behind him. "What does the number twenty signify?"

This was met with silence.

Dougie then cast an eye over his team and said, "It starts now and it doesn't end until we catch this killer."

As the officers returned to their desks, Dave strode towards Morven carrying a large pile of folders.

"We'll talk to Janet tomorrow," he said. "She's home from the hospital. In the meantime, I suggest you read the witness statements." He plonked the files on the desk next to Ross's with a thud, adding, "After you've done that, see if Ross has a use for you."

As Dave strutted off, she caught Ross's eye and they shared a pained smile.

"C'mon," said Ross, "let's get a coffee and then I'll give you a tour of HOLMES."

If not for Ross, thought Morven, she might well have run for the hills.

Chapter 11

Kerry took out her anger on a carrot which she diced furiously into tiny pieces. Her husband perched beside her on a stool and listened as she recounted her meeting with Professor McLaughlan.

"Stonewall and their ilk are harming research and stifling free intellectual debate," said Kerry, "and anyone who dares to question their approach is shut down with allegations of bigotry."

Andrew collected up fallen chunks of carrot and rinsed them under the cold tap. "I don't disagree but are you sure you know what you're doing?"

She ceased chopping, put down the knife and looked at him. The two had met in their twenties at the university chess club, and they'd married soon after graduating. While Kerry had gained her PhD and reared two children, Andrew had climbed the ranks in an investment bank. Now, as a VP, his role demanded long hours and regular travel, meaning family time was precious. Kerry worried about him carrying extra pounds, the result of his sedentary job, and tried to cook fresh healthy meals whenever he was home.

"No, I'm not sure" she said, "but someone's got to make a stand. Academia should be a safe space for discussion but, because of people like Owen, everyone's afraid to question this ideology. But nothing should be off limits, and all knowledge should be open to scrutiny."

She'd described the professor's reaction to her insistence that William must phrase the question in his study to be about biological sex, not gender identity.

Kerry picked up the knife and began chopping again, sending slices of onion flying.

"You don't need to convince me," said Andrew, "I'm just worried about the consequences for you. I've read about academics being hounded out of their jobs for exercising free speech."

Kerry scooped up the onion and added it to the bubbling soup mixture. "What's the worst that can happen?"

"You don't want to lose your job."

"Gender critical views are protected so it's not like they can fire me."

Andrew looked unconvinced. "They can make your life unpleasant though."

Kerry stirred the pot with a wooden spoon. "I love working at Lothian." She slammed the lid on the pot and turned to face him. "But when did we become an Orwellian 'Ministry of Truth' that tells students what to think, instead of how to think?"

Andrew slipped his arms around her waist and pulled her to him. "I love it that you care enough to speak up."

"Academia is the one area that must always hold the line and allow open intellectual enquiry."

"As long as you're aware of what you're up against." He chuckled, "I'll wager that when Kuzi's PhD proposal naming you as primary supervisor lands on McLaughlan's desk, he'll have a purple fit."

"That's how these activists operate. They want us so afraid of losing our livelihoods that we'll stay silent."

He trailed kisses from her neck to her collarbone. "Unfortunately for them, they've absolutely no idea how stubborn and brilliant my beautiful wife is." His mouth dipped lower just as their daughter appeared.

Erin stopped dead and stared at her parents in wide-eyed disgust. "Eew," she groaned, "that's minging."

She spun on her heel and fled, leaving Kerry and Andrew squealing with laughter.

***

Morven had just gotten out the bath and put on pyjamas when the doorbell went. She peeked out the bedroom blinds to see Natalie on the doorstep, her mop of brown curls instantly recognisable.

Pulling on her dressing gown, she rushed downstairs.

"Thought you might need this," said Natalie handing her a bottle of red wine.

Forgetting her exhaustion, Morven laughed, "I'm glad to see you, the house feels lonely without Ollie."

She immediately regretted her words, aware Natalie also returned to an empty home since splitting with her long-term partner Linzi.

"How is he?" asked Natalie.

Morven shrugged. "As far as I know, he's fine but he's not replying to my messages. I think they call it ghosting."

"Ooh listen to you, one day in CID and you're all urban dictionary."

Morven giggled; Natalie always cheered her up.

They sat at the kitchen table, sipping the wine and chatted about Natalie's latest disastrous dating attempt. In her early forties, she'd been finding it increasingly difficult to meet other women. Recently, she'd signed up to a popular dating app for lesbians and Morven asked if she'd swiped right on anyone suitable.

Natalie put her head in her hands. "They're all trans women," she moaned. Spotting her friend's bewilderment, she added, "Men who identify as women."

Morven felt she ought to know this since Natalie had been vocal about the clash between trans rights and women's rights for several years, to the extent she'd joined a campaign group.

Still confused, Morven asked, "But they're still attracted to women?"

"Yes, so they claim to be lesbians although they're male and fancy women. When I pointed out to one of them that I wasn't interested because I'm same sex attracted, he accused me of being a sexual racist and had me blocked on the app."

Morven couldn't believe what she was hearing. "What the hell's a sexual racist?"

"Well, apparently, if lesbians don't want to sleep with men who identify as women, this is akin to racism."

Morven shook her head in disbelief and let Natalie rant on about how it was an encroachment on her boundaries. When they finished the bottle, Morven opened another. When Natalie inquired about Morven's first day, it was her turn to put her head in her hands and groan.

"You'll never guess who they've partnered me with?"

Natalie gave a quizzical look. "Who?"

"Dave bloody Newton."

Natalie gasped. "No, surely not. You mean Dave as in 'Blackford Gate' Dave?"

Morven nodded and took a large gulp from the glass Natalie handed her. They'd been friends for long enough that Natalie knew the story well.

After Morven had passed her probation, she and Dave had worked together briefly. They'd both been part of a raid on a haulage company called Blackford Logistics which operated out of a unit on the Strathmurray industrial estate. The business was a front for drug smuggling and Vice had discovered they were expecting a large shipment of heroin. What no one realised was that Blackford were also trafficking Albanian criminals so, when four truckloads of armed men spilled out into the estate, the operation went to rat shit.

Morven and Dave gave chase but found themselves cornered by two knife-wielding thugs. She had been knocked semi-unconscious and Dave slashed across the throat. Although he survived with Morven's help, to this day, Dave maintained that, had he been partnered with a male officer, his injury would never have occurred.

"Aye, the very same Dave," said Morven.

"But I thought he didn't like working with women?" said Natalie, still gawping.

"So did I but maybe Dougie didn't get the memo."

"And how is he towards you?"

Morven rolled her eyes, "Exactly as you'd expect. But everyone else seems pleasant enough."

"Jesus," said Natalie, "and I thought my day was crap."

Natalie was a senior midwife at the local hospital. They'd become friends after Morven and Mark had moved in next door to her and Linzi, before Ollie was born. Since Natalie's mother had passed away, she had reduced her shifts and worked part time for Morven helping with childcare. The arrangement suited Natalie who'd never been able to have children, and she was a godsend for Morven.

"What happened?" asked Morven taking another swig. The wine was working its magic and she felt relaxed for the first time in days.

Natalie's stories were often amusing and sometimes tragic. Morven's favourite tale was of her removing a ring piercing with pliers from the labia of a woman about to give birth.

"A state-of-the-art cock-up is what's happened."

Natalie produced her mobile and showed her a photograph of a computer screen. Morven peered at it, realising that it was a system for recording a newborn baby's discharge summary. Next to fields for names was one for 'Gender Identity' with a dropdown menu listing everything from non-binary to pangender.

"What the hell," said Morven, zooming in on the picture, "is this for real?"

"Too right it's for real. The NHS spent millions on this new IT system, yet I can't enter a baby's sex, only its gender identity." Topping up their glasses, Natalie said, "It's absolutely ludicrous."

Natalie explained that the system was designed to record vital health information which is shared with GPs, health visitors and other hospitals, and forms part of the patient's permanent NHS health record.

"What are you going to do?" asked Morven.

"I've asked for a meeting with management because this is downright dangerous. Of all the places where it's imperative to know a person's sex, healthcare is it."

Natalie produced a leaflet about breastfeeding from her handbag and passed it to Morven. As Morven scanned it, Natalie said, "Not once does this mention 'mother'. Instead it uses the terms 'birthing parent' and 'chest feeder' and all in the name of inclusivity in case we offend any men."

Natalie swallowed the remainder of her glass. "I've had enough Morven. Leaflets are one thing, but this IT system is quite another."

"What are your colleagues saying?"

"Everyone's too scared to say a word. There's a climate of fear when it comes to this. If you dare to say anything you're branded a transphobe."

Natalie put down her glass and stood up. "But to hell with it, I'm blowing the whistle."

Chapter 12

Morven arrived early for work next morning to find Dave already at his desk.

He glanced up, and said, "Afternoon."

"It's not even seven o'clock," she snapped.

"Get out of the wrong side of bed, did we?"

Christ, he knew how to push her buttons and it seemed to amuse him. Muttering obscenities in her head, she stalked off in search of coffee. After the wine she'd drunk, she'd had a disturbed night's sleep, her dreams filled with jumbled images of postmortems on sexless babies.

Ross was in the kitchenette and he greeted her with a disarming smile. "Back for another fun-filled day?" he chuckled.

"Just try and keep me away," she laughed.

They returned to their desks and Ross spent the next couple of hours patiently helping her input data into HOLMES. He explained how the system collated information to provide officers with a real-time view of live operations, and to manage serious and complex crime investigations. Morven regretted not spending more time reading the manual Cavendish had given her.

Mid-morning, Dave sidled up to her desk and announced it was time for them to speak to Janet.

"I'll just pop to the loo," said Morven grabbing her handbag, "I'll meet you in the car."

"Women," muttered Dave, striding off with his suit jacket slung over his shoulder.

Ross met Morven's eye and smiled, "Why do I get the feeling there's going to be another murder."

"A brutal and bloody one," she said with a wink.

Oh God, did I actually just wink at Mr Eye Candy?

***

Half an hour later, Morven and Dave sat in overstuffed armchairs in Janet's living room. The central heating was on full blast and the room felt oppressive and suffocating. Bundled beneath a blanket in a wingback chair, Janet seemed even more frail than Morven remembered. The right-hand side of her face drooped slightly, and her pallor was grey.

Janet's daughter Meghan had shown them into the modern terraced house. The room was furnished in antiques and chintz more suited to a period property, and every shelf and surface was cluttered with family photographs and blank-eyed china figurines.

Meghan brought a silver tea tray laden with patterned porcelain cups and fingers of shortbread, and then departed. Morven nibbled on the shortbread, the first food she'd had all morning, and produced her pocketbook, content to let Dave do the talking.

"Take your time," said Dave to the elderly woman, "and please say if you get tired."

Janet returned a crooked smile, a residual sign of the stroke she'd suffered, and her cup rattled in its saucer.

"Can you tell us about the protest against Drag Queen Story Hour?"

"Oh that," slurred Janet, the corner of her mouth turning up.

Was it disdain or as a result of the stroke, wondered Morven.

Janet wiped her mouth of drool and continued. "That was Mike's idea. He was always looking at ways to grow visitor numbers. There have been deep budget cuts and he was worried the library would close and we'd be made redundant."

"What sort of things did he try?" asked Dave.

"Various initiatives — author visits, gaming sessions, 'computing for the terrified' lessons — but nothing that really increased footfall." Janet took another slurp of tea and gazed at them through cloudy eyes. "Young people don't seem to want to read anymore. Despite our best efforts to instil a love of literature and learning, they prefer YouTube, TikTok and Netflix."

You could be describing my own child.

"How did drag queen story hour come about?" he asked.

"Mike spotted the advert in a trade publication and contacted him ... I mean her ..." Janet gave a mirthless laugh. "You know what I mean."

"Did Barry ... err, Iona Dick .... visit the library before the event?"

Janet pulled a face at mention of Barry's stage name before explaining that everything had been arranged over the phone. Mike had advertised the event in the press, on their web site, and put up posters in the library. He'd also had flyers printed by an online company and dropped around local businesses.

"Did you receive complaints before the day of the event?"

"Not that I'm aware of, so it was a shock when all these protesters showed up and started shouting at us." Janet's blue-veined hands trembled and Dave asked if she was alright to continue.

Janet nodded, "It was horrible, like we were under siege. And the worse part was the abuse we got from people we knew. It was so bad, we'd to shut our doors. It's the first time we've ever had to do that."

"What did Barry do?" asked Morven.

Janet told them that he was already in costume with his makeup on, and had to be escorted by the police from the building to his car.

"People were throwing things at him," she said.

Morven knew this, having read the incident report. She asked, "Did Barry seem surprised at the turn of events?"

Janet pursed her lips. "Turns out it's not the first time it's happened to him. I just wish his agent had warned us beforehand."

Dave showed Janet photographs taken at the protest and pointed to a couple of women holding placards, "We've been able to identify many of the protesters but not these two. Do you know who they are?"

"No," said Janet, "I've never seen them before."

"Were any more angry or aggressive than the others?" asked Morven.

Janet stared at Morven. "They were all angry and aggressive. I feel anxious just thinking about it."

Morven glanced at Dave, who took the hint and thanked Janet for her time. He left his card in case she thought of anything else.

They drove back to the station saying little. When the car was stationary at lights, Dave asked, "You ever been to a drag queen story hour?"

Morven laughed. "Funnily enough, yes I have."

He looked her wide-eyed. "Seriously? What did you think?"

She told him how she'd once taken Ollie to a show when they were on holiday at the sea side. "He was really young and to be honest, he loved it, it was all glitter, fairytales and daft wigs."

He shook his head. "But what possesses a grown man to dress up in women's clothes and read stories to young children?"

"Well, when you put it like that ..."

"I wouldn't take my daughter," he said. "I guess it's the job, I've come across too many perverts and paedos."

The news surprised Morven. She didn't know he had a daughter, and it was the first time he'd revealed anything personal. She wondered what Cavendish made of the child. She didn't fancy the girl's chances with her as a stepmother – she was straight out of a Grimm's fairytale.

"What age is she?" asked Morven.

"Nine. Lives with her mother. And Ollie?"

"Fifteen. Lives with his father."

Dave glanced at her but said nothing. A pall of damp silence hung in the air.

***

"McNab's last patient," said Bill, "was a man called Gavin Templeton."

DI Bill Arnold paced in front of the murder wall and pointed to Dr McNab's picture. He explained that he had interviewed Templeton who denied seeing the doctor, despite the surgery's internal booking-in system showing him as registering for his appointment. The medical staff confirmed that, on arrival, patients entered their date of birth into the system which let the doctor know they were waiting.

Bill said, "Templeton claims he was still at work and his alibi checks out. We have CCTV of him leaving his work at six, and his wife confirmed he was home by half past. They went to Nando's and then the cinema, and we have footage of him at both venues."

"Which begs the question," said Dougie, "just who the hell was in McNab's surgery? Answer that and we'll have our killer."

Bill reported that they'd interviewed other patients in the waiting area and the staff but no one had been able to give a description beyond a vague 'male in black joggies and hoodie, average height and build, in his thirties or forties'.

The arrival of the Assistant Chief Constable and the Press Liaison Officer heralded the end of the meeting. Morven returned to her desk and began sifting through everything connected to McNab, although by now she knew the contents by heart.

When Ross placed a mug of coffee on her desk, she gave him a grateful smile ... and tried not to stare too long. He held her gaze. The moment was brought to a halt by the ringing of Morven's desk phone. Seeing it was from Rob, she immediately picked up.

After brief chit chat, Rob explained they'd received a call from a detective in Sussex Police informing them about the discovery of a body in a flat in Brighton. The officer had identified the dead man and found messages on his mobile requesting that he contacted Strathmurray police. She asked the name of the deceased.

Morven gasped, "Bloody hell."

***

Lothian's Ethics and Integrity Committee convened every fortnight to oversee policies, procedures and practices across the University. When a school had an application that they deemed risky or where they lacked expertise, they escalated it to this cross-faculty group for consideration. Kuzi's recycled PhD proposal on detransitioners was one such case.

With her stomach twisting in knots, Kerry accompanied Kuzi to the classroom where the committee met. She wished Kuzi luck and they entered and took a seat. About a dozen members sat around tables arranged in a rectangle. At the end sat the committee chair, Professor Clements from the Faculty of Science, who invited them to take a seat and he made the introductions. Present were Professor Owen and Dr Edwina Taylor, the Head of Diversity, Equality and Inclusion.

Clements invited Kuzi to make her pitch and Kerry listened with a mixture of nerves and excitement. From her own research, Kerry knew there was a dearth of data on what happens to transgender patients long-term after they receive interventions. It was an area so understudied that if Kuzi could get approval for her research, it would have an enormous impact.

Kuzi had rehearsed her presentation with Kerry and together they'd pre-empted questions and objections. The committee also had a copy of her proposal in front of them. Kuzi spoke clearly and confidently.

After outlining her qualifications, training and experience as a clinical psychologist, she spoke passionately about her therapeutic work with sufferers of gender dysphoria and transgender people. She reported how young girls with Rapid Onset Gender Dysphoria (ROGD) now made up the majority of her clients. Many had underlying mental health problems and some were autistic, and she described the challenges in dealing with them. Professor Owen scribbled notes in red ink on his sheet as she spoke.

Kuzi explained that the context for her PhD proposal was the increasing number of people reverting back to their natal sex who were presenting in her clinic. Her colleagues reported a similar spike in the detransitioners they were seeing, and this trend concerned them.

"Part of the problem," said Kuzi, "is the woeful lack of research around detransitioning despite the growing numbers. There are so few studies and of those published, many are either deeply flawed, outdated or from disreputable sources."

Kerry spotted Owen underlining text in the document, his eyebrows knotted. He caught her eye and cast her a baleful look.

"What's needed," said Kuzi, "is thorough independent, peer-reviewed research to understand the reasons for what we're seeing."

Kuzi outlined the methodology she intended to employ, and explained the difference between 'desisters' who stop identifying as transgender after socially transitioning, and 'detransitioners' who revert back following medical intervention. She talked about how gender clinics rarely followed up with patients after treatment, and how little support there was for those who detransitioned. She spoke at length about the need to differentiate between adolescents who were simply exploring gender diversity, people with a long history of gender dysphoria, and those who'd progressed to hormones and surgery.

Indicating Kerry, Kuzi added, "This is where Dr Connelly's expertise will be invaluable."

Kuzi had asked the course leader from her master's degree to act as second supervisor and she'd recruited a panel chair from the same institution. Both had taken some persuasion, fearful of a possible backlash. The committee were happy with these appointments, and Kerry took this as a positive sign.

When asked about funding, Kerry reported this had already been secured from the Equality and Human Rights Commission and from the British Academy, which amounted to almost £30,000. At this news, Professor Owen's lip curled in disdain.

Kuzi concluded her presentation with the assurance her study would make a valuable contribution to the understanding of detransitioning. She thanked the committee for their time and asked if there were any questions. Professor Owen remained silent while a general discussion followed about anonymising participants. Kerry and Kuzi had anticipated this but she was nevertheless impressed at how well Kuzi fielded queries.

Dr Taylor, Head of DEI, inquired about the definitions Kuzi intended to use. She said, "I note you define women as adult human females but surely that excludes men who identify as women."

Kerry resisted the urge to roll her eyes at her crass stupidity. She replied, "It would be impossible to research detransitioning without first establishing what a participant's biological sex is. However, Kuzi's survey will also record gender identity so we can determine how long a person's transition was for, prior to reverting."

Owen shifted his weight and gave a small cough. The knot in Kerry's gut tightened.

He said, "You use the words 'desisting' and 'detransitioning' yet these are value-laden terms. They imply regret but that may not always be the case."

Unfazed, Kuzi said, "These terms are the most widely understood ones in current literature, so I went with them. However, I'm happy to substitute them."

Owen wasn't appeased. "It smacks of bias."

Kuzi gave a tight smile. "Not at all. If therapists like me are to truly help people who swapped gender and then changed their minds, it's crucial we understand the reasons for their decision. Whether it's due to regret or not is what we aim to discover."

Kuzi then shared heart-breaking stories from her clinical work of people living with the irreversible effects of transition, without access to services and support. She reported the harrowing case of a suicidal man who'd found it too difficult to pass convincingly as the opposite sex, and who'd been harassed and bullied.

Another woman had detransitioned after being made ill by what Kuzi described as the 'industrial level' of hormones she'd had to take. The drugs had left her with a deep voice and a beard. Kuzi also mentioned the tragic case of a 22-year-old woman who'd taken testosterone from the age of 15 and had her breasts removed, only to later realise she'd made a dreadful mistake.

"Well, this is all very interesting," said Owen with a dismissive wave, "but our focus must be on the ethical aspects of such a study and that's what concerns me most." His eyes bored into Kerry's. "You *claim* the number of detransitioners is rising but where's your evidence?"

Kuzi answered. "I've seen a steady increase in my clinic over the last few years, as have my colleagues. The online Detransition Subreddit has over fifty-two thousand members, so one aim of the study is to establish whether this observation is true or not."

"Supposing it is," said Owen, focussing his ire on Kerry, "what message would that send? You *claim* the purpose is to help patients but what about the political fallout?"

Kerry took a deep breath. "We're academics seeking the truth. Politics is of no concern."

Owen spat, sending a mist of spittle across the tabletop, "It's the primary concern. A study such as this on transgender people has political undercurrents. It undermines the notion that gender identity is innate, and your findings could have a negative impact on the way trans people are treated."

Professor McLachlan, Head of Faculty, spoke for the first time. "Professor Owen has a point. We're under pressure to fill places and generate income. Engaging in a politically sensitive piece of research carries a risk to the university's reputation."

Astonished, Kerry said, "This institution exists to encourage discussion, research, dissent even. We must be free from political constraints to challenge ideas."

"You're being naïve," said Owen. "It's perfectly clear your underlying premise is that gender identity is of less importance than biological sex and, as such, the research risks being smeared as transphobic."

Kerry sighed. "That's simply not the case. Politicising the debate like this only polarises it and shuts it down. If academics are too afraid to conduct gender-based research, then women, children and adolescents will suffer."

There was muttering amongst the committee members. Finally, McLachlan thanked them both and said he'd be in touch soon with the committee's decision. As she and Kuzi filed out, Kerry felt the eyes of every member upon her.

Chapter 13

The day after they learned that the body of Barry Mills had been found, Dave and Morven took EasyJet's early 'orange eye' flight to London, and then an hour-long train journey to Brighton. Dave spoke little and slept most of the way, while Morven perused a copy of the forensic pathologist's report. It made grim reading.

They were met at the station by DI Steve Bartlett who drove them to the apartment where Barry Mill's body had been found. Bartlett, a squat bloke in his forties with a cockney accent, passed them photographs of the crime scene to peruse on the journey.

Gawping at a picture showing how the body had been found, Dave let out a low whistle. He handed it to Morven who clamped a palm over her mouth.

"Good God," she said, "what a dreadful death."

"It's the most bizarre one I've come across," said Steve, "and I've seen a few strange ones over the years, especially in these parts."

Morven glanced up briefly as Steve drove them past the domes and minarets of Brighton Pavilion. It was a cold crisp day and, after the gloomy weather they'd endured in the north, Morven was glad of the sunshine.

As she and Dave sifted through the photographs, Steve explained that the flat where Barry had been found was owned by a couple who worked in Dubai for most of the year. While abroad, they rented it out through a holiday letting agency that managed the property. Barry had booked the apartment for two weeks, as he did every year, but this time he'd failed to return the key to the office. The cleaner from the agency, a young Polish woman, had found him.

Steve parked in an elegant street lined with Regency townhouses boasting white stucco façades, tall windows and ornate balconies. Blue and white police tape was wrapped around the iron railings of a black and white tiled perron.

At the top of the steps, Steve passed them each a face mask. "You'll want this," he said, "we've aired the place but the smell's still dreadful."

Morven found out what he meant after Steve entered and they were assaulted with a putrid odour. Dave ferreted in his jacket pocket and offered them each a mint. Steve led them through the property which had a neutral colour scheme, warm wooden flooring and beautiful period features. Morven wished her home looked like this.

She caught a glimpse of a designer kitchen before they climbed the stairs to a bedroom on the second floor. She recognised it from the photographs and braced herself. The sickly-sweet stench was stronger here and Morven covered her mask with her palm and sucked hard on the mint. Dave sent her a look as if to say, 'Are you going to puke?' and she shook her head. He pressed the packet of sweets into her palm and she nodded a grateful thanks.

The room was tastefully furnished with an iron bedstead and antique nightstands. The door to a small ensuite shower room lay open. Steve opened an adjacent door to reveal a walk-in wardrobe. The light flickered on automatically to illuminate a 4 x 6 space with a few empty shelves and a hanging rack. The dark stain on the beige carpet was the only indication of what had been there — that and the number 20 spray-painted in red on the back wall.

"When the cleaner found him, the heating was on full blast and all the windows were shut," said Steve. "The pathologist said it speeded up decomposition."

Morven felt nauseous.

"And the suitcase was locked?" asked Dave pointing to the stain.

Steve nodded. "The zip was padlocked on the outside, and the keys were inside, under the body. The cleaner tried to move it but it wouldn't budge and then when she saw what was oozing out of it…" His words trailed off.

Steve went to the bedroom window and pulled it up as high as the sash would allow. The fresh air was welcome.

"Mills was naked," said Steve, "so I thought it was another autoerotic death gone wrong. We see them occasionally; usually some guy suffocating or hanging himself by accident when his failsafe hasn't worked." He pointed to the graffiti, "But that message is suspicious and the cleaner said it wasn't there before."

"Aye," said Dave with a sigh, "there's no doubt about the connection."

Steve said, "Pathologist reckons he was drugged, then stuffed into the suitcase and left to suffocate."

For Barry's sake, Morven hoped he hadn't been conscious inside that suitcase.

Before leaving, they wandered through the property. Only the master bedroom had been slept in and only one set of towels used in the bathroom. Discarded women's clothes were strewn over the side of the bath, and Steve told them the SOCOs had found semen inside the shower cubicle, on the tiled floor, and over the bathroom cabinet. The clothing and ejaculate samples had been sent to the lab.

Across the hall, in a second bedroom, a long auburn wig lay draped over the back of a chair. The dressing table was covered in trays of makeup and bottles of perfume. The closet was lined with dresses and high-heel shoes, and the drawers stuffed with lacy lingerie. All the clothing was in large sizes. Semen had also been found in the ensuite.

Downstairs in the kitchen, there was little food in the fridge but plenty of wine. The glass recycling bin overflowed and a half-full bottle of Malbec lay open on the counter next to a wine glass smudged with pink lipstick.

"The next-door neighbour said she saw a stout woman with long dark hair enter, but that was almost a fortnight ago. That may have been the last sighting of Mills."

Barry wasn't the first cross-dresser Morven had encountered. She'd once arrested a transexual in the changing rooms of Marks & Spencer's after staff discovered him trying on ladies' underwear, masturbating and ejaculating all over the mirrors. As a young probationer, she also recalled pulling over a truck in a service station that was being driven erratically. The driver had refused to get out of his cab and when he finally climbed down, he was wearing stockings, suspenders and stilettos, and little else.

Morven wondered what possessed some men to do this. She'd learned that their victim was divorced and had grown-up children, so she doubted he was homosexual. She'd read about auto gynephiles or AGPs — men aroused by the image of themselves as a female — so perhaps Barry could only get himself off when dressed as a woman?

When they'd finished at the property, Steve drove them to the local station and took them through the files, and they examined the bagged evidence lodged in the custodial department.

Later, over a pub lunch, he shared stories of unusual cases he'd come across in Brighton, including the arrest of a man who liked to dress as a cat and rub himself against elderly people. Dave regaled them with a tale from his student days when he'd had a flatmate who used to wrap his feet in clingfilm for several days and then, when they were suitably ripe, their pervy neighbour would pay for the privilege of smelling them. Morven didn't eat much, but the discussion helped to lighten the mood until it was time to head back to the airport.

Emotionally and physically exhausted, she slept the whole journey home.

***

The day after the committee meeting, Kerry entered the faculty staff room, a soulless space with shabby furniture. It was morning and a group of her colleagues sat chatting. They stopped when she appeared. She nodded in greeting but people looked away and no one responded. A silence so heavy it was almost palpable descended as Kerry made herself a coffee. Flicking her gaze towards the group, she caught some exchanging snide looks. Gradually they all got up and left, leaving Kerry on her own.

Kerry trudged down the corridor towards her office, mug in hand. A small group of undergrads lingered outside one of the classrooms. As she approached, they stopped talking. One of the students, a heavyset guy with a ginger beard and orange dungarees, shot a hostile glance at her as she passed, and they began whispering. She recognised him from her first-year class because, during the ice breaker at the start of term, he'd announced that he identified as a non-binary pansexual. Kerry remembered because she'd had to look the terms up. At least there were no 'furries' in her classes, unlike in the Politics department where they had a lad who dressed up as a cat and called himself Marmaduke.

She caught one word of the group's conversation: "Terf."

Ignoring them, Kerry reminded herself that she'd chosen this course of action and she'd known there would be repercussions. She entered her office and switched on her computer. There was an email from Professor Clements, the committee chair, addressed to Kuzi which Kerry was copied on.

The email thanked Kuzi for submitting her proposal and informed her that, unfortunately, the committee had decided to reject it. The grounds given were that the research was 'politically incorrect' and might cause criticism which would reflect negatively on the university. Clements added that, although they acknowledged the potential benefits of such a study, they felt it was better not to risk offending people.

Kerry read it three times in disbelief.

***

Still tired after travelling up and down the country the previous day, Morven accompanied Dave on a visit to speak to Barry Mills' ex-wife.

Sonya Mills owned a florist in Strathmurray's High Street. Morven had never been in the shop but she'd often seen her adverts for wedding flowers and memorial wreaths. Tall zinc tubs full of unseasonal blooms sat outside on the pavement, and the window was festooned with a bright floral display in stark contrast to the pewtery sky above.

The clang of a bell mounted above the door announced their arrival and Dave and Morven found themselves in a small shop filled with the scent of lilies. There were no customers but they could hear a radio playing in the back.

Sonya Mills appeared from behind a rich velvet curtain, the beginnings of a smile vanishing quickly. She was tall with long auburn hair and looked to be in her early fifties. Dave produced his warrant card.

"Wondered when you lot would show up," she said. "Suppose you'd better come through."

They followed her to the rear where Sonya was assembling a long garland of roses on a table. While she worked, Dave explained that Barry's death was being treated as a murder investigation. Uniform had broken the news earlier to Sonya who was still registered as Barry's next of kin.

"I'm up against the clock," said Sonya, "this is being collected in an hour.

As she wove pink and white blooms together, she showed little emotion beyond irritation, and Morven wondered if it was because of their interruption or Barry's death.

"I'm not surprised the stupid bugger's dead," she said. When Morven asked what she meant, she said, "Well, it's not normal, is it, the way he behaved." Sonya picked up some stems and snipped off the ends with secateurs. "The dressing up was only the half of it; he was convinced he was an actual woman."

"And you think that's what got him killed?" asked Morven.

Sonya paused and looked at her as if she was daft. "Course it was. I keep reading in the papers how many trannies ... I mean transsexuals ... are attacked and killed."

Morven resisted the urge to correct her since no trans-identified people had been murdered in Scotland and, statistically, they were amongst the safest in society unless engaged in sex work.

Sonya said, "So yes, the silly bugger probably went too far this time and that's what got him killed."

"Can you tell us about your ex-husband," asked Morven, "it'll help us build up a picture of him."

Grimacing, Sonya pulled a recalcitrant stem through the garland. "Technically, we're still married. He refused to give me a divorce and I couldn't afford a lawyer. But we separated years ago."

"When did you last see him?" asked Dave.

Sonya paused for a few moments. "Hmm, must be six months ago." She explained that she and the children no longer had anything to do with him.

Dave asked about her movements over the last couple of weeks and she told him pointedly that she'd been running the shop six days a week for twenty years.

"How long were you married?" asked Morven.

"Ten years." She stabbed a rose into the garland, adding, "And his nonsense started on our honeymoon."

As Sonya worked, she explained how Barry's fetish had manifested itself. It had begun harmlessly enough with him painting his nails and using her hair products. He then experimented with makeup, progressing to wearing lingerie beneath his normal clothing. After their daughter was born, his compulsion to cross dress went into overdrive and Sonya had once found him in her maternity clothes while he bottle-fed the baby.

"I tried to understand him, I really did, and for a while it worked. We'd an arrangement he'd only cross dress upstairs on weekends."

This had worked for a time until Barry demanded to dress as a woman in front of the kids and be called Hazel, and he gradually frittered away their savings on his wardrobe and accoutrements. He kept pushing the boundaries of what was tolerable, and his behaviour caused countless arguments. He always dismissed Sonya's concerns insisting it was just harmless fun, leaving her feeling like she was being the unreasonable one.

Sonya pricked her finger on a thorn and winced. "The final straw," she said, "was when I found him going through the bathroom bin for my used sanitary products. I kicked him out after that."

The bell sounded and Sonya left for a few moments to take a delivery. Morven and Dave exchanged a look that conveyed their bewilderment and sympathy.

Dave muttered, "Christ, this business is getting stranger by the minute."

When Sonya returned, she glanced at the time and began working at the table again.

Morven said, "It can't have been easy for you or your family."

Sonya gave a dark chuckle. "It wasn't but, compared to some trans widows, I had it easy."

"Trans widows?" said Morven.

Sonya explained this was the term given to wives whose husbands had transitioned. Many were married to fetishists like Barry who are aroused by dressing and acting in stereotypical female ways. In cases where the husband fully transitions, these women find themselves like widows.

Morven asked if she'd received any support and Sonya told her how a social worker had put her in contact with a pro-trans organisation that pressured her into putting up with what Sonya described as the 'un-put-upable'. In the end, she found support on an online forum for trans widows.

"I lost friends through it," said Sonya bitterly. "I was accused of being unsupportive, and my sister-in-law even asked why I refused to identify as a lesbian after Barry transitioned." Sonya shook her head and scoffed, "Like being a lesbian is something you can just switch on."

The beautiful garland had finally taken shape and Sonya carefully placed it inside a plastic bag.

"For a wedding," said Sonya. "I hope the bride has more luck than me."

Chapter 14

> Hi Kerry, can you meet in the Coffee Cabin at 10:30? Will explain when I see you. Sam x

Running late after a tutorial, Kerry hurried through the downpour to the Coffee Cabin to meet her colleague. The café was the closest one off-campus and Kerry wondered whether the location Sam had chosen was significant. Inside it was warm and welcoming, if somewhat shabby. She spotted her at the rear and slid into the seat opposite. As she peeled off her wet coat, a waitress appeared and Kerry ordered an espresso.

"What's going on?" asked Kerry.

Sam offered her a look of sympathy. "I thought you should know," she said.

She passed Kerry her phone. On-screen was the home page of a closed Facebook group set up by Professor Owen. According to the description, the group's purpose was to tackle the rising levels of transphobia in the university. It cited Kuzi's 'controversial' proposal and the fact that Kerry was named as the primary supervisor.

Kerry scrolled through the posts in disbelief. She recognised the names of colleagues she'd once regarded as friends who were calling for her to be reported for 'hate crimes' and fired from her job. One person had shared a template letter of complaint, another had contacted the local press, and one colleague's post described Kerry's presence on campus as 'harmful'.

Disbelief turned to anger and then hurt and tears welled behind her eyes. She handed Sam back her phone as their server appeared with the coffees. Kerry turned away and dug in her handbag for tissues.

"I'm so sorry," said Sam, after the waitress had gone.

Kerry shook her head. "I'm glad you told me. It's better to know."

"I got the invite this morning. I haven't posted anything but I'm screenshotting everything for you. What they're doing is cowardly and unacceptable and you'll be able to sue them."

Swallowing the lump in her throat, Kerry mumbled her thanks. "I expected some pushback ... but not this."

Sam reminded her to contact *Real Women Scotland*. "You also need legal advice," she said, scrawling down the name of a website on a scrap of paper which she gave to Kerry. "This organisation has helped other women who've lost their jobs for expressing gender critical beliefs."

"I never imagined being one of them," said Kerry.

Sam reached over and squeezed her hand. "None of us imagined it."

***

It was late Friday evening and the CID office was still busy. Morven finished inputting the latest details about Barry Mill's murder into the computer which 'Brighton Steve' had shared. She sent a quick email to thank him and wish him a pleasant weekend.

She glanced at the framed photograph of Ollie next to her screen. It had been taken a couple of years ago in happier times when they'd holidayed in Dunbar on the East Coast. She wished she could rewind, back to those carefree and laughter-filled days. She hadn't heard that sound in a while and the thought made her sad. Ollie had continued to ghost her on social media and decline her calls, and the only information she got was monosyllabic answers from Mark confirming their son was alive.

The thought of the weekend made her chest tighten. She was supposed to have Ollie stay, but Dougie had asked the team to work overtime. Conscious she was 'the new girl', and with Dave making her feel she wasn't up to the job, she needed to rearrange it with Mark. Desperate to spend time with her son, yet unable to let the team down, Kerry felt torn.

She'd been putting off the call to her ex all afternoon and now there was no avoiding it. Her throat felt thick as she dialled his number. He didn't answer. Sighing, she got up to stretch all the stiffness out of her limbs. She gazed out of the window at Strathmurray below. Rain sheeted against the glass and the howling wind made a mournful, moaning sound as it whipped around the building.

Her first week in CID had felt like the longest of her life, but also one of the most exhilarating. Working from dawn to dusk, she had read every witness statement and explored every possible connection to the victims in HOLMES. But still the team were no further forward. There had to be a connection so why couldn't she see it? Was she simply too exhausted to realise what was staring her in the face?

The sound of Ross yawning pulled her from her reverie.

"Want caffeine?" she asked.

"I'll come with you," he said, stretching.

They traipsed to the kitchenette and while they made coffee, they talked about what they were not doing this weekend. He'd been planning to take part in a karate competition and they chatted about martial arts. Morven revealed she'd done Judo when in her teens and he encouraged her to take it up again.

She laughed, "I'd struggle with Yoga these days, never mind Judo."

"Nonsense," he said, "a young thing like you."

She met his gaze and wondered if he knew she was older than she appeared. Natalie had always insisted she could pass for ten years younger but she'd never believed her.

She changed the subject. "I'm supposed to spend the weekend with my 15-year-old son but he'll have to stay at his father's."

Ross chuckled. "You don't look old enough to have a teenager."

"Flattery will get you everywhere," she giggled.

Jeez, I really must stop flirting with him.

***

Kerry checked her work email with trepidation. After Kuzi's proposal had been rejected by the committee, Kerry had sent a polite email to the Chair requesting they reconsider. She cited the university's own charter which was about 'fostering an environment conducive to helping early career researchers'. So far, she'd received no reply.

There was a message from McLachlan with next term's timetable. Kerry opened the attachment listing the staff members assigned to each module. Only one item, 'Statistics for Social Scientists', appeared against her name while others in the department had been allocated multiple key roles. Thinking this an oversight, she replied to McLachlan asking what other modules she'd be teaching.

A new email with an official-looking subject line arrived in her inbox from an address she didn't recognise. She opened it.

from:	**Cordelia Monk** <Cordelia.Monk@lothianuniversity.org>
to:	Kerry.Connelly@lothianuniversity.org
subject:	Updated Privacy Policy

```
You deserve to be fucked with a broken beer bottle
you Nazi fucking TERF!
```

Kerry covered her mouth with her hands and gasped. She deleted the email and then recalled it from Trash so she could show it to the IT department. A ping alerted her to another.

> from: **Joshua Bland** <Joshua.Bland@lothianuniversity.org>
>
> to: Kerry.Connelly@lothianuniversity.org
>
> subject: Late assignment

```
You need to be correctively raped you brainless
cunt. I know where you live!
```

Pressing a fist against her mouth, Kerry slammed shut the laptop. She felt the gorge rise in her throat and swallowed it down.

Taking her computer, she hurried downstairs to IT on the first floor. Terry was hunched over a computer and he looked up as she approached. In his thirties, Terry looked like a typical basement dweller with a complexion the colour of wallpaper paste, long greasy hair and 'gamers' hands. He glanced up and smiled.

Kerry felt a flush creep across her face as she explained what had happened and showed Terry the emails. He did a quick search on the user names to determine that neither Cordelia Monk nor Joshua Bland were students or staff at Lothian.

Terry said, "I suspect these are external addresses and not internal. I'll make some adjustments at the firewall to prevent them getting through." He gave her a sympathetic look. "You might get a few more in the meantime but just delete them."

She nodded, conscious her hands were trembling. He asked if she was okay.

He stammered, "I can walk you to your car if you're worried."

Kerry fought back the tears that were threatening, thanked him and left. She took the lift back up to her office.

Someone had tacked a note onto the outside of her door. Handwritten in red ink were two words: Connelly OUT!

***

Morven felt completely drained and depleted both emotionally and physically, not helped by having worked more shifts at the weekend. And, to make matters worse, Ollie was still refusing to speak to her.

So, it wasn't a good start to her Monday morning when the gaffer emerged from his office with news that another body had been found, this time in Edinburgh. The local DI to whom he'd spoken revealed information about the crime scene that left Dougie in no doubt it was connected to their case.

Wearing an un-ironed shirt, Dave appeared at Morven's desk armed with car keys. "Ready Morv?"

With a Herculean effort of will, she mustered the energy to trudge after him to his car. The damp and cold of the day seemed to seep into her bones and she struggled to get warm, even with the heater turned up. As they hurtled along the motorway past mist-shrouded hills towards the city, a weary silence filled the Audi. Forty minutes later, Dave pulled up outside a large mansion in the salubrious Morningside district.

The first thing Morven noticed as she entered the property was not the body but the smell of alcohol. The forensic teams were busy photographing and swabbing every angle and surface, but they couldn't capture the stench.

The victim, a swarthy middle-aged man, was tied to a wooden dining chair in the centre of the living room. His head was thrown back and an empty bottle of whisky had been rammed deep into his gullet. The number '20' was written across the front of his shirt in red felt-tip pen, and his clothes were covered in vomit. Around his ankles, lay discarded booze, like the spillover from a bottle bank after the weekend. Vodka, gin, whisky, brandy. Morven counted the empties.

Twenty.

The house was immaculate except for the presence of the corpse. Tastefully furnished and decorated, it exuded wealth. A new top of the range Mercedes was parked in the drive and the paintings adorning the walls were originals. The deceased was well-dressed in tailored shirt and gabardine trousers, his suit jacket draped over a nearby sofa.

Dave, who'd been speaking with the local DI, appeared at Morven's side and surveyed the scene. Stabbing his fingers through his gelled hair, he cursed.

"Do we know who he is?" asked Morven.

"Doctor Alessandro De Garcia. He's some sort of specialist. Divorced, lives alone. Colleague reported him missing when he didn't show up for work and uniform found him."

Just then Dr Hellberg, the forensic pathologist, bustled past in forensic overalls and gave a flinty nod. Morven had a horrible feeling of déjà vu. Hellberg cast an eye over the surroundings and then took the temperature of the body before examining it in more detail. She paid particular attention to the head and neck.

"Any guesses as to how long he's been dead, Doc?" asked Dave.

With a look of mild irritation, she muttered, "It's a guess but around twelve hours."

Morven did the calculations, realising De Garcia must have died around midnight.

Hellberg added, "As well as the obvious trauma, there's some bruising on his face and neck indicative of gripping injuries, but these may take some time to show." She crouched to examine the cable ties securing the victim's ankles. "He doesn't appear to have resisted his bindings."

"You think he was already drunk when he was tied up?"

"Or drugged, but you'll need to wait for the tox report."

Dave and Morven left Hellberg and wandered through the rest of the house. It was clean and tidy and appeared to have been occupied only by De Garcia. The only sign of family was photographs of the victim with a woman and young girl. The rooms, although beautiful, lacked any homely touches or accessories, and the place had the sterile feel of a show home.

There was ample food in the kitchen and a well-stocked wine cellar, and the only spirits an unopened bottle of whisky. There was nothing to indicate the doctor was anything other than a moderate drinker.

In De Garcia's home office there was an antique desk which took up most of the space. Forensics had already bagged the laptop as evidence. Dave rifled through the papers on the leather-topped surface while Morven inspected the certificates on the wall. One caught her eye.

"He's a consultant endocrinologist," she said, reading the award.

"And what's that when it's at home?" asked Dave rummaging through the drawers.

She explained that they treat hormonal problems like diabetes, overactive thyroid and fertility issues. Dave paused what he was doing and frowned, and she asked what he was thinking.

"He's the second doctor to be murdered. There's got to be some sort of connection but how does this relate to a librarian and a drag queen? None of it makes sense."

When Dave struggled to open one of the drawers, he ran his fingertips along the underside of the desk and retrieved a small key. "Works every time," he muttered, unlocking it.

Inside was a small photo album which Dave flicked through. Raising an eyebrow, he gave a long, low whistle which drew Morven to his side.

She peered over his shoulder to watch as he flipped through pictures of men having intercourse with morbidly obese women. One showed a naked 500lb woman sat on top of a slender male, her flesh smothering him. Another featured the same couple, her lying face-up on a sofa, with him up to his plums in her as he rammed a donut into her mouth. The same pair doing it doggy style with him clawing handfuls of her thighs. Similar images showed men being suffocated by the limbs of enormous women. The last photograph featured De Garcia being fellated by a grossly overweight woman with long dark hair and pendulous breasts. His head was thrown back, his expression one of ecstasy.

Dave's ears turned red. He cleared his throat and said, "De Garcia is also the second victim to have a kink."

Morven said, "You think this is the connection?"

He shrugged. "Out of four victims, two are doctors, and at least two have a fetish." Running a hand over the stubble on his chin, he added, "I guess it's something." He turned to look at her. "You got a better idea?"

She glanced at the framed certificate again and pondered for a moment. A theory had begun to take shape but she wasn't certain enough to share it yet. Dave gave her a quizzical look and she shook her head.

Dave bagged the photo album and said, "Let's talk to De Garcia's colleagues and family and find out what kind of man he was."

Chapter 15

Kerry hurried along the corridor aware she was a few minutes late for the department meeting. She'd been with Terry in IT who'd wanted to install security software on her laptop since some abusive emails were still appearing in her inbox. Like everything computer-related, it took longer than expected.

Outside the meeting room, she glanced at the time. Only three minutes late. With a deep breath, she gave a knock and entered. To her dismay, Professor Owen was chairing the meeting and he was in mid speech. He stopped talking and glared at her as she entered mumbling an apology.

With a contemptuous glare, Owen barked, "In future Dr Connelly, kindly show us the courtesy of turning up on time to these meetings."

Kerry felt every eye on her, and her cheeks burned with humiliation. "I'm sorry," she said, "IT were helping me with—"

Owen cut across her words and returned to his speech. Kerry crumpled onto a chair and fought the urge to cry. After a few minutes there was a tap at the door and Rebecca Lister, a junior lecturer, entered. Owen said nothing as she took her seat.

For the next half hour, Kerry kept her gaze downwards and tried to concentrate on what was being said. Her mind kept returning to Owen's public admonition of her and the disparity in the way she'd been treated. His mention of her name pulled her from her trance and she glanced up to find everyone staring at her.

Owen said, "Dr Connelly, if you'd been paying attention, this is the part of the meeting where we share our progress. Perhaps you'd like to contribute."

Swallowing, Kerry quickly gathered her thoughts and rambled about the progress of her statistics classes. She shared the news that she'd been successful in a grant application for a new server and software application which would be available to students next term.

She summed up with, "Kuzi's proposal to study transgender detransitioners was rejected by the Ethics Committee but I've asked them to reconsider, given the importance of the research."

Her words were met with a cavernous silence, and a sea of blank faces stared back. Kerry was certain her own face was a shade of volcanic red.

With a deep, judgemental sigh, Owen turned from her to Dr Lister and asked for her progress report.

***

The first person that Dave and Morven interviewed in connection with the murder was Karen Simpson who had worked for Dr Alessandro De Garcia for almost seven years as his personal secretary. She worked out of an office in a private hospital in a leafy suburb of Edinburgh.

An overweight woman in her late thirties, Karen had long brown hair and an attractive face. She wore a billowy blouse cut low to reveal a large bust. Morven thought she resembled one of the women in the photo album. They broke the news to her that her boss had been found dead and she became upset.

Dabbing her puffy eyes with a tissue, Karen said, "I can't believe it. What an utter waste of a brilliant man."

Dave asked about her role and she explained that she managed De Garcia's diary, and arranged consultations with patients, treatments and follow-up appointments. Most of her day, she said, was spent on the phone or updating spreadsheets and databases.

He inquired about De Garcia's patient list and asked Karen to check if their other victims were on it. There were no matches and she didn't recognise the names. As the printer spat out a copy of the list, Morven asked about the types of patients De Garcia saw. Through her tears, Karen explained that, like many consultants, De Garcia divided his time between the NHS and private practice.

"He sees ... saw ... a variety of people. Most of his private patients were women with fertility problems, while many on his NHS list were struggling with their weight."

"What other conditions did he treat?" asked Morven.

Karen referred to her computer screen and rhymed off a few other conditions including diabetes and thyroid problems. She said, "He also treated gender dysphoria." When Dave asked what she meant, she said, "People who want to change sex. He'd a few who he prescribed puberty blockers or cross-sex hormones to."

Dave asked why she'd been concerned when De Garcia hadn't shown up for work.

"It was so unlike him," said Karen. "He never misses an appointment, and when he didn't answer his mobile or home phone, I knew something was wrong." She blew her nose loudly in a tissue.

Dave asked if there had been any complaints against Dr De Garcia.

Karen shook her head. "He was highly regarded by his patients and colleagues."

"When did you last see him?" said Dave.

Swallowing, Karen glanced away as if thinking hard. "Err ... last Friday."

"Anything unusual about his behaviour? Did he seem stressed or anxious?"

"He was always stressed," she sniffed, "he was extremely busy and the job took its toll."

"Were you and De Garcia in a sexual relationship?" asked Dave. His directness surprised Morven as much as it appeared to surprise Karen.

When the woman broke down in tears, Morven shot her partner a withering look. Dave shrugged as if to say, 'well, I had to ask.' Grimacing at his lack of tact, Morven politely suggested he fetched them all a coffee from the machine in the waiting area.

Passing Karen a fresh tissue, Morven apologised for his abruptness.

"It's just such a shock," she wailed.

When she'd calmed a little, Morven asked how long they had been together.

Fresh tears sprung to Karen's eyes. "Almost two years. His divorce had gone through and well ... it just sort of happened."

"Was it common knowledge?"

Sobbing now, "No, we kept it a secret. He didn't want his ex and his kid to know."

Morven asked how Karen had felt about that, and she admitted it had caused tension between them as she wanted more commitment.

"Friday night, said Karen, "was the first time we'd gone out publicly as a couple." She explained they'd had dinner in Edinburgh and then returned to De Garcia's place where they'd spent the weekend together. She'd left on Sunday afternoon around four o'clock.

She began to weep again, "He asked me to move in with him."

Poor cow, was that his idea of commitment?

She asked about De Garcia's relationship with his ex-wife.

"Civil as far as I know," sniffed Karen, "they made an effort for the sake of the kid. She's remarried."

"Any idea why they spilt up?"

Karen hesitated, went to say something, and then stopped when Dave returned with the coffee. "You'll need to ask Maria about that."

***

"Is Simpson the woman in the photograph?" asked Dave.

They were driving back to the station for Dougie's meeting. As Dave negotiated the traffic, Morven flicked through the photographs to find the one of De Garcia being orally pleasured by a large woman with long dark hair. Although she couldn't see the face, her resemblance to the doctor's secretary was striking.

Morven examined the picture carefully. "It certainly looks like her. The hair's similar and she's ample enough."

Dave kept his eyes fixed on the road. Morven could swear his ears were still pink.

"You didn't ask her?"

"Of course not, she was upset enough without me accusing her of blowing her boss."

Colour spread from Dave's ears down his neck turning him crimson. He gave an embarrassed laugh and said, "I'd have straight up asked her. Honestly, you should have left the questioning to me."

Morven was in no mood for his nonsense. "We're a team Dave. We both contribute. It's not a competition."

Morven flicked open the sun visor and examined herself in the mirror. Her exhaustion was evident in her red-rimmed eyes and she swiped it shut.

Mockingly, he said, "Yeah, yeah, team players. But you'd be no use in a proper fight."

Her frustration which had been simmering beneath the surface erupted into full-blown anger. She clenched her fists in front of her face and yelled, "Can you just stop being a complete and utter twunt for five minutes. Is that too much to ask?"

Her explosion surprised her as much as it did Dave. He gasped and pulled the car into the layby next to Junior's van. After killing the engine, he gaped at her in wide-eyed astonishment and she twisted away from him so he couldn't see her tears. She regretted shouting, but he deserved it.

"Morv," he said in a low voice, "I'm sorry if I went too far and upset you."

His gentle tone made her cry even more and she let out a sob. "You're only saying what you really think, what you've always thought." She turned to face him, "Why did you agree to this partnership when you have absolutely no respect for me or any other female officer?"

His mouth fell open. "Jesus, is that what you think?"

"Of course I do, you've made that abundantly clear, and it all stems back to Blackford. You blame me for what happened, for not being physically strong enough."

Dave tipped his head back and exhaled loudly. "Christ almighty." He said nothing for a while and then he gazed at her. "You're right. I did ... and I was a complete dick."

She swallowed hard, certain she'd misheard.

He spoke quietly. "I came close to dying that day and it scared the hell out of me. I didn't know if I could continue in the job. But none of it was your fault. You saved my life. I see that now and I'm sorry."

Taken aback by his apology, she mumbled, "I'm sorry for yelling, it's been a tough day."

"It's been a tough week and, for what it's worth, I think you've handled it incredibly well, given what we're dealing with. Nothing has fazed you."

She wiped her eyes with the back of her hand.

In a sincere tone, he said, "And I do respect you Morv. I always have."

It was her turn to gawp as Dave exited and strode towards Junior's van, leaving her to wonder why it mattered what he thought of her. Knowing this was a watershed moment in their relationship, some of the weight she was carrying seemed to lift slightly.

After fixing her eye makeup, she followed him out to the van. The smell of fried food was intoxicating and her stomach reminded her that she'd hardly eaten. With a contrite smile, Dave handed her a roll piled high with bacon and potato scone, and a cup of coffee.

"Peace offering," he said.

She thanked him and they ate in companionable silence. After his other customers had gone, Junior wiped his hands on his dirty apron and leaned his elbows over the counter.

"Hear you've got a serial killer on your hands," said Junior regarding them in turn.

Dave pulled a face. "Just the press putting two and two together to make five."

Junior grinned. "So that's a yes then." When neither Morven or Dave replied, he added, "Amazing the stuff I learn here. Folks seem to think I'm deaf or stupid.

Just last week I'd a couple of lads standing right where you are, openly discussing a new smuggling route."

"Oh aye," said Dave, "what're they smuggling?"

Junior winked. "Now that would be telling officer."

Dave fished out a few notes from his wallet and passed them to him.

Junior stashed the money in his trouser pocket and leaned in closer. "Turns out the Kennedys have started bringing drugs in from the Netherlands."

"By truck?" asked Dave.

"Nope, sea. Boat's operating at night somewhere off the East Coast."

Dave nodded thoughtfully. Morven drained her coffee and thanked Junior.

When she and Dave turned to go, Junior called, "I'll keep an ear to the ground about the other thing."

"Aye, you do that," said Dave, "If we've a serial killer on the loose, I want to know."

They returned to the car and as Dave pulled out into the traffic, he chuckled. Morven asked him what was funny.

"I've been called many things," he said, "but never a twunt."

They hooted with laughter.

***

After lunch, Kerry closed her office door, took a deep breath and checked her In-box. Fortunately, whatever Terry had done to her laptop seemed to have stopped the steady stream of vitriolic messages. She opened an email from McLachlan.

from:	James McLachlan <James.McLachlan@lothianuniversity.org>
to:	Kerry.Connelly@lothianuniversity.org
subject:	Departmental meetings

```
Dr Connelly,
```

Professor Owen has asked me to remind you of the need to be on time for departmental meetings.

Furthermore, going forward we would also ask that you do not mention Kuzi's PhD proposal at these meetings or in email. The issue of trans rights is difficult for numerous members of staff and many find your views akin to racism i.e. toxic and harmful.

Regards,

James McLachlan

Head of Faculty

This was almost as bad as the abuse and Kerry let out an involuntary moan of despair.

Chapter 16

Maria De Garcia lived in a large traditional villa in Colinton, a leafy suburb of Edinburgh. She was an elegant, dark-haired beauty whose family originated from Venezuela. A lawyer, she'd met De Garcia when they were at university and they'd married young. Sitting at the marble-topped breakfast bar in her elegant kitchen, Morven noticed, despite the pregnancy bump, Maria appeared much slimmer than in the photograph of her in her ex-husband's home. Dotted around the house were recent wedding pictures of Maria with her new husband.

Maria explained that, after the divorce, she and De Garcia had shared custody of their daughter Conchita. She'd last seen her ex-husband when he'd dropped Conchita home the previous weekend, and they'd arranged for him to collect her a fortnight later.

Maria dabbed her eyes with a tissue. "Poor Conchita, she'll be so upset. She adored her father." Looking at Dave, she asked, "Was it a heart attack?"

"We won't know until after the postmortem."

"He worked so hard," she said tearfully, "always under too much pressure."

"Was your ex-husband a heavy drinker?" asked Dave.

His abrupt question startled her and she bristled. "Why do you ask that?"

If Dave doesn't tread carefully, thought Morven, Maria will flick into 'lawyer mode' and they'll get nothing out of her.

Morven said, "He appeared to have consumed a lot of alcohol."

"He rarely drank. I mean maybe a glass of wine with a meal but he was never a drinker." She paused as if wrestling with her thoughts. "You think it was suicide?"

Dave asked, "Did he have any enemies? Someone who wanted to do him harm?"

Mouth agape, Maria shot to her feet. "Are you saying he was murdered?"

"Please don't upset yourself," said Morven, shooting Dave a warning look, "these are routine questions we have to ask when there's a sudden death."

Maria sat again and turned her attention to Morven. "No, Alessandro was a good doctor and a loving father." She dabbed her eyes again.

Dave said, "Where were you this weekend?"

"Oh my God," she gasped, "am I a suspect?"

Morven repeated. "Just routine questions."

Glaring at Dave, Maria said, "My husband and I spent the weekend celebrating our wedding anniversary at Stobo Castle."

Raking his fingers through his hair, Dave said, "We need to ask about your relationship with your ex."

Maria shot him a look that could curdle milk. "Well, that's not a routine question."

Realising Dave was antagonising her, Morven interjected. "How about DS Newton makes us all a cuppa and you and I have a chat in the living room?"

She appeared to weigh her options and nodded.

Scowling, Dave filled the kettle while Maria led Morven towards a snug decorated in a Highland Cosy theme.

Morven settled into a high-backed chair upholstered in grey tweed. "When's the baby due?" she asked.

"I've three months to go," beamed Maria, rubbing a palm over her swollen abdomen. She fixed Morven with a keen gaze. "I'm not an idiot you know. You clearly have your suspicions about Alessandro's death."

"Which is why I need to ask you some fairly personal questions." When Maria didn't object, she ventured, "We found some photographs amongst your ex-husband's things. Erotic pictures."

Maria put her head in her hands, "Oh God, I knew it. I knew he'd do something foolish."

Morven stayed silent hoping she'd say more. She did.

"He had a thing for large women." She spread her hands wide to convey just how big. "The fatter the better." Fresh tears sprung to her eyes. "I wasn't aware of it when we got married. I only found out later."

"When did you realise?"

"Alessandro was what you'd call a 'feeder'. It was endearing at first, I thought he was just taking good care of me, cooking me wonderful meals and taking me out to dinner. But then, when I tried to lose a few pounds, he got annoyed. Told me he preferred me chubby. I put on a lot of weight although I knew it wasn't healthy. When I fell pregnant, well he took the 'eating for two' thing to a whole new level."

Glancing towards the kitchen, Maria leaned forward and in a low voice said, "And the bigger I got, the more interested in sex he became."

Morven offered a sympathetic smile. "Probably not what you felt like doing in the latter stages of pregnancy."

"Exactly. And then, after Conchita was born, he didn't want me to stop breast feeding or to return to my previous shape. His obsession grew until it spiralled out of control."

"When you say out of control?"

Maria paused for several long moments as if battling with painful memories. "I discovered him on one of those live-streamed porn sites. The woman he was watching was huge. After that, all the jigsaw pieces fell into place."

She stopped talking when Dave approached with mugs which he placed on the coffee table. When he lingered, Morven cast him a 'why the hell are you still here?' look and he retreated to the kitchen.

Turning to Maria, Morven said, "That must've been difficult for you."

She nodded, "I thought I could handle it but it was the beginning of the end. I knew I could never satisfy him in that way."

In a soft voice, Morven asked, "Do you know if he ever went further than watching porn?"

"Like going with other women?"

Maria sniffed, "I'm fairly sure he visited a prostitute. I found a card in his pocket once."

"Can you remember her details?"

She shook her head. "No but the address was out in the sticks somewhere. A place called Strathmurray."

***

Darkness had fallen by the time Kerry left work. Carrying a box file full of student assignments for marking, she picked her way over the frozen car park. There were few vehicles and her Volkswagen Golf sat alone beneath a broken lamp post, in front of a line of trees.

Spotting the leaflet tucked under the windscreen wipers of her frosted car, she felt a quiver in her stomach. It was the same poster with 'Connelly OUT' which had appeared all over the campus. She scrunched it up and stuffed it into her pocket. She heard a rustle in the bushes which sent an icy chill down the back of her neck.

Placing the box file on the bonnet, she fumbled in her handbag for her car keys. Suddenly, two men emerged from the treeline and ran towards her. They were short and stocky and wore dark clothing and woollen hats. Kerry's heart thudded in her chest as she frantically searched her coat pockets. She found the keys but, in her haste, dropped them. The men were just feet away as she scurried to unlock the car. Throwing her things onto the passenger seat, she leapt in and locked the door just as one of the guys reached the driver's side and thumped on the glass.

She let out a scream and started the engine. The other man appeared at the passenger window. He pointed a camera at her and its flash blinded her for a few seconds. She rammed the car into reverse but couldn't see through the misted rear glass to pull out.

"Hey, wait," shouted the guy next to her, slapping a palm on the window. "We're Press." He showed her his photo ID and yelled, "We just want a statement."

The camera's fluoresce lit up the inside of the car again, startling her. Kerry gathered her courage and lowered the window an inch.

"What the hell are you doing?" she shouted. "You nearly scared the living daylights out of me."

He took a step back. "We only want to talk to you and get your side."

Glaring at him with suspicion, she said, "My side of what?"

"The reports that you're using your position to pursue transphobic research."

She glared at him in disbelief. "Who told you that?"

The photographer stepped around to the driver's side and pointed the camera at her again.

"Stop doing that" she yelled, covering her eyes with a hand.

"What do you say to accusations you're hateful and intolerant of trans people?"

She'd heard enough and pressed her foot on the accelerator and reversed. She lurched to a halt as the reporters dashed towards her, and then sped from the car park. Feeling as though her heart was about to burst through her chest cavity, she watched in the rearview mirror as the two men grew smaller.

She was still trembling when she arrived home but her feelings of fright had turned to anger at being accosted in a dark carpark. If they hadn't been reporters … she pushed the thought away, too afraid to go there. But it reminded her of stories she'd read about the violence and intimidation levied against people in the name of 'trans rights'. She'd watched videos of women being punched at speaking events and seen photographs of SNP politicians at a rally posing in front of a sign stating 'decapitate TERFs'.

She put her key in the front door. The house was in darkness. Andrew was on a business trip and the children at friends. She'd been looking forward to enjoying an evening to herself but now she craved her family around her. Maybe the kids were right and they should get a dog. A large one.

After flicking on the hall light, she double locked the door before removing her coat and shoes. Then she checked every room, put all the lights and television on, and made sure the windows and doors were secure.

***

On the drive back to the station, Morven repeated her conversation with Maria to Dave.

"Finally, some connections," said Dave. "The librarian worked in Strathmurray, as did the GP. The drag queen was also doing a gig there, and it sounds like the consultant had a prossie there."

Incredulous, Morven said, "A prossie? Didn't you do the DEI class?"

"Well, what would you call her?"

"I believe the correct term is sex worker."

Dave snorted with derision. "Aye, whatever, but the point is Strathmurray connects all the victims, meaning the killer's probably local. And two victims had a kink — Barry the trannie and De Garcia the chubby chaser."

Morven berated him for his choice of words which made Dave laugh, and she realised he was trying to goad her. Determined not to take the bait, she said, "You think the others had a fetish we don't know about?"

He grinned. "Now you're thinking like a detective."

Back at the CID offices, Dave made a bee line for Ross who was hunched in concentration over a laptop. His face fell when he looked up to find Dave looming over him.

Indicating the machine, Dave said, "Is that De Garcia's?"

Ross nodded. "There's something you should see." He hesitated and glanced at Morven. "It's not pretty though ... just saying."

"Trust me," said Dave, "after what we've just witnessed, it's nothing we can't handle."

Ross launched a video file. A grainy black and white image appeared showing De Garcia and Karen Simpson, his secretary, romping naked around his living room. Armed with a riding crop, the doctor was pretending to chase her and she was squealing with laughter. He caught her meaty upper arm and turned her so she was side-on to the camera. He smacked her backside hard with the whip and she cried out. He then bent her over the back of the sofa and pushed her face into the cushions. Then, gripping the whip between his teeth, he grabbed her hips and rammed into her, making her arch and gasp.

"Tell me you want it, bitch," hissed De Garcia, his eyes fixed on the camera. He shoved her head back down.

Simpson's muffled reply spurred him on and he pounded into her at a ferocious pace. With each thrust, he kept his wild eyes on the lens.

"Ugh," said Morven, unable to watch any more. "She doesn't know she's being filmed."

Ross switched it off. "I'll spare you the rest but there are dozens more like this taken over several months, and I suspect all have been recorded without her knowledge."

"Do they all feature corporal punishment?" asked Morven.

Ross nodded. "That one was tame. In some, he beats her black and blue."

"Jesus," muttered Dave, shaking his head. His face was bright red.

Dave asked Ross to take another look at Mike Carrigan's digital background and that of Dr McNab to determine if either had had an unusual predilection. Ross assured him he'd already scoured their devices but he'd explore the darker corners of the internet.

Turning to Morven, Dave said, "And I need you looking for every sex worker," — he emphasised the term — "that De Garcia might've been in contact with in the Strathmurray area. You know his preference so that should make the task easier."

Dave sauntered off towards the Chief DI's office leaving Morven and Ross to share a mutual, long-suffering look. She logged onto the computer next to Ross and began trawling for known prostitutes within a five-mile radius. The list was long and she recognised a few faces. She discounted most of them based on body type until she'd winnowed the names down to just three. One candidate stood out from the rest; a hefty woman of indeterminate age called Lorna Singer. Lorna's public Facebook profile showed numerous photographs of her and her three young children, and older posts revealed she'd spilt with her husband. It never ceased to surprise Morven what personal information people shared so publicly.

Ross asked Morven if she wanted coffee and she accompanied him to the kitchenette. He inquired how her search was going and she told him what she'd found.

"Want me to check if she's on some of the streaming sites?" said Ross. "She'll be using a false name and her face might not be visible, but if she's getting paid for content, I'll find her."

"Where did you learn this stuff?" asked Morven.

Ross gave an enigmatic smile. "Misspent youth."

After returning to their desks, it took Ross only minutes to discover Lorna on a popular streaming platform advertising sexual services. He beckoned Morven over and she wheeled her chair next to him. Listed under the sobriquet 'Chubby-CumBunny', Lorna offered her subscribers private messaging, livestreaming and customised videos.

Ross played her most recent teaser video which showed Lorna naked on all fours on a bed facing the camera with her enormous ass in the air. The mirrored wardrobes behind her left nothing to the imagination. Morven pulled a face which made Ross snort with amusement.

"And this isn't hidden behind a paywall," said Ross, "anyone, even kids, could stumble across it." Then, with a mischievous grin, he rubbed his hands together. "Right, let's find out what's on offer."

Signed in under the username 'WhackaHole', Ross messaged Lorna to ask if she was into water sports.

"Is that what I think it is?" asked Morven, unable to keep the disgust from her tone.

Ross laughed. "Yes, but personally I prefer the surf and waves variety."

An image of Ross in a wetsuit sprang to mind and she battled to dispel it. A reply from Lorna appeared.

> [ChubbyCumBunny] Yes, want to watch me squirt in your face?

Morven groaned in revulsion as Ross's fingers flew over the keyboard. He sniggered as he typed.

> [WhackaHole] Then I'll want to spank you

> [ChubbyCumBunny] Yes please sir, the harder the better

Morven stopped Ross before he could reply, "Okay, I've seen enough. We can safely say she'd appeal to De Garcia."

Ross turned to her, eyes glinting. "Aww, I was enjoying that little exchange too."

"Aye, a little too much." She joined in with his infectious laughter.

God, that smile, those eyes...

Dougie emerged from his office, the worry lines between his eyebrows deeper, and asked for everyone's attention. The room fell silent, and the atmosphere felt charged as he and Dave explained about De Garcia's penchant for large women.

Feeling like every eye was upon her, Morven piped up to say that they'd likely identified the sex worker who De Garcia may have been a client of.

"We'll interview her tomorrow," said Dave, "in case she knows the other victims."

Dougie turned to Bill Arnold who was leading the investigation into the GP's murder. "We need to know if McNab also had a kink." And then to Dave, "Same goes for Carrigan."

"We've found nothing yet," said Dave, "unless cardigans are a thing?"

Dougie didn't smile. "I don't care if he was into knitted sweaters with belts, if he'd a fetish, we need to know about it." Addressing Ross, "Do whatever digital digging you need to, I'll worry about the warrant."

After the meeting ended, Dave approached Morven's desk. "Good work detective."

Jeez, two compliments in one day. Wonder what he's after?

Dave glanced at the clock and announced he was going home. When Morven grabbed her coat a few minutes later, Ross sent her a smile that made unfamiliar parts of her tingle.

Chapter 17

The following morning, Morven battled the urge to vomit into the nearest sink. Wearing scrubs and Wellington boots, she huddled with her grave-looking colleagues in what was becoming the all-too-familiar surroundings of the mortuary's examination room. The mint she sucked did little to disguise the stench of alcohol wafting through the air after Dr Hellberg had drained the contents of De Garcia's stomach. The pathologist had removed the empty bottle of whisky from the deceased's mouth and it had been bagged and put aside.

Hellberg held up a glistening red-brown organ and transferred it to the scales. "Perfectly healthy liver," she announced, "no signs of cirrhosis."

"So, he wasn't an alcoholic?" said Dave.

"Unlikely, despite the amount of alcohol in his gut but, until we get the results from the lab, we'll not know how much was in his system."

As Hellberg continued, she gave a running commentary of her thoughts and findings to the officers. Because De Garcia had drank on an empty stomach, the alcohol had been absorbed rapidly through his intestinal lining into the bloodstream and brain. The spirits he'd ingested had a high absorption rate meaning he'd have become inebriated quickly.

"As you're aware," said Hellberg, "the blood alcohol limit for driving in Scotland is 50mg per 100ml blood. At 300mg to 100ml, even habitual drinkers are in danger of dying because at these levels the medulla is affected."

Hellberg then took an electric saw and began cutting through the cranium and the smell of heated bone filled the air. She removed the brain from De Garcia's skull and examined it.

Don't puke, don't puke.

She held it up and pointed at it. "This is the part that helps control vital processes like heartbeat, blood pressure and breathing. Above 300mg of alcohol, the heart slows to the extent that oxygenated blood can't reach the organs, and the brain can no longer adjust breathing. Keep drinking and death is the inevitable consequence."

She placed the brain into a stainless-steel dish and addressed her audience. "However, in this case, death was caused by suffocation from the obstruction in his throat. The bottle has been rammed in with considerable force, enough to tear his oesophagus and windpipe. You can see the finger bruising around his jaw where he was held."

Morven covered her masked mouth with her hand in an attempt to quell the sick rising in her own gullet.

"Was he alive when it was done?" asked Dave.

Hellberg's eyebrows knitted together. "He was likely unconscious."

For De Garcia's sake, Morven hoped she was right.

***

Lorna Singer lived in a modest semi-detached home in the private Strathmurray Park estate. A popular locale for families, the house had been extended above the garage at the side. Number 48 had a blue door and a front garden littered with children's bikes. The clouds loomed low as if a heavy grey blanket had been draped over the town suffocating any hint of light.

Dave rang the bell and a colossal shape appeared behind the frosted glass of the door. Morven recognised the woman who answered from the teaser video. Her hair was tied back in a pony tail and she wore a baggy pink tracksuit. Dave flashed his warrant card and asked if they could come in, reassuring her that her family was fine.

Lorna waddled into a small living room where toys were strewn over the furniture and floor. She cleared a space on the sofa for them and invited them to sit.

"Sorry about the clutter, she said, "I've not had a chance to tidy up." She spoke with a strong east coast accent. "So, what's this about?" She glanced nervously at the carriage clock on the mantlepiece. "My kids will be home from school soon."

"It's about your side hustle," said Dave.

Lorna blanched. "But I'm not doing anything illegal, and I pay my taxes." Looking close to tears, she added, "It's the only way I can keep a roof over our heads."

"We're only after information," said Morven. "We need to know if you recognise any of these men." Pushing aside some Lego, she placed photographs of the four victims on the coffee table.

Lorna stared hard at the pictures and then looked uncertainly from Morven to Dave.

"You're not in trouble Lorna," said Morven, "but if you know any of these people, you must tell us."

Tentatively, Lorna pointed to De Garcia. "Him, although I haven't seen him for months."

"What about the others?" asked Dave. He showed her a picture of Barry dressed as Iona Dick. "Recognise him now?"

Lorna shook her head.

Morven asked her about De Garcia and she confirmed he'd been a personal client for several years. He used to visit her home every Wednesday morning during term time, and she'd often find him parked outside when she returned from the school drop-off.

"Neighbours think I'm a massage therapist." She mused, "Suppose I am, of sorts."

Dave cleared his throat. "What ... err ... services did De Garcia want?"

Morven noticed he'd flushed pink again. For a tough detective, it was kind of endearing.

Lorna hesitated for several moments and then said, "I'll show you."

They followed her into the hall where she unlocked a door that led into what was once a garage. She flicked on the light to reveal a room painted a deep shade of red and carpeted in black. A mahogany fourposter bed with a silky crimson cover dominated the space. Silver manacles were attached to each post.

On the wall opposite was a large wooden cross with bindings for hands and feet where a person could be splayed out. A large metal dog crate with a water bowl bearing the word 'slave' sat in one corner. In the other, was a loo seat on a box with a hole cut into the side big enough for a head to fit through. Morven guessed this was for 'water sports'. The room had unusual furniture which, at first glance, looked like weight-lifting benches.

Every wall was adorned with leather whips, chains, paddles and handcuffs. A large glass cabinet displayed trays of what appeared to be stainless steel instruments of torture, and various shapes and sizes of dildos and butt plugs. Dave examined a padded leather bench in the corner.

"It's a spanking chair," said Lorna. "Most of my clients come to me for a BDSM experience. Fifty Shades of Gray has a lot to answer for." She picked up a leather riding crop. "Some enjoy a bit of punishment; others like to give it."

"And De Garcia?" asked Dave, "what was he into?"

"Oh, he liked to dish it out, a little too hard for my liking. He was also heavily into flesh worship." When Dave looked questioningly at her, she added, "He made the most of my folds."

Dave blushed a deeper shade of pink.

"Do you think he was capable of hurting someone?" asked Morven.

Lorna shook her head. "It was all consensual play." After a pause, she said to Morven, "Has something happened to him?"

Dave said, "He was found dead."

Lorna's mouth fell open. "Oh my God, that's dreadful."

"Can you think of anyone who might have a reason to harm him?" asked Morven.

She shook her head. "Was he murdered?" When neither answered, she said, "I didn't know him, he was just a client. I provided a service he couldn't get at home."

"Do you think his wife knew?"

"Doubt it, I'm very discreet, I have to be. Can you imagine if folk knew there was a dungeon on their doorstep?"

"How'd he pay you?" asked Dave.

"Cash. All my personal clients pay in cash. Only the web site has an online payment facility."

"We're going to need a list of all your clients," said Dave.

Lorna was about to object but stopped herself. Tears sprung to her eyes and she sniffed, "This'll put me out of business."

From outside, there was the sound of footsteps and young children approaching. Lorna appeared anxious.

Morven said in low voice, "We'll also do our best to be discreet."

***

Kerry sat at the kitchen table, with a copy of the local newspaper open in front of her. A photograph of her frightened face stared back at her beneath the headline 'Academic accused of transphobia at Lothian'. She read the story with a mixture of anger and incredulity.

The reporter, a nasty weasel called Robert Ingram, had done a hatchet job on her that was so one sided that it broke every rule of journalistic fairness and objectivity. In it, she was described as a 'gender-critical academic' who, according to an unnamed university spokesperson, was causing disruption at Lothian by advocating for 'controversial anti-trans research'. Beneath Kerry's photograph was a picture of a student wearing a T-shirt emblazoned with 'no more dead trans kids'. An anonymous member of the university's LGBTQ+ Society was quoted as saying 'Dr Connelly's presence on campus is toxic'. The article said Kerry had declined to make a statement.

Kerry rarely drank and never on her own; she'd always been a social drinker and only in moderation. This situation, however, called for copious amounts of alcohol. She opened a bottle of red wine and poured herself a large glass. She was on her own since Andrew was away on business and the kids were out. Usually, she enjoyed this part of the day when she got a chance to unwind, but now she felt anxious and alone.

She checked the time and dialled her husband's mobile number. The unfamiliar dialling tone reminded her he was travelling and wouldn't be home until later. When it went to voicemail, she hung up thinking Andrew had enough to worry about without her adding to it.

She refilled her glass and re-read the article. She then checked Lothian University's LGBTQ+ Society web page and wished she hadn't. There was a post about the newspaper article with numerous comments beneath, many labelling Kerry transphobic and trans exclusionary. One called for all students to stand in solidarity with the trans community and demand that she be de-platformed and removed from her position.

Kerry knew she should stay away from Twitter but it was hard to ignore it when she suspected awful things were being said about her. Far better to assess the damage so she could plan how to defend herself. It was worse than she expected. Much worse. In amongst the 'Shut the fuck up TERF' messages was one she simply couldn't ignore:

```
Next time you show your fugly face on campus, I'm
going to slit your fucking TERF throat
```

***

On the drive back to the station after interviewing Lorna, Dave said, "De Garcia was a big guy, so how did the killer get him into that chair?"

Morven reminded him there was little evidence of the doctor having resisted his bindings. "He must have been pretty drunk, but how do you get a doctor who hardly drinks into that state?"

In unison, they both said, "You drug him."

Dave said, "We need to know what he was doing and who he was with before he arrived home, or if anyone visited him."

Morven said she'd check his diary and examine CCTV from the neighbourhood.

"Tomorrow" said Dave, "another squad will take over this part of the investigation. Go home, get some sleep."

She was exhausted but sleep was the last thing on her mind; she wanted to examine the footage from the streets surrounding De Garcia's home. In any case, there was nothing and no one to go home to.

Ross was still at his desk when they arrived back at the office. Dave packed up soon after and gave Morven a wave as he left mouthing 'go home'. She and Ross worked in silence for another hour, by which point everyone had gone. Ross popped his head round and asked how she was getting on.

"No sign of De Garcia or his car on CCTV or ANPR. The nearest CCTV to his home isn't working. It's like the killer knows."

Ross frowned and asked if she'd eaten. She shook her head. She'd had nothing all day and couldn't face food after the postmortem. She told him about Hellberg's findings and their hunch that De Garcia may have been drugged.

Ross gave her a disarming smile. "Fancy a curry?"

She laughed. "I could murder a curry."

***

Ross suggested a restaurant located a short walk from the station. It was pelting with rain and they ran, crouched, through the deluge. Morven hadn't set foot inside this place for many years and it had changed significantly. No longer a greasy cafe, it had been gentrified with opulent furnishings, upholstered banquette seating, and a pricey cocktail list.

They chose a quiet corner table close to the open fire. Red embers glowed in the grate and the smell of woodsmoke filled the air. Morven's stomach rumbled as she perused the menu. Ross ordered red wine which went straight to her head, reminding her of Hellberg's lecture on the absorption of alcohol.

Over curry and a second bottle of Shiraz, she learned that Ross, after dropping out of the Royal Dick Vet school, had completed a computer science degree. He had worked in the cyber division of The Met but, following an acrimonious divorce, he'd returned to his home town and applied to Police Scotland. His mum had passed away and his father now lived in England with his second wife.

Through a mouthful of naan bread, Morven said, "For low pay and long hours? You could earn a fortune in the private sector."

Ross shrugged. "I enjoy the work and I feel I'm making a difference." He fixed her with an aquamarine stare. "So is life in CID everything you hoped for?"

They burst out laughing. When he asked how she was getting along with Dave, she told him about how they'd previously worked together.

"What's the story with the scar on his neck?" asked Ross. Her expression clearly told him he'd hit a nerve. "Ah, sorry," he said, "it's none of my business."

She took a large gulp of wine and debated whether to say something or not. Now that she and Dave had cleared the air, it somehow felt disloyal to discuss it. But where was the harm, this was Ross after all. She described what had happened on the night that had almost ended Dave's life and her career.

"Bloody hell," said Ross, topping up her wine. "You'd think he be a bit nicer to you. You saved his life after all."

She shook her head. "Dave's got some rough edges but he's alright."

Ross looked doubtful. "His attitudes towards women belong in the '70s, not in modern policing."

Morven shrugged and took another slug of wine. "The service Dave and I joined has changed a lot over the years. Back then, sexism was overt. Now it's just buried beneath the surface with a coat of DEI gloss over it."

He reached for her hand. "I hope you don't think I'm like that." A frisson skated down her spine at the feel of his touch. He grazed his thumb over her knuckles and their eyes locked.

She swallowed hard, aware the wine had gone straight to her head. Her lower body clenched at the longing in his gaze. She thought about pulling her hand away but couldn't; it felt like a current ran between them. Slowly, he leaned towards her and placed a kiss on her lips and she responded.

The kiss escalated.

Chapter 18

Kerry awoke screaming from a nightmare in which she was being chased by a man in a black balaclava wielding a knife. Andrew sat bolt upright and put his arms around her until she'd calmed down.

"Shh, it's just a dream" he soothed. He held her shoulders and fixed her with his gaze. "Hey, this is not like you. Are you going to tell me what's going on?"

"Oh, it's nothing, it's just work stuff."

"It's not nothing when it's affecting you like this." He indicated the bedsheets which were twisted into a ball and drenched in sweat. "Talk to me."

She told him everything, and he listened in stunned silence until she reached the part about the death threats.

"You have to report this to the police," he said.

She shook her head. "They won't do anything. It's just words after all, it's not like actual violence."

He gawped at her. "You need to take this seriously. All it takes is one broken person to …" He let his words trail off. "What are you going to do?"

"Tough it out. I'm not going to let Owen and his cronies push me around. People like him think they have the moral high ground and if they shout loud enough, they can silence us."

Andrew smiled. "You're so stubborn Mrs Connelly."

Grinning, she said, "It's Dr Connelly to you." Her title was a longstanding joke between them.

He hugged her tight. "God, I couldn't bear it if something happened to you."

She mumbled into his chest, "Nothing'll happen but I'm screenshotting everything in case that makes you feel better."

Andrew reached for his phone. "Not really, but I know what will."

Frowning, she asked what he was doing and he said he was setting himself a reminder to have security cameras installed outside their home.

"It'll give us both peace of mind," he said.

Kerry wasn't so sure. Impotent rage was no match against the righteous on a mission.

***

Morven awoke in a strange bed feeling like she'd been run over by a truck. A headache thrummed behind her eyes and her stomach felt like she'd been drinking diesel. Her head and tummy weren't the only places she was sore, and she winced at the memory of what she and Ross had done. All night.

She turned to gaze at him as he slept, feasting her eyes on his handsome features, the high chiselled cheekbones, the soft flawless lips, and the thick eyelashes fanning over his cheeks. The bedroom was in disarray with clothes strewn across the floor and condom wrappers. Several of them.

She vaguely recalled the taxi ride to his apartment and them tumbling through the door. They'd stripped one another on the way to the bedroom where Ross had wasted no time in burying himself inside her. The delicious ache in her lower regions reminded her of just how much they'd enjoyed one another.

Pulling on his t-shirt, she padded into the bathroom and drank straight from the tap. She washed her face, rubbed toothpaste on her gums and found paracetamol in the cabinet. In the kitchen, she filled the kettle and while she waited on it boiling, she snooped around the open-plan room. Although the Victorian property boasted high ceilings and period features, the furnishings were modern. Behind the sofa was a weight bench and a sports bag containing a white cotton suit of the type martial artists wear.

Morven peered at family photographs on the wall showing a much younger Ross with a couple she presumed were his parents. She smiled at pictures of him as a chubby baby, a mischievous toddler, and as a gangly teenager. A girl appeared in some, presumably a younger sister given the resemblance, but she was absent in later pictures.

Ross approached from behind, wound his arms around her waist and pulled her towards him. She could feel him hard beneath his robe.

He kissed her neck and mumbled, "Come back to bed."

She sniggered as he pressed himself against her bottom. "Who's the girl in the photos?" she asked.

"My sister." He turned Morven towards him, lifted the t-shirt and trailed kisses from her stomach to her breast.

"Where is she now?"

He stopped and looked at her, his expression one of sorrow. "She died."

Morven whispered, "I'm so sorry, I'd no idea."

With a rueful smile, Ross took her hand and led her back to the bedroom.

***

Morven popped home to shower and change before heading into work. On the drive to the office, images of their lovemaking played over and over in her mind. She couldn't remember the last time she'd had sex but, whenever it was, it'd been nothing like that. Jeez, the things he'd done...

Ross was already at his desk and she greeted him with a curt nod and then spent the next hour trying to ignore him. However, every time she caught his eye, he appeared to be gazing at her. With each attempt to focus on her task, her thoughts wandered back to his bedroom.

Mid-morning, a message pinged on her computer.

[Ross Forsyth] Can't concentrate!

> [Morven MacLeod] Is this wise on work kit?

> [Ross Forsyth] I'm the tech guy, don't worry :-)

> [Morven MacLeod] I can't concentrate either

> [Ross Forsyth] Only 1 cure

> [Morven MacLeod] ???

> [Ross Forsyth] Replay later?

She glanced up to see his shoulders shaking with mirth. Against her better judgement, she typed:

> [Morven MacLeod] I need to go home ... but you could come to mine ;-)

He replied with a smiley face and she sent him her address. It was difficult to focus after that, so it was almost a relief when her partner appeared.

"The tox report is back," said Dave, "De Garcia was drugged with Rohypnol."

Morven nodded. "And surprise, surprise, there's no CCTV."

Dave then asked for her help to bring the new squad up to date with the latest developments. She spent the rest of the morning in the briefing room going over the details of the cases, and the afternoon inputting information into HOLMES.

And anticipating what the evening held in store.

***

Kerry drove through the busy morning traffic towards the campus, her night thoughts still shrouding her. She had slept badly and her eyes felt tired and gritty. Her gut churned at the prospect of the reaction from staff and students following the publication of the news article and the resulting twit-storm.

She'd reported the online death threat to the police and emailed McLachlan to let him know about the abuse she was receiving. She also complained about the public posts on the University's LGBTQ+ website and asked if he could arrange to have these taken down.

Unsurprisingly, McLachlan responded with an insincere string of cliches along the lines of 'don't worry, it'll all blow over'. His lack of support and failure to acknowledge the malign nature of the comments and tweets she was receiving left her disappointed. Surely, he must realise the chilling effect this would have on academic freedom, and on her personally.

Andrew had also advised her to raise a formal grievance since the posts and comments were on Lothian's servers and they had a responsibility towards her. She'd been reluctant at first, until she revisited the website and saw the latest vitriol levied against her. She submitted the grievance citing the worst of the abuse plus the death threat. So far, she'd heard nothing from the police.

The alarm company had fitted two security cameras, one at the front of her home and another at the rear. They also installed panic buttons inside close to the front door and in the main bedroom. The mere sight of them was a sobering reminder of the attacks Kerry had read about on gender-critical women.

She parked as close to the campus as possible, beneath a working lamppost. On the walk to the entrance, she spotted a dozen 'Connelly OUT!' posters. She kept her head down but her stomach felt like it was full of writhing snakes. She decided to forgo her usual coffee and took the lift to her office. Her door was plastered in posters, and the sight of them brought tears to her eyes. She ripped them off and binned them.

She shut her door and sat at her desk and fretted until it was time for her first class. The lecture theatre seemed busier than usual and a hush descended as she made her way to the lectern. As she set up her laptop to display slides for today's topic, a young lad coughed the word 'TERF' loudly, and a low ripple of laughter followed.

Kerry's cheeks burned but she ignored it. Keeping her eyes on a fixed point above her students' heads, she launched her presentation on the concepts of mean, median, and mode. She navigated to the next image but the PowerPoint application glitched so, instead of a slide showing these statistical measures, a picture of a noose appeared. This was accompanied by sniggering from a large group of young men seated in the back two rows.

A prickle of unease crept up her spine at the realisation that these students were not known to her. In fact, she recognised few of the faces glaring back at her. Most were male — despite their gaudy clothes and makeup — and she wondered where all the females had gone. Keeping her expression neutral, Kerry switched to the next slide and continued as though nothing had happened.

After defining the mean, she moved to the next slide to show the formula. A black and white sketch of a woman hanging from a rope filled the screen. Kerry watched in horror as large red letters appeared beneath it that spelled out 'Dead TERF'.

Hands on hips, she glared at the lads and yelled, "Suppose you think that's funny?"

Her words were met with defiant stares. The atmosphere in the room had shifted to something sinister. Kerry swallowed and felt the hair on the back of her neck lift. She glanced at the exit which suddenly seemed a long way off.

One of the group, a young man with rainbow-coloured hair, eye makeup and face piercings, began thumping his fist on the desk in front. The others copied him and stamped their feet, filling the theatre with a rhythmic and thunderous beat. Every structure reverberated under the impact, amplifying the sound and sending an almost primal, tribal signal through the room.

Kerry's heart pounded against her chest wall in time with the tempo. Hands shaking, she shut her laptop and yanked out the cables.

Then a chant went up, "Connelly out, Connelly out ..."

The room became a living, pulsating entity fuelled by hatred.

Kerry ran from the theatre on legs that felt like jelly, and she didn't stop running until she reached her car.

And there, she found gouged deep into the paintwork of the bonnet the words 'Die Cis Scum'.

***

A couple of days later, Dave and Morven were driving back after interviewing another sex worker in Strathmurray when the call came into his mobile. From the tone of Dave's voice, Morven could tell immediately that something was wrong, and she pulled the car over into a layby. Dave scribbled down an address and ended the call.

"Oh God," he groaned, "we've another victim, a woman this time."

"What makes you think it's one of ours?"

He turned to her, his expression grim. "The number twenty's written on her bedroom wall." Dave lowered the window letting a blast of cold air into the car and he sucked in a breath. "Forensics are there now. It sounds pretty gruesome."

She'd never seen him look so rattled and a feeling of dread crept up her spine. They swapped a look as if to say 'what the hell's going on'. Dave input the address into the satnav and she swung the car into the traffic and sped towards the opposite end of town. As they drove, Dave repeated what he'd been told about the crime scene by the first responders. The victim was a young female, and she'd been discovered at her home by a colleague who'd called to give her a lift to work. Dave went quiet after that.

Fifteen minutes later they arrived at a quaint row of stone-built terraced cottages with brightly painted front doors. A uniform stood outside one and several police vehicles lined the road. Further up the street, a group of neighbours gawked from beyond a line of police tape and behind them, the media circled. Morven pulled up next to the SOCO's van.

After checking in with the officer stationed outside, they pulled on paper oversuits, gloves and shoe covers and entered a tiny vestibule. The hallway beyond was decorated in rich bohemian reds with bright prints and tapestries adorning the walls. The theme continued into a small living room which was jampacked with squashy sofas, velvet cushions, and trippy tapestries. The small fireplace was littered with incense burners and joss sticks that imbued the cottage with the scent of lavender and jasmine. Morven was reminded of the local hippy dippy shop, the one she'd done for selling cannabis under the counter.

From the rear of the property came the sound of weeping where, Morven assumed, the colleague was being comforted by an officer.

"Up here in the bedroom," came a voice she recognised. "I hope you've a strong stomach."

Morven's gut roiled as she followed Dave up the narrow staircase and into the bedroom. The vision that greeted them was like a scene from hell. Lying on the bed was the naked body of a young woman, her chest cavity laid open like a field-dressed deer. One of her organs had been stuffed into her mouth. There were blood splatters on almost every surface of the room, and the mattress and carpet were saturated in a black-red pool. The room was the worst thing Morven had ever seen.

Hellberg was crouched by the bed and she gave the briefest nod of acknowledgement. Morven tore her eyes from the horror to the wall above the corpse where the number twenty had been daubed in large crimson numerals.

A wave of nausea hit her and she darted into the bathroom and puked in the toilet. After emptying the contents of her stomach, she rinsed her mouth and joined Dave on the small upstairs landing. She half expected a sarcastic remark but instead he gave her a look of sympathy and asked if she was alright.

She nodded. "I just didn't expect ... that." She couldn't bear to look beyond the bedroom door.

Running a hand over his chin, he said, "Me neither. I've seen a few things over the years but nothing like this." After a pause, he suggested they got some air before continuing.

They returned to the car and stood outside in shocked silence. After a few minutes Dave asked if she wanted to sit this one out but she declined. So, like a couple of ghostly apparitions, they rejoined the pathologist upstairs where Hellberg was packing up her case.

"So, Doc," said Dave, "what can you tell us?"

The doctor pursed her lips and glanced out the window to the street below. After a few moments, she turned to him. "It's always hard to be accurate but I'd say she's been dead for about six to eight hours."

Dave glanced at his watch. "So, she likely died around midnight or the early hours of this morning."

Hellberg nodded. "I'll know more at the PM."

Morven swallowed down the bile rising in her throat and pointed to the gaping chest wound. "Was she alive when …?" She couldn't finish the sentence.

Hellberg offered her a sympathetic look. "Judging from the arterial spray, I believe she was." Pointing at the organ which had been removed and bagged as evidence, the pathologist added, "that's her heart."

Morven clamped a hand over her mouth to stifle an involuntary gasp.

Dave came to her side and murmured, "Hey, why don't you wait in the car."

"No." Morven forced herself to look at the body. "I want to catch whoever did this."

He nodded.

"She was alive," said Hellberg, "but quite possibly unconscious when it was done." She pointed to a wound on the back of the woman's head which Morven hadn't noticed due to all the gore. "She's been struck with a blunt object."

"How much strength would it take to open her up like that?" asked Dave.

Morven forced herself to look at the gaping chest cavity.

"It'd require some power but with the right tools, maybe not as much as you think." Hellberg pointed to marks on the breastbone. "Some type of electric saw has been used. This hasn't been done with a manual blade, and again it appears as if your killer has some medical knowledge."

The doctor met Dave's gaze. "I know what you're asking and yes, in my opinion, a woman could have done this."

They gazed at the victim in silence until Morven broke it. "But stuffing her heart in her mouth … I mean what type of person does that?"

"A crazy one," muttered Dave.

Hellberg drew their attention to tell-tale spattering on the wall which indicated where the fatal injury had occurred, and cast-off staining from where the killer had raised the weapon again.

"This killing has all the hallmarks of a ritualistic one," said Hellberg matter-of-factly. She glanced at the wall. "Why the number twenty?"

Dave shrugged. "That's what we intend to find out. Once we know that, we'll have our motive."

The pathologist concluded her examination and they accompanied her out to her car.

As Hellberg put her cases into the boot of the vehicle, Morven asked her, "How do you bear it? Doesn't it upset you?"

"Emotion has no place in my profession," she said. "My job is to seek the truth with detachment." Then, with a parting nod, "I will see you at the postmortem."

They watched as she drove away. Dave then turned to Morven and asked if she felt up to speaking with the colleague of the deceased. When she nodded, he rewarded her with a genuine smile, one of few she'd ever gotten from Dave.

"You've balls," he said, "I'll give you that."

As he walked away, she thought, *No, I'm a woman, I don't have balls.*

Chapter 19

Using the security camera app on her phone, Kerry watched and listened as the police constable examined the letters scratched into her car and took pictures of it with his phone. The two officers, a huge guy and a small woman of south-Asian descent, had finally pitched up two days after she'd reported the damage to her car. Harassment and intimidation were clearly not their top priority, which was understandable given media reports of a serial killer the press was calling 'The Strathmurray Slasher'.

The policeman looked up and down the street and chuckled. The audio from the camera was clear and Kerry could hear everything being said.

"Why are you laughing?" said the female officer.

"I was remembering the last time Morven and I were in this area and we caught Murphy." He shook his head, "God, I'll never forget that shift."

Kerry wondered what he meant.

Scrutinising the 'Die Cis Scum' message etched into the paintwork, the WPC asked, "What does 'cis' mean?".

Her partner tapped his phone and said, "According to Professor Google, it's short for 'cisgender' meaning someone who has a gender identity that corresponds to their biological sex."

The woman frowned. "So, like most people."

He gave a small shrug. "Guess so." He glanced directly into the security camera. "Right, let's go talk to the real professor."

Kerry quickly closed the security app on her phone and hung back out of sight until the officers buzzed the doorbell. She unlocked the front door and slipped back the bolt her husband had added for extra security. The policeman introduced himself as Constable Rob Fraser and his partner Usha Patel. Kerry invited them to take a seat in the living room and the officers politely declined her offer of coffee.

Rob had a gentle manner which she didn't expect in a man of his size. She thought he must be six foot six.

With a kindly smile, Rob said, "So, would you like to tell us what happened and why someone might have vandalised your car?"

Kerry gave a deep sigh and then told them everything. She explained about her PhD student's research proposal, the reaction to it from staff and students, the newspaper article, and the online abuse. She described the incident in the lecture theatre and how she'd fled in terror. The two officers listened intently, and somewhat incredulously. At one point, the woman shook her head in disbelief and appeared to bite back what she wanted to say.

"Do you know the people involved?" asked Rob.

"I've never seen any of them before and none of my female students were present. It was very odd."

Patel scribbled furiously in her pocketbook as Rob continued to question Kerry. She told him about the journalists accosting her and she pinpointed on a map where she'd left her car that morning at the university.

Rob said, "I understand you recently reported an online death threat."

Kerry nodded. "Yes, but no one's been in touch about that yet."

He nodded. "Well, given that the online world seems to have spilled into the physical realm, I'll make sure this becomes a priority, and someone from CID will be in contact."

Kerry thanked them. After they left, she locked and bolted the door and set the perimeter alarm.

***

After peeling off their forensic suits, Morven and Dave joined the victim's colleague in the kitchen. The young woman sat with a female officer at a pine table piled high with mismatched tea cups and plates. She gazed up at them with red swollen eyes magnified behind enormous glasses. The uniform took CID's arrival as her cue to leave.

Mid-thirties with short auburn hair, she was dressed in yellow dungarees and a purple top which blended with her surrounding's equally whacky colour palette where green walls battled with orange cabinets and blue tiles. It reminded Morven that her own kitchen needed redecorating. Perhaps in a more muted tone.

Trembling in the corner of the room sat the ugliest dog Morven had ever seen. The size of a Cocker Spaniel, but nowhere near as cute, it looked like a cross between a wallaby and a Chinese Crested. It had straggly grey fur and what appeared to be faded cigarette burns on its rump. The woman spotted Morven looking at the creature.

"That's Mugly," she said, "Claire rescued him from a crack den."

To Morven's surprise, Dave crouched in front of the dog and extended his hand. "Hey boy," he said softly. The dog sniffed him and thumped its tail on the floor.

"He's a whole lot of ugly," she said, "but very friendly."

"So ugly, he's cute," said Dave stroking the dog's head.

Dave and Morven took a seat beside the woman, and he explained that they were from CID. He said, "I know you've already spoken to our colleagues but we'd appreciate it if you'd talk to us."

She nodded and blew her nose noisily into a tissue. Her name was Sandra and she told them she was a community officer with Strathmurray Housing Association. The victim's name was Claire Angus, a youth worker employed by a charity that provided services to the Association.

Sandra explained that she'd called to collect Claire that morning as they were attending a conference together. Mugly was barking frantically and when she got no answer at the front door, she tried the back which was unlocked. She discovered her friend's body upstairs. This set off a fresh batch of tears and Morven offered her another tissue.

Claire had lived alone and worked evenings and weekends at 'Strathmurray Connect', a youth engagement project aimed at building relationships with young people. Her job was to organise group activities and workshops to develop skills and promote personal development.

"She was a wonderful mentor and role model," sobbed Sandra, "the kids adored her, and she loved her work."

"Did she have any who were particularly challenging?" asked Morven.

Sandra nodded. "Most of them, that's why they're referred to the project. Some have dreadful homelives — drink, drugs, domestic abuse. Others have been in and out of care; several have been in prison."

"Any who'd do her harm?" prompted Dave.

She shook her head. "I can't imagine anyone doing ..." She began weeping again.

"We'll need a list of her clients," said Morven.

Sandra explained that they got referrals from Social Work which they then passed onto Strathmurray Connect. She gave them the address of the charity's headquarters. When Dave asked who their contact was in the Social Work department, she frowned.

"I'm not sure," said Sandra, "The woman we used to deal with died suddenly."

Morven's ears pricked up and she asked what Sandra knew about her death.

She dabbed her eyes. "Pat Duncan was her name. She worked in Children's Services. Tragic accident apparently. Sad really, she wasn't that old."

When more tears fell, Morven made Sandra a strong mug of tea with two sugars. The name she'd given them, Pat Duncan, sounded familiar and Morven wondered if this was the same social worker who'd helped Ollie after he was assaulted at his previous school.

Once the colour in Sandra's cheeks had returned, Dave produced head shots of the other victims which he laid out on the table. He asked her if she recognised any of them.

Shaking her head, she said, "Only what I've seen in the newspapers."

Glancing around the kitchen, he said, "This is a nice pad, but I can't imagine a youth worker's salary covers the rent."

"Her grandmother left it to her when she died. Claire also worked part-time in a coffee shop." Sandra sniffed, "She said it helped pay the bills."

"What about boyfriends?" said Dave, quickly adding, "Or girlfriends?"

"Peter, her partner." Then Sandra clapped a hand over her mouth and wailed, "Oh God, they don't know. They're in London."

Morven wondered about the use of 'they'; just how many partners did Claire have?

Morven assured Sandra the police would handle all communications, and she jotted down Peter Sneddon's details. Dave asked about the relationship and Sandra told them the couple had met through work, and that Peter was employed by another charity. He and Claire had only recently got together but already there'd been talk of moving in. She began crying again.

"Poor Claire," she sobbed, "she didn't have an unkind bone in her body."

Morven pushed the box of tissues towards her. *Clearly someone thought otherwise.*

The dog barked and wagged his tail, and Dave went back over to pet him.

"What'll happen to Mugly?" asked Sandra. "I've got three cats otherwise I'd have him."

"Perhaps Claire's partner will take him?" ventured Morven. She hoped so, the dog had clearly suffered a hard life.

Sandra shook her head. "Peter hates the dog, hated the way Claire showered him with affection. They used to argue about it."

Morven stopped herself from pointing out that it was Claire's house, not Peter's. She was already forming a picture of this guy and it wasn't favourable.

"Did Claire have family?" asked Morven.

"No, she was an only child and both her parents are dead. Her grandmother was her only relative."

Morven sighed. "We'll call the SSPCA, they'll find him a home.".

Dave scratched behind Mugly's ears and was rewarded with a lick. "Doubt it, not looking like that he won't."

To Morven's amazement, he lifted the dog into his arms and it burrowed its head under his chin for a cuddle which made him smile. "I wish I could take you home bud," said Dave, "but I can't."

Dave sat with Mugly on his lap for the remainder of the interview. Morven hadn't realised her partner was such a soft touch. Afterwards, they thanked Sandra, gave Mugly a farewell pat and headed out to the car.

Dave started the engine but didn't budge. He turned to look at Morven. "God, that was like a trip to hell. Are you okay?"

She nodded although she didn't feel okay. Instead, she felt a profound sadness at the way that young woman's life had been ended, and the fact someone could do that to another human being. Suddenly there was a thud against the car which made her jump. She looked out to see Mugly pawing at the driver's door. The young WPC was trying to catch him but he was dodging her attempts.

Dave opened his door and the dog leapt onto his lap, licked his face and then jumped into the back seat. Chuckling, Dave waved the constable away, saying, "It's fine, I'll drop him at the Cat and Dog Home."

Dave and Morven then turned in unison to look at Mugly who was sitting up panting as if to say, 'Where to next?'

Dave petted him and made cooing noises. "Aww, he's such a friendly wee guy," he said. "I wish I could keep him."

The Ice Maiden would turn your ball sack into a mitten if you took the mutt home.

Watching the interplay between man and dog, Morven decided Dave Newton was less of an arsehole than she'd previously thought.

***

Open Letter concerning transphobia

We, the undersigned Lothian University faculty and staff, write to express our concern about the anti-trans research nominated by Dr Kerry Connelly. We are committed to the inclusion and acceptance of trans and gender non-conforming people and we condemn Connelly for using her position at Lothian to advance the idea that biological sex is more important than gender identity.

Trans people are discriminated against and marginalised in society, and studies such as the one Connelly is promoting will only amplify these harms, serving to restrict trans people's access to life-saving medical interventions, encourage harassment, and reinforce the patriarchal status quo.

We believe in the principles of academic freedom but with this freedom comes responsibility and it should never be used to harm vulnerable people. Transphobic fearmongering and attacks on marginalised people should not be mistaken for valuable scholarship.

We oppose members of our profession using their academic status to further gender oppression. We denounce transphobia in all its forms, and hereby publicly implore the executive team to withdraw support for Connelly and create a more inclusive culture, in which trans, non-binary and genderqueer people are able to thrive and be respected for who they are.

***

Kerry stared at the letter in disbelief as she read it for the umpteenth time. Sam had phoned to let her know about its publication on the university's website, and she'd been at pains to point out that she'd had nothing to do with it. The letter was signed by dozens of academics and staff, including Professor Owen. Not only was his signature on it, but his influence was also all over it. The letter ended with a call to others to add their support.

Kerry held her head in her hands as she scanned the names of colleagues she'd regarded as friends. Each one read like a physical blow. Even Professor Aitken had added her signature which was a bitter stab as she'd always been so kind. Kerry knew the list would continue to grow as news of the letter spread like wildfire through the university.

Highly damaging and humiliating, the letter made Kerry out to be a monster who was using her position to wage a campaign of hate and misinformation against trans people. It suggested that her true aim was to pursue a transphobic agenda rather than legitimate research, and that she was somehow deceptive and dishonest. Kerry wondered what had happened to one of the key tenets of academia: critique the idea, not the person.

By condemning her publicly in this way, the letter had torpedoed Kerry's name and her professional reputation. And even if she stuck it out at Lothian, it hurt that so many signatories were people she would be expected to work with. How could she possibly continue to do her job knowing her colleagues were so hostile to her, her research and her beliefs? Emotionally, as well as professionally, Kerry knew it was untenable.

This changed everything. She was being socially expelled from the academic community and publicly denounced as a transphobe. Forever tainted, her academic career was over. Worse still, the letter would also serve as a warning to others who might share her beliefs.

She'd expected pushback but had thought it'd be more of the same: the cold shoulder, the whispering, the complaints behind her back. She was prepared for that but not for a moment did she think her colleagues would sign a public letter attacking her.

With a heavy heart, Kerry drafted her resignation realising that the trans mob had once again succeeded in silencing dissent.

Chapter 20

The Strathmurray Connect charity operated out of an office above a community centre in town. Morven drove them there in silence and parked in the lot at the back of a fast-food joint. The dog was fast asleep in the back seat and they left him.

As she stepped from the car, a fat rat scuttled away towards a line of commercial bins. The area was a well-known haunt for sex workers and drug addicts and Morven knew it well from her days on the beat.

"Dare say you've been here a few times," said Dave as they passed a line of charity shops and shuttered units daubed in graffiti.

"Aye, it gives me that warm coming-home feeling," she said stepping over the remains of a takeaway that looked as though vermin had been at it.

Dave stopped and looked at her. "You miss it?"

She rolled her eyes to the sky. "Considering what we're dealing with right now, I'd give my left arm to be back chasing spoon burners."

He fixed her with a penetrating blue gaze. "You were wasted in uniform and, as tough as things are just now, CID's where you belong."

He strode away leaving her speechless.

Jeez, an actual full-blown compliment from Newton.

The retail units either side of the community centre were closed for good, their windows empty and only the café opposite seemed to be doing any real trade. The entrance was strewn with rubbish and smelled of stale piss.

Dave and Morven climbed the stairs to the second floor and found the Strathmurray Connect office at the end of a shabby corridor. A woman in her sixties sat at a desk. She'd short grey hair, wore a twin set, and had glasses attached to a gold chain. The office was lined with old-fashioned metal filing cabinets and its walls were covered in educational posters. Morven would have sworn she'd stepped back in time, were it not for the shiny new laptop on which the woman typed.

Dave showed her his warrant card and explained they were investigating a sudden death. The woman introduced herself as Joyce Stroud, the office manager, and she appeared flustered by the intrusion. She cleared a pile of dog-eared folders from a couple of chairs and invited them to sit.

Dave inquired about the charity's work and Joyce explained they provided 'support workers to service providers'. The business jargon she used meant Morven was no clearer in her understanding of their role.

"Does that include the Strathmurray Housing Association?" asked Morven.

Joyce nodded. "We run several projects for adults and young people."

"Tell me about the youth groups," said Dave.

Joyce retrieved a file from one of the cabinets and handed it to Dave. "We've two groups, one on the Strathmurray estate and another over in Ladyburn."

Dave flicked to the Strathmurray section and scanned a list of names which Joyce said were the current 'service users'.

Dave passed her the file but Morven didn't recognise any of the names.

"How long's the group been going?" asked Morven.

"Several years," said Joyce, "ever since Claire joined. She's the youth worker who runs the service." She paused and looked at them. "Has something happened to her?"

Dave said, "Have you a list of the previous kids who've been though the programme?"

She shook her head and sighed. "We'd a break-in a few weeks ago. The thieves stole the computer which had all the information on it. We lost almost everything."

"What about backups?" he said.

Joyce appeared embarrassed. "We didn't keep any. Didn't think we needed to."

Morven stifled a groan and pointed to the laptop. "What about this computer?"

"Oh it's brand new. It was gifted to us by Clownfish after the robbery. I'm inputting all the paper records into the new system." With a sheepish look, she added, "It's automatically saved into the clouds."

"That was very generous of them," said Morven with a reassuring smile. "They're the LGBTQ+ charity, yes?"

Joyce nodded, fingering the chain around her neck. "We partner closely with them and they fund some of our work."

Dave asked who her contact at Clownfish was and Joyce said it was a young man called Peter Sneddon.

"He's a friend of Claire's," said Joyce. After a long pause, she whispered, "It's Claire, isn't it? That's the reason you're here."

Dave nodded.

Joyce covered her face with her hands and wept. "Oh, I just knew something like this would happen. The types of people she deals with. Drug addicts, alcoholics, ex-prisoners." She looked up through wet lashes. "She cared about all of them."

Morven leant across the desk and touched her arm. "We need you to help us identify all the clients who've passed through Claire's groups over the years. Do you think you can do that?"

Joyce took a balled-up tissue from the sleeve of her cardigan and wiped her eyes. "I'll do my best." She stopped to think for a moment and then said, "You could ask Eddie. He was a friend of Claire's who occasionally gave talks to the young people."

Morven jotted down Eddie's details and thanked Joyce. Dave gave her his card and they left.

Back in the car, Mugly was still fast asleep. Dave stretched over and stroked his head. He said, "So Sneddon's charity is bank-rolling the youth groups." After a pause, he said, "I wonder why they're called Clownfish?"

Morven said, "I know this because of all the nature programmes Ollie used to watch. Clownfish are one of the few creatures that can change their sex."

Dave rolled his eyes to the ceiling and muttered, "Aye, because us humans are so like fish."

***

On the way to Eddie Stewart's home, they called into a pet shop where Dave bought a leash, two bowls and a packet of dry dog food. Morven was tempted to point out that it would have been easier to visit the Cat and Dog Home but decided this was far more amusing. After feeding Mugly, they took him for a walk near the loch. It was late afternoon and the sun was beginning to slide from view.

"Peter Sneddon sounds like he's worth a look," said Morven.

"Aye, I'm always suspicious of people who hate dogs," replied Dave, stroking Mugly's head. "I'll get Bill's team on it until they appoint another squad. At this rate, every detective in Scotland will be assigned to this case."

They heard a commotion by the water and turned to see a mother and toddler feeding the ducks. A swan, its wings partially extended, was threatening a duckling which was paddling frantically to get away. With a flurry of feathers and angry quacks, the mother duck positioned herself between the swan and her young. The woman tugged her child away from the chaotic splashing and squawking, as the hen defended her offspring and drove the swan away. As the flotilla of ducks glided off, Morven pondered on the instinctual drive of a mother to protect her offspring, even against a more powerful adversary.

She said, "I wonder what Eddie used to give talks on."

Dave shrugged. "Gen Z nonsense probably. Climate change, mental health, gender identity and critical race theory. Take your pick."

Morven was surprised he knew about critical race theory which she'd only heard about from Ollie who often banged on about inherent racial bias. However, Dave could have been describing her son and she felt a sudden need to defend him. "That generation have had it hard with Covid and all the political and financial upheavals."

"Bunch of whiny snowflakes if you ask me." Dave gazed over the serene loch. "But I do worry about what sort of world my daughter's growing up in."

"It's no easier with a son," she said.

Mugly began barking at a squirrel and they coaxed him back to the car. When Dave produced a dog chew from his pocket, Morven tried hard to contain her laughter.

***

Dave parked outside Eddie Stewart's home, a modern bungalow in a salubrious area of Strathmurray. Eddie was a handsome man in his early forties, with short brown hair and a neatly trimmed beard. He was dressed in sports gear and looked as though he spent a lot of time in the gym. Black Celtic tattoos snaked upwards from his wrists before disappearing beneath the material of his t-shirt which strained against muscular biceps. Spotting the electric drill in his hand, Dave took a slight step back.

"Sorry, I'm doing some DIY," said Eddie. He placed the drill at his feet beside a hammer.

Dave gave him a spiel about making routine inquiries about the death of a young woman, assuring him she wasn't a relative. Eddie invited them inside and they followed him through to a tastefully furnished living room with a spectacular view over Strathmurray. A wedding photograph of Eddie and his bride sat on the mantlepiece alongside pictures of their two small children. Kid's toys were neatly stacked in storage boxes, next to a partially built IKEA shelving unit. They sat on a plush sofa opposite Eddie.

Speaking in a deep baritone voice, Eddie said, "What's this about?"

Dave showed him a picture of Claire Angus and explained she'd been found dead. Eddie appeared shocked and asked what had happened.

"That's what we're trying to find out," said Dave. "We got your details from Strathmurray Connect. They said you knew her."

Eddie stroked his beard. "I haven't seen Claire for ages. I was an occasional speaker at one of the youth groups she ran."

"Can I ask what you gave talks about?" asked Dave.

With a hard obvious swallow, Eddie turned his head away and gazed out of the window. Several moments passed before he met Dave's eyes. "I'm transexual," he said. "I was born a female but transitioned in my twenties. I used to talk about my experience with her LGBTQ+ group."

Morven opened her mouth and immediately closed it again. Without breaking stride, Dave inquired about the last time he'd attended the group. Eddie reckoned it was at least two years ago, and Dave asked why he'd not been back.

Eddie shifted his weight and cleared his throat. "We'd a difference of opinion."

When asked what he meant, he explained that he'd raised concerns that the kids in the group were too young and were transitioning too rapidly. Claire was unhappy at Eddie dispensing advice to wait until turning eighteen before making such a life-altering decision.

Eddie said, "When I got my diagnosis of gender dysphoria, it helped me to understand how I was feeling but these kids aren't waiting for professional confirmation, they're self-declaring, and some at a really young age."

"Did you argue?" asked Dave.

He paused for a long moment and Morven worried he'd clam up. Finally, he said, "We had a disagreement but we parted on good terms. Claire meant well even if her methods were questionable."

Eddie described how he'd begun his own transition aged 24. At five years old, he'd known he was meant to be a boy. The idea hadn't been pushed on him; he instinctively *knew*. His social and physical transition was gradual and he'd received treatment through the NHS at a gender clinic in London. He recalled sitting nervously in the waiting room with only one other person.

"Sex change was very uncommon back then," he said.

Dave glanced at the family photographs. "It obviously worked out okay for you."

"It cured the gender dysphoria but it still didn't make me a real man. My wife and I had to use a sperm donor. It's not been all rainbows and butterflies, and that's what I wanted those kids to know."

"How was that received by the group?" asked Morven.

Eddie shook his head. "Honestly, it was full of young girls wanting to be boys, who've all been indoctrinated to believe people can actually change sex."

When Morven asked why he thought that was, he said without hesitation, "Social media. It's a contagion if you ask me, like anorexia and fainting fits."

He told them about a woman on TikTok with four children under the age of 12 who were all either trans or non-binary, and how she regularly posted pictures of them draped in rainbow flags. Eddie said, "If that's not pathological virtue signalling by the parent, then what is?"

Eddie rose and gazed out of the window. Looking at his strong jaw and powerful physique, Morven found it hard to believe he was a biological female.

"They're not being honest with these kids or their parents," he said. "They tell them the drugs are safe and any changes are reversible, which is simply not true. Testosterone is a really powerful hormone which has profound effects on the body, especially on a female one." He turned to face them. "These girls have no idea what it will do to them."

"Can you remember the names of any of the kids?" asked Dave.

Eddie didn't but he said he'd photographs that Claire had taken with him and the group at Christmas parties. He offered to dig them out and send them. Morven asked if Claire had invited other speakers to fill in after Eddie had given notice.

"I don't know, but I wouldn't be surprised if Clownfish were involved, they've got their tentacles in everything."

"The trans charity?" said Dave. "Why d'you say that?"

"Clown Show, more like." He practically spat the words. "Organisations like them are the ones pushing this agenda and none of it's grounded in science or reality." He took a deep breath and regained his composure. "Anyway, I can't be sure if they're involved, I'm not part of that community anymore."

When Morven asked why that was the case, he gave a bitter laugh. "I'm an old trannie and my views aren't popular these days. I've been attacked for speaking out. I've even been branded 'tru scum'."

He explained this term was volleyed at older transsexuals like himself who'd undertaken a traditional pathway involving therapy, hormones and gender re-assignment surgery to make them 'pass' in their chosen gender. The TRAs — as he referred to the new breed of trans rights activists — dismiss this approach, insisting there is no need for a gender dysphoria sufferer to undergo any treatment or present as a member of the opposite sex. Instead, it was enough to simply have an inner feeling of gender identity.

"Quite frankly," said Eddie, his nostrils flaring, "they're a bunch of groomers. Teaching kids that biology doesn't matter and gender is just a social construct is downright dangerous. And as for transitioning children, that's tantamount to abuse."

Eddie strode to the mantlepiece and picked up the photograph of his daughter. "I mean, how can you possibly make a decision like that until you're an adult?"

Morven wondered whether his anger at those involved in what he described as 'grooming' was motive enough. Dave must have been thinking the same thing as he asked about Eddie's movements on the day that Claire died. Eddie appeared taken aback at the question and hastily flicked through his diary.

Dave and Morven swapped a look that screamed 'person of interest'.

Eddie showed them the calendar entry. "I was at home all day with my wife and kids."

"One last question", said Morven. "May I ask what you do for a living?"

"I'm a paramedic," he said. "I work at Lothian and Borders hospital."

Dave thanked him and they departed. As they pulled away in the car, Morven spotted Eddie watching them from the window.

***

Back home, all Morven wanted to do was sleep for a week. After getting home late, she felt the need to shower. The memory of the crime scene coated her like a layer of grime. After, she consumed a tasteless microwave meal for one which sat in her stomach like a lead weight. She'd been about to go to bed when her mobile rang.

What fresh hell is this?

Sighing, she answered it. It was Danny Galbraith, the custody sergeant.

"Sorry to bother you at this hour Morven," he said, "but I thought you'd want to know we've got your ex-husband in the cells."

Morven was suddenly wide awake.

Chapter 21

Morven scanned the charge sheet that Danny had handed her, shaking her head with incredulity.

"Who the hell reported this?" she asked.

Danny explained that an anonymous call had been made to emergency services and a couple of young officers whose names she didn't recognise had responded and arrested Mark. Morven read the list of charges with disbelief. Her ex-husband was many things but not this. Never this.

Danny led her to a cell and she peered through the inspection hatch to see Mark slumped on a plastic mattress with his head in his hands. Danny unlocked the door and Mark glanced up. His eyes were red and puffy and he appeared to have aged ten years. The custody sergeant left them and she perched on the cot beside Mark.

"You're the last person I expected to see here," she said. "What the hell happened?"

Mark shook his head. "I wish I knew because, I swear to God, I don't know what's going on in our kid's head." He looked at her. "Have you spoken to Ollie?"

"Briefly, but he didn't say much, only that you'd argued. He's staying with one of his mates tonight."

Mark explained what had happened after he'd got home from work that evening. Ollie had been in a strange mood, but he'd been acting odd for a while so he hadn't paid it much attention. However, during dinner, Ollie suddenly blurted out that he was 'transfemme' and wanted to socially transition to being female.

"Whoa," said Morven, "what did you say?" She thought she'd misheard.

Mark repeated it and Morven gawped in disbelief.

Wide-eyed, she said, "Transgender ... as in he thinks he's a girl?"

Mark nodded and explained that Ollie felt he'd been born in the wrong body and, from now on, he wished to be addressed as Olivia. He insisted they use female pronouns 'she' and 'her' when addressing him and made no mention of the 'deadname' Ollie. Morven struggled to take in what Mark was telling her and she kept asking him to repeat information.

Despite Mark's own shock and confusion, he'd remained calm and had asked only a few probing questions about why his son had arrived at this decision. Ollie claimed that it had been on his mind for some time and he'd been presenting as a female at school.

"Since when?" gasped Morven.

Mark shrugged. "First I've heard of it."

They sat in silence for a while, Morven trying to make sense of what he'd told her.

"So, how did you end up in here?" she asked.

Mark explained that when he'd expressed concern about Ollie's decision and offered to arrange counselling for him, a full-blown argument had ensued. Ollie said some nasty, spiteful things and the outburst culminated in him accusing his father of transphobia and storming off to his room.

As Morven listened, she grew more and more anxious. She'd sensed something was up and she'd long suspected her son was confused about his sexuality. She'd expected him to come out as gay. But knowing this wouldn't change how she felt about him, and she'd have supported him. She was certain Mark would too. But trans? Never this.

She glanced at Mark who looked haggard in the glare of the fluorescent light. "When did the police show up?"

Mark told her that later, when he and Brittney had gone to bed, Ollie had been in his room gaming and chatting to his mates online. Just after midnight, the police knocked at the door and woke the household. After a brief discussion with Ollie, they arrested Mark on charges of domestic abuse and took him to the station for questioning.

"Did you know about this?" asked Mark.

Morven's mouth fell open and she tried to contain her anger. "Of course not, why the hell would you even think that?"

They sat without speaking for several long minutes during which time her annoyance faded to sympathy. She spoke softly, "I'll bring you a coffee, then I'll sort out this mess and take you home."

"You can do that?" His relief was evident.

She blew out a hard breath. "Quite frankly, no one here's got a clue why you're here, least of all me. I love our son dearly but right now I could wring his bloody neck."

Mark placed a hand on her arm. "Morven," he said, "I'm worried about Ollie's mental state and I don't know how to handle this." He paused then added, "And Brittney ... well, she's got enough to deal with and I'm not sure I want this stuff around our younger kids."

As much as Morven resented Mark's wife, she couldn't blame her for wanting Ollie out of her home. How were young children who were only just learning the difference between cats and dogs supposed to make sense of a boy claiming to be a girl when he clearly wasn't?

"It's fine," said Morven, "I'll fetch him home."

He gave her a grateful smile. "You always were a lot better at this kinda stuff."

She stifled the urge to point out he'd never stuck around long enough to deal with 'this kinda stuff'. The knot in Morven's gut tightened. "I'll talk to him," she said, "once he's calmed down. Hopefully it's just a silly teenage fad."

Trying not to dwell on what Eddie had said earlier about social media contagion, Morven left in search of the custody sergeant to sort out Mark's release. As she strode towards Danny's desk, she'd a sudden flash of realisation.

She knew how all five victims were connected.

***

Kerry wasn't sure what a 'Terf' was supposed to look like but it wasn't the attractive sixty-something woman on-screen. Her name was Jemma and she was a volunteer with *Real Women Scotland*, the organisation Sam had told her about. Kerry had perused their web site but, until recently, hadn't contacted the group.

After the open letter was published, Kerry decided to email RWS and explain what had happened to her at Lothian University. Jemma had gotten in touch straight away.

Today's Zoom call, Kerry knew, was to vet her to ensure she was a biological female who shared the organisation's values. Infiltration by trans rights activists was a constant threat that groups such as RWS had to guard against. Jemma explained RWS comprised of an informal network whose aim was to defend women's rights and foster free speech. Although based in Scotland, they collaborated with other similar UK-wide groups on various matters such as promoting clarity about biological sex in law, policy and language.

Jemma said, "We've several members in your area who I can put you in touch with. We use the Signal messaging app because it offers good privacy and security."

A tingle of unease crept up Kerry's neck as she pondered on whether she'd need Signal's enhanced features. Why did simply speaking up for her rights make her feel like a subversive? Kerry asked what she'd be expected to do.

"It's entirely up to you and your group," said Jemma. "You can do as much or as little as you want. We adhere to the principles of non-violent direct action though."

Jemma described the numerous actions the group had been involved in, including protests outside the Scottish Parliament about the Gender Recognition Reform Bill. The GRR legislation would allow any male, aged 16 upwards, to acquire a female birth certificate purely on his say-so, and vice versa. RWS had campaigned against the Hate Crime Act, a draconian bill to ensure gender-critical opponents are criminalised.

RWS had also been involved in demonstrations when the violent double rapist Adam Graham (aka Isla Bryson) was being housed in a women's prison in Scotland. And further action had been taken by the group after the horrific attack on a schoolgirl by the cross-dressing paedophile Andrew Miller.

"If you get arrested," said Jemma, "I'm afraid you're on your own."

Another sobering thought. Undeterred, Kerry requested to join her local group.

After the call ended, she smiled to herself. In the war against women, it felt good to fight back.

***

"It's a medical pathway," said Morven. "It's what connects them all."

It was early Saturday morning and she and Dave were stood in front of the murder wall which had been relocated to the larger conference room. Mugly sat at Dave's feet. She'd made them each a coffee, hoping the caffeine would dampen her exhaustion. After freeing Mark from the cells, she'd barely slept a wink.

When Dave frowned, she said, "It's a journey to changing your gender."

"What, like a sex change?" Dave's eyebrows knitted together as he appeared to think this through.

"General Practitioners," she said, "are the gatekeepers to accessing gender reassignment treatment and specialists such as endocrinologists who prescribe puberty blockers and cross-sex hormones."

Dave pointed to Mike's picture. "I can see where the doctors fit in, but what about the librarian and the drag queen?"

"By inviting a drag queen along to the library, Mike was helping peddle the idea to young children that you can be born in the wrong body. That's what the protest was about." Then, indicating Barry's photograph, she added, "and he's living proof that some people present as the opposite sex."

Dave added, "And the youth worker ran a queer group funded by Clownfish which supports all things transgender."

"Precisely," said Morven.

Sipping his coffee, Dave mulled it over for a while and then said, "Okay, supposing you're right, this means the killer is targeting people who're helping others alter their gender." He pointed to the photograph of the protesters outside the library. "It certainly gives this lot a motive beyond waving placards." Indicating the victims' pictures, "But why target these particular individuals? Is he choosing them at random based on their jobs or are they somehow all connected?"

"Perhaps they've all come into contact with someone who's transitioned," said Morven, "but we've yet to find a connection between McNab and De Garcia's patients." Almost as an aside, she added, "None were responsible for Eddie's transition, I checked."

"We need to go through their lists again," said Dave. "There's got to be something, even if it goes back several years."

"I'll speak to Ross, see what he can dig up." She looked at Dave, uncertain of whether to say what else was on her mind. Then, after a few moments, "There's something else." When he gave her a puzzled look, she said, "It might explain the increasing level of violence. Maybe the killer saw Mike and Barry as somehow less culpable than the professionals dispensing drugs and advice."

"There's certainly been an escalation," acknowledged Dave, "although I don't imagine Barry's death was particularly pleasant."

Morven stabbed a finger at De Garcia's photograph. "But if this truly is the motive, the journey may not end with hormones."

Dave gave a resigned nod. "So our killer's not done."

Just then Dougie emerged from his office. He pointed at the dog, pulled a face and barked, "What the hell is that, and what's it doing here?"

Mugly sprang up and wagged his tail so hard his whole body twisted with the effort.

"I've not had a chance to drop him at the dog pound yet," said Dave, without a trace of conviction.

The gaffer looked at him like he was nuts. "Get one of the uniforms to take it. It cannae stay here."

"Got time for a quick word, sir?" asked Dave.

Morven's stomach gave a lurch at the thought of what the gaffer would make of her theory.

"Come see me in an hour," muttered Dougie, "I've the brass and the press breathing down the back of my neck." He pointed at the dog, "That should give you ample time to get rid of Yoda."

***

Morven and Dave made use of the extra time scrutinising her hypothesis that a medical pathway connected the victims. She knew it was sketchy at best but they had little else.

Dave made no effort to disturb Mugly who lay curled up under his desk. The animal had already attracted some admirers. A young DC took him for a walk and returned with dog treats, and another donated a portion of homemade chicken casserole.

After an hour, Dave and Morven approached Dougie's door. The Chief DI was pacing back and forth on the phone but he beckoned them in as he wrapped up the call. Dougie's suit was crumpled and he had a five o'clock shadow although it was still morning. His desk was a mess of coffee cups, case files and reports and Morven wondered if he'd pulled an all-nighter.

"That was the Chief Constable phoning from the golf course," said Dougie flopping into his chair. "He wants to know why there haven't been any arrests." He looked questioningly at Dave. "Tell me you have something."

He said, "Morv has a theory you should hear."

After taking a seat, Morven took a deep breath and repeated her idea. Dougie listened and then asked many of the same questions Dave had. She told him Eddie Stewart was a person of interest but Dougie said a new squad was being assembled to investigate Claire's murder who would pick this up. After she'd finished, he slumped back in his chair and folded his arms, appearing to consider it.

He exhaled loudly. "It's flimsy at best, and the brass will hate it."

"I agree there are holes," said Dave, "but you've got to admit it has merit."

Dougie leaned forward and looked from one to the other. "Listen, if we take this line and we're wrong and it comes out later we were targeting the trans community, we'll be crucified. It'll be the end of all of our careers."

Morven said, "No one's suggesting a transgender person is responsible — Eddie might be innocent — only that our victims have all played a part in the pathway to transition."

Dave said, "Plus it's the only explanation we have so far that offers a possible motive and a connection between the victims."

Shaking his head, Dougie said, "You've yet to give me either." He picked up a sheaf of papers from his desk and turned to a page. "Meanwhile, upstairs have announced yet another diversity, equality and inclusivity initiative. This one's all about how we should determine the pronouns of those we arrest."

He read an extract aloud in a mocking tone, "It is important to respect a person's gender identity by using appropriate terms of address, names and pronouns."

He pulled a face and looked at them. "And you'll be delighted to know you've all to attend unconscious bias and hate crime training." Exasperated, he stabbed a finger at another document. "And next week, the Chief Constable is unveiling a Pride mural to symbolise that this is an inclusive place." He threw the documents onto the desk with disdain and rose, saying, "That's the political climate we currently find ourselves in so, without more evidence, I cannot sanction this line of inquiry."

Dave said, "But if Morv's right and it later emerges that we dismissed the idea, we'll still be vilified."

He shook his head. "I'm not willing to take the risk. This has the potential to turn toxic, so unless you bring me evidence, I suggest you pursue other avenues."

He opened his door signalling that the meeting was over. As they trudged out, Dougie reminded them to attend the training sessions. "No excuses," he called, before closing his door.

Dave muttered so only Morven could hear, "Hate crime, really? In the middle of a bloody murder investigation."

She followed her partner to the kitchenette. There was no one else around but she kept her voice low. "So what do we do now?"

Dave huffed out a breath, "Aye, that was disappointing but not entirely surprising. But the more I think about it, the more I suspect you're onto something."

"We'll get our arses kicked if we pursue it," she whispered.

He flashed her an impish smile, "I'm up for a good arse kicking if you are?"

Morven laughed, realising she had underestimated Dave Newton.

***

Morven parked outside Natalie's home. It was early evening but already dark and the rain sheeted against the windscreen. She pulled up the hood of her jacket and took a moment to prepare before making a run for the front door, unsure of the welcome she'd find inside from her son.

Natalie answered and Morven, dripping wet from the short dash, followed her into the kitchen. Natalie flicked on the kettle and then, after looking at Morven properly, asked if she'd eaten. The remains of a roast dinner rested in a tray on the cooker and, in normal circumstances, Morven would have taken no persuading. Natalie was a good cook but she'd no appetite.

"Where is he?" asked Morven sitting at the table.

Natalie set a mug of strong tea and a packet of biscuits in front of her. "Spare room. I've hardly seen him. He spends all his time on the computer talking to his friends." She looked at Morven over the rim of her mug. "What's up, he's acting really odd? And what's with all the makeup, is he auditioning for a musical?"

"Hasn't he told you?"

When Natalie shook her head, Morven said, "You'd better sit down."

Natalie slipped into a chair and wrung her hands in that way she always did when anxious. Keeping her voice low so as not to be overheard, Morven told her about how Ollie had come out as transfemme.

Natalie gawped at her and whispered, "Good God, Morven."

Morven repeated the dreadful argument Ollie had had with his father, his arrest, and how she'd hoped to have a conversation with her son about the implications of his decision. Morven had spent every spare moment researching the health implications of medical transition, and what she discovered was horrific.

"You're surely not going to go along with it?" gasped Natalie.

"I'm hoping to convince him to wait 'til he's older before making any life-changing decisions."

They heard footsteps on the stairs. They swapped a look and Natalie rose and went to the sink to rinse her cup.

"Hello love, how are you?" said Morven when Ollie appeared.

Ollie scowled and slid into the chair opposite. He wore a flowery strap dress over a white tee-shirt and he'd applied thick blue eyeliner. Morven tried not to stare. Natalie offered some excuse about needing milk and departed. Morven heard the front door close and a car engine start.

"Want a cuppa?" said Morven.

"Spoken to Dad?" Ollie's words sounded like a challenge, not a question.

"Well, I'd to bail him out last night." She'd aimed for a neutral tone but fell way short. "I thought we might have a chat."

With a baleful look, he snarled. "If you've come here to talk me out of it, forget it, I've made my choice and you need to respect it."

Morven forced herself to count to five in her head before responding. "Of course I'll respect your decision but you need to understand I've concerns." When Ollie said nothing, she launched into the speech she'd prepared in her head. "Adolescence is a very confusing time—"

Ollie shot to his feet, the chair making a horrible screeching sound on the tiles. "I bloody knew you'd be like this," he yelled. "It's my life, my body, my identity."

Looking at her son, Morven didn't recognise the person screaming at her. He was different, someone she no longer knew.

As he stalked off, Morven caught his wrist. "Please just hear me out."

Glaring, he wrenched his arm from her grip. "LEAVE ME THE FUCK ALONE!"

Morven wept. Ollie's assertion he was trans felt like he'd destroyed the foundations on which her life had been built — she had a son, not a daughter. She was still weeping when Natalie returned. Her friend took one look at her, produced a bottle of wine from her shopping bag, and poured her a large glass.

Natalie perched beside her. "What are you going to do?"

She shook her head. "What can I do? He won't talk to me."

Natalie regarded her over her glass. "Well, you'll have to do something because there is no way I can simply stand by and watch while that lovely young boy destroys himself."

Chapter 22

Beamer lived in a quiet estate built in the sixties in the 'arts and crafts' style. Trees lined broad avenues where winding pathways led to quaint cottages nestled in mature gardens. Before Beamer's heart attack, Morven had visited on a couple of occasions and each time she'd wished she could afford a house here too.

She stood on the front porch, admiring the traditional craftsmanship of the carved wooden columns either side, and rang the bell. Beamer's wife Jane greeted her, the delicious scent of home baking accompanying her. Morven handed her a bouquet of flowers and Jane thanked her. She led Morven across the rich hardwood floor of the hallway and into a spacious living room which overlooked a manicured lawn.

Beamer was napping in an armchair beside a stone fireplace, a novel resting on his chest. The television was on low, tuned to a nature programme Ollie often watched. Morven was grateful it wasn't showing continuous coverage of the investigation since every traditional and digital platform was saturated with updates, speculation, and analysis.

"Look who's here to see you," said Jane.

Beamer opened his eyes and rewarded Morven with a generous smile. He'd lost weight, and his face was pale and hollow. She tried not to let her concern at his appearance show. He placed the book down and eased himself out of his chair.

"Please don't get up," she said.

He plopped back down as if the effort had been too much. Morven leant over and gave him a light peck on the cheek, and then sat opposite him.

"It's good to see you," he said. "I'm sick to the back teeth of daytime telly."

"I would have visited earlier but—"

He dismissed her apology with a wave. "I want to hear every last detail of the case." His eyes sparkled with interest.

She gave a dark chuckle. "Huh, that might take a while."

Indicating the book he was reading, he said, "Well, it's not like I'm busy."

Beamer excused himself to use the bathroom and she examined the paperback he was reading, a spy thriller called *Operation Mincemeat*, which told how the Allies had deceived the Germans during the Second World War. She remembered seeing the film. She placed the book down beside a newspaper with the sensationalist headline *Strathmurray Slasher Strikes Again*. The media interest had been intense since the discovery of McNab's body to the extent the team were overwhelmed with the influx of tips, rumours and speculation generated by the coverage.

Morven's attention shifted to the nature programme which showed a male wading sandpiper bird performing an elaborate courting ritual. She watched as another male, mimicking a female, fooled the other sandpiper into mating with him instead.

Beamer reappeared and switched it off. He scrutinised her and asked how she was bearing up.

"You've had a baptism of fire," he said. He picked up the newspaper, a national title, and said, "Cases like this are as rare as hen's teeth and few officers ever come across a serial killer. Yet here you are, in at the deep end on your very first day in CID."

She exhaled loudly. "I can't even begin to tell you how crazy it's been. And it'll only get worse until we catch him."

Jane appeared with a tray laden with coffee and freshly baked scones that reminded Morven of how little she'd eaten recently. Jane handed her husband a plate of sliced apple and he rolled his eyes.

"Am I not even allowed a scone, wummin?" he said, stretching for one.

Jane playfully swatted his hand away and placed the tray out of his reach.

After she'd gone, Beamer said, "Honestly, this recuperation business is doing my nut in. I feel like a useless old horse put out to pasture." He rose from the chair, grabbed a scone and with a wink, said, "So, tell me everything."

Morven did and he listened intently as she outlined each case, interrupting occasionally with probing questions. When she shared her theory about how she believed the victims were connected, Beamer gave a low whistle.

"Good grief," he said, "you'll have to tread carefully, that's a political minefield."

Biting into a scone piled high with jam and cream, she mumbled, "That's what Dougie's worried about. He doesn't want us focussing attention on the trans community."

"Aye, the brass won't like it one bit. Not when there's folk like Cavendish championing all that Diversity, Equality and Inclusion rhetoric." He paused. "Don't get me wrong, we ought to reflect the community we serve, but I'm not convinced bringing in the likes of Stonewall is the right way to go about it." He looked at her and said, "Can you believe they rewrote our parental leave policies to remove the word mother?"

Incredulous, she shook her head and took another mouthful of Jane's baking. "Has Rob been to see you? How's he coping under the new regime?"

"Aye, popped in last week. He's moaning his face off about Cavendish and the Snowflake Brigade as he calls them. But him and Patel seem to be getting on well." Dougie wiggled his eyebrows.

Morven snorted in amusement.

Beamer's eyes twinkled with mischief. "You'll no doubt have heard the rumours about Cavendish and Dave?"

That had her attention and she pulled her chair closer. "No, what's the latest gossip?" She wasn't sure who enjoyed office tittle-tattle more, her or Beamer.

"They've split up. Cavendish has been in tears. The ice-maiden has a heart after all."

Morven gawped at him. "Dave never mentioned it, at least not to me." She felt a pang of sadness at him not telling her. Despite their history, she thought they'd cultivated a good working relationship, especially under the circumstances. Still, they were colleagues — nothing more — and at least this explained some of Dave's recent behaviour.

"So, who dumped who?" she asked, leaning forwards.

"According to Patel, Dave did the leaving." Beamer grinned. "He's gone up in my estimation but he's probably scuppered his chances of promotion."

"Explains the dog," she said. She told him about Mugly and how he still hadn't taken the creature to the dog pound.

Beamer said, "I think you're right though; these killings are personal and whoever's behind them has an axe to grind with each of the victims."

Morven gave a heavy sigh. "But why aren't we finding a connection? All we've got is my flimsy theory and a few fetishists."

Beamer tapped his temple. "I'm going to have a think about what you've told me. I need something to keep the old grey matter active. Between us, we'll figure it out."

She hoped he was right. Beamer was looking tired and she needed to go home for a nap since Ross was coming round later. They'd been seeing one another regularly and anticipation of the night ahead was the only thing keeping her going.

As she rose to leave, Beamer said, "Look after yourself Morven. Cases like this can take their toll and we've lost good officers due to burnout, stress, and emotional exhaustion.

If only he knew that the investigation was only the half of it.

***

The following morning, nothing was mentioned during Dougie's meeting about Morven's theory, and she didn't dare raise it. At one point, when the gaffer asked for an update from her, she caught Dave's eye and he gave an almost imperceptible shake of the head.

Dougie introduced the new squad taking over responsibility for the investigation into Claire's murder. It was headed up by a young DS called Toby Larson who'd been fast-tracked to detective status as a graduate with a Law degree from Edinburgh University. The clean-shaven and sharp-suited Toby looked like the living personification of LinkedIn.

Toby introduced his team and explained they were still getting up to speed with the wider investigation but they'd already begun to delve into Eddie Stewart's background and alibi.

Pointing to his picture, Toby said, "Eddie is a trans man who knew Claire through her LGBTQ+ youth group."

Dougie said, "Remind me, what's a trans man?"

"A female who identifies as a male." There was a hint of condescension in Toby's tone.

"So, he's not a man," said Dougie looking baffled. "I thought Eddie was a trans woman."

"No, a trans woman is a man who identifies as a woman."

"Oh for Chrissakes," said Dougie, "I'm confused." With a red marker pen, he wrote the definitions of trans man and trans woman on the whiteboard.

Bill Arnold then got to his feet and explained he'd interviewed Claire's partner, Peter Sneddon, in connection with her murder. "Sneddon's got a cast iron alibi," said Bill, "he ... or should I say *they* ... were on a work trip."

Dougie frowned. "What's all this he/they nonsense. How many Sneddons are we talking about?"

With a wry grin, Bill said, "Sneddon is non binary, sir."

"What the hell does that mean?" asked Dougie.

Bill chuckled. "Apparently, *they* don't identify as either male or female."

"So what is he?" Dougie was looking more bemused by the second.

"*They*," mocked Bill. "*They* have no gender at all or have a mix of genders."

"Oh for fuck's sake," bellowed Dougie, "this is weapons-grade bananas." He grabbed the pen again and added the definition of non binary beneath the other definitions.

Laughing now, Bill said, "Do you want to add agender, bigender, gender queer and gender fluid to the list?"

With a strangled cry, Dougie turned to face the team. "What the hell is wrong with these people? If *they* don't know what sex they are, *they* only need to look in their underwear."

When the muted laughter abated, Dougie ceded the floor to 'the tech guy'.

Clearing his throat, Ross said. "I've been broadening my investigation of all the victims' devices and I've found something interesting ... and rather alarming."

Ross cast his computer output onto the large television screen and lines of code appeared which looked like gobbledegook. He highlighted a line which he explained pointed to a kiddie porn site on the dark web. "I found this buried deep on McNab's home machine."

His words were met with groans of disgust.

"Aw Jesus," exclaimed Dougie, "so the good doctor was a paedo?"

Bill Arnold said, "Which means we've another fetishist, if you can bear to call paedophilia that."

Dougie nodded. "Exactly. Which means three out of our five victims have a predilection. This can't be a coincidence people, there's got to be a link." Addressing Ross, he said, "I want every machine belonging to the librarian and the youth worker forensically examined. And if we need extra bodies on it, let me know."

You'll get more bodies if you stray down this path, thought Morven with dismay.

Dougie wrapped up the meeting and returned to his office, followed by Dave who closed the door. Morven watched them arguing and Dave waving his hands around. She spotted Bill Arnold taking a marker pen and, next to the definition of a trans woman, writing 'bloke in a dress'.

Ross approached her desk and Morven pulled her gaze to his.

"Sorry I didn't warn you about McNab," he whispered, "I only just discovered it." He flicked a glance at Dougie's office where a barnie was in full swing. "I guess that's put the kibosh on your theory."

The previous night, after a marathon sex session, she'd shared her theory with Ross who'd listened with interest. She tried to hide her disappointment at Dougie's disregard for it. With a rueful smile, Ross returned to his desk.

But Morven couldn't let it go. She dug out the autopsy report for Patricia Duncan, the social worker who'd made the referrals to the youth project run by Claire Angus. Pat, as she was known, had been found dead at her home after a neighbour became unwell and was taken to hospital. Carbon monoxide poisoning was detected and although the neighbour made a full recovery, Pat was not so lucky. Blood tests from the postmortem showed she had a 61% CO content, well above the fatal 50% threshold.

An investigation by the Health and Safety Executive found that Pat's gas boiler, which had been installed in the 1980s, was producing high levels of CO that had affected her and the adjacent property. Further inspection revealed the boiler hadn't been serviced for some time and was in a dangerous condition. The flue had also been stuffed with newspaper and the ventilator was blocked with dust. As a result, Pat's landlord was facing charges.

After scanning the photographs taken during the investigation, Morven pondered on the report. Pat's death appeared to be the result of an entirely preventable fatal accident and there was nothing to suggest foul play. Her landlord had failed to ensure the boiler was serviced and maintained, and annual safety checks carried out. And it had been assumed that Pat had blocked the flue in order to prevent a draft.

But Morven didn't believe in tragic coincidences.

She phoned Dr Hellberg the forensic pathologist and left a message on her answerphone. Hellberg returned the call minutes later and Morven outlined her concerns about Pat's death.

"Send me the file, I'll take a look," clipped Hellberg.

Morven thanked her and emailed over the autopsy and HSE reports.

***

Kerry spotted a woman waving from a table in the small family-run bar. The charming pub was one of Edinburgh's finest, known for its quirky décor and curios. It also offered private little nooks and crannies at the rear, perfect for furtive meetings such as this.

"You must be Kerry," said the woman, extending a warm handshake. "I'm Natalie."

They'd been messaging each other in the *Real Women Scotland* group chat and Kerry was delighted when Natalie had suggested a drink. It was a chance to meet people who shared her belief that women's rights and the right to freedom of speech and association were under threat from radical trans activism, and who were prepared to speak out.

"It's so lovely to put a face to the name," said Kerry sliding into the seat opposite.

A waitress appeared and Kerry ordered an orange juice since she was driving. She and Natalie exchanged small talk until their drinks arrived. Natalie checked her phone and spotted a message from Amruta saying she'd be unable to make it as one of her children was sick.

"That's a pity," said Natalie, "Amruta is really passionate about the cause."

They discussed rumours of a possible RWS event coming to Glasgow in the near future. Natalie explained that, because of security concerns, the dates and locations of these were never shared too far in advance.

"Have you been to any events before?" asked Natalie.

Kerry shook her head. "I understand they can get quite lively."

Natalie chuckled. "Aye, that's one word for it. The TRAs always target us so don't be alarmed if there's a bit of jeering and jostling. We always get a good turnout in Glasgow though, so security will be tight."

Having read about attacks on women attending similar gatherings, Kerry hoped a bit of jeering was all she'd encounter from the trans rights activists, if she was brave enough to go. She asked Natalie why she'd become a member of RWS.

Natalie explained she was a midwife and, over the years, she'd become increasingly concerned about the impact gender ideology was having on her profession and within the wider healthcare system. The 'cult', as she called it, had crept in slowly and stealthily until almost every part of the NHS was infested.

Natalie said, "First, we were beaten into submission with Equality, Diversity and Inclusion training and mandatory pronouns. Then came the erasure of women's language from maternity care."

She described how staff were expected to refer to women as birthing parents and chest feeders.

"Not only is this language dehumanising and demeaning," said Natalie, "but it makes no sense to our patients. In this country, the average reading age for healthcare language is eight years old."

"Eight?" gasped Kerry.

Natalie nodded. "Less educated mums or those who speak English as a second language simply don't understand terms like gestators, birth-givers and menstruators."

She also described the end of single-sex wards and the impact this had on women. "It's not just about safety," she said, "it's about privacy and dignity."

She bemoaned the fact that women who objected to receiving intimate care from trans-identified males were called transphobes, often by other women. Natalie said she'd recently complained to management when software was introduced by the hospital that recorded the gender identity of newborn babies, rather than their sex. Kerry shook her head in disbelief.

Natalie said, "It's imperative we record data accurately, especially sex."

She told Kerry about a case where a trans man, whose sex was recorded as male on her health records, presented in A&E with severe abdominal pain. The patient was pregnant but this was discovered too late and the foetus died.

"Equipment is designed differently for males and females," said Natalie. "There are cases of trans men being intubated with tubes designed for males resulting in serious injuries to the airway."

Kerry asked what direct action Natalie had been involved in and she revealed she'd been a long-standing member of another women's rights group. However, she'd become increasingly frustrated by the lack of action and progress.

"Writing to newspapers and signing petitions is all very well," she said, "but nothing will change unless we march on the streets like the trans activists do. We need stronger action to put an end to this madness before more women and children get hurt."

Kerry wondered what she meant by 'stronger action' but before she could ask, Natalie glanced at her watch and announced it was time she caught the bus home.

"I'll look forward to seeing you at the RWS event," said Natalie, putting on her suffragette scarf. "We should meet up beforehand. It's safer if we stick together."

Wondering what she'd gotten herself into, Kerry's stomach gave a lurch.

Chapter 23

It was late evening and Morven lay in bed wrapped in Ross's arms. Since their first night together, they'd been banging away like a cludgie door in a gale at every opportunity. So, when Mark had messaged to say Ollie was spending the night at a friend's house, Morven and Ross had made use of every room and item of furniture in her home. The bedclothes were knotted around her and she pulled the duvet over them. Despite the afterglow, her worries about Ollie and her anger at Dougie's decision still rankled and this must have shown on her face. Ross asked if she was okay.

She slid her hand down his torso making him smile. "I'm better than okay."

He flipped her onto her back and kissed her hard. When he broke away, he asked, "You hungry? I could get us a takeaway."

She wrapped her legs around him and pulled his pelvis towards her. "I can't believe you're thinking about food."

"I need sustenance woman," he chortled, rolling off of her, "a man cannot live on hair alone."

She swiped at him with a pillow but he ducked out of the way. Laughing, he grabbed her wrists and pinned her to the mattress like a butterfly on a board.

"Chinese or Indian?" he murmured through kisses.

"Scottish," she sniggered with the heady sensation of being a teenager again.

But the sex was incredible and better than anything she'd experienced with her husband or previous partners; not that she'd had many. Perhaps it was because she was older and more accepting of her body. As a youngster, she'd hated that her curves hadn't conformed to the ideals portrayed on the glossy covers of magazines. The demands of her job had kept her fit, but there was no hiding the stretch marks and effects of gravity. Ross didn't seem to mind though.

He rose and began pulling on his clothes. She marvelled at his body: the broad chest with a dusting of hair, bulky upper arms, and powerful taut thighs.

"Enjoying the view?" he asked, eyes twinkling.

Her phone buzzed on the bedside table and she checked the screen. Her horny feeling vanished. It was Ollie letting her know he wouldn't be home next day as they'd planned, and that he intended to remain at his mate's. It was the first message she'd had from him in days. She tried calling but he didn't answer, so she texted him. His reply was swift.

> [Ollie] Please respect my decision and understand that right now I need time and space apart from you and dad.

The constriction in Morven's chest tightened, like something pressing heavily on her. She tried phoning the friend's mother but there was no answer and she suspected she was already in bed.

"Everything alright?" asked Ross, perching beside her.

She looked at him, trying to decide whether to tell him or not. But, if they were ever to be more than fuck buddies, he ought to know, so she told him about Ollie's announcement and her concern about what it might lead to.

Blanching, Ross gently took her hand. "Christ almighty Morven, you must be worried sick." His voice was a mere whisper.

The tears she'd been holding back finally fell. She described Ollie's belief that all his unhappiness was due to being born in the wrong body, and her fears of what he might do. Ross listened patiently without interruption, and it felt good to share the burden she'd been carrying around.

He asked about Ollie's computer habits and she told him about the hours he spent gaming and chatting online, and her apprehension about the content he was being exposed to.

"You're right to be concerned," said Ross, "God only knows what he's viewing." After a moment he said, "Want me to look at his machine?"

Her initial reaction was to decline because it was clearly an invasion of her son's privacy, but if Ollie was being lured into believing that changing his gender would be a magic 'cure all' for his unhappiness, she needed to know. This was more important and she was confident Ross could examine the device without leaving a trace.

"OK," she said, "I'll get the food while you do your thing."

Morven led Ross to Ollie's room and showed him the computer.

***

What Ross discovered on Ollie's computer was far worse than anything Morven had expected.

Long, emotional threads from transgender activists about how they'd felt the same way prior to transitioning and how happy they were now. Teenage girls delighting in the irrevocable effects that testosterone was having on their bodies: a deep voice, facial hair, muscle mass and the constant urge to masturbate. Young women expressing hatred for their breasts alongside others parading double mastectomy scars like badges of honour. Influencers telling their followers how hot and trendy it was to be trans. Adverts from unregulated clinics offering hormones without a prescription and payment plans for surgery.

But the most disturbing and hurtful of all were the posts made by Ollie about how bigoted and unsupportive his parents were, and how much he hated his life. It made hard reading and Morven wept bitter tears.

Ross brought her a mug of tea and wrapped an arm around her shoulders. "It's an echo chamber," he said. "Everyone in it is immersed in the fiction that you can change your sex. No one dares question it and if they do, they're kicked out the cult."

She sipped her tea. "I don't know how to handle this. I can't stand by while he harms himself, but if I push back, I'm afraid it'll only make him more determined."

Ross scrolled through Ollie's emails and opened one. "There's something else you should see."

Her gut clenched as she read Ollie's enquiry to one of the clinics requesting a price list.

Morven buried her head in Ross's chest and sobbed.

***

After they'd eaten, Ross returned to his own flat saying he'd a plumber coming next morning. Despite her mental, physical and emotional exhaustion, Morven lay in bed unable to sleep. Although it had felt good to share her worries, she was consumed by an overwhelming sense of confusion, anger, sadness and shame. Her son hated his family and his life, and that could only be a reflection of her and Mark's shortcomings as parents. After the divorce, she'd strived to fill the father-shaped gaps in Ollie's life but clearly she'd failed.

Morven wasn't ready for this new 'truth' that Ollie could become a girl. How could she hold fast to her conviction that humans cannot change sex in a kind and respectful manner that wouldn't alienate her son? How could she impart her own beliefs without him flying off the handle and doing something impulsive? Ollie was like an unexploded bomb which was about to go off at any moment, and she felt utterly helpless in the face of his emotion. If she affirmed Ollie as female, she might salvage their relationship, but to do that she'd have to embrace a fiction.

Morven considered her own lived experience as a woman, in the roles of daughter, wife and mother. She could understand why young girls today might want to opt out of womanhood. Females were at the mercy of their bodies and every age seemed like a new assault: periods, pregnancy, breastfeeding, menopause.

But she also remembered the many wonderous moments of being a woman: a lover's touch, discovering she was pregnant, the flutters and kicks of a developing baby, the visceral agony and exquisite joy of giving birth and meeting your child, and the toe-curling pain of breast feeding. And, as difficult as some of these experiences were, she wouldn't have missed any of them for the world.

How could anyone seriously believe that sex was a choice of identity and not a biological reality? And how do you say to a young person suffering from gender dysphoria to 'give it a few years and everything will work out fine'? Because most of the time it does.

Should she go along with Ollie's new identity in the hope it was just a passing fad he'd grow out of? But if Ollie did seek hormones and surgery, she could not watch him poison and mutilate his body in the hope of finding happiness. She loved her son and wanted him to be happy but Mark was right — this path would lead to a lifetime of medicalisation and misery.

No, she refused to affirm a lie and to do so would be immoral. It would be akin to telling an anorexic they were fat and watching them starve to death.

***

Next morning, Morven drove to work feeling weary to her core. She'd endured a sleepless night and now every movement felt like an extra effort. She'd a pounding headache and felt nauseous. Was this the burnout which Beamer had talked of?

Unable to face the office yet and now that it had stopped raining, she trauchled to the coffee shop at the top of the street. Inside, the shop was warm and smelled of freshly baked bread which reminded her she'd not eaten. After ordering a latte and a chocolate pastry, she perched on a stool by the window and checked her phone. She spotted four missed calls from Beamer and a voicemail. She listened to his message which asked her to call him urgently. He ended it by saying, "I know what twenty means."

She immediately phoned him back and Beamer answered on the second ring. Without preamble, he said, "It's Operation Mincemeat, that's what made me realise."

Oh God, how many meds has he taken?

"Sir, I'm sorry but you're not making any sense."

"Listen," said Beamer, "during World War II there was a group of the best counterespionage and intelligence experts called the Twenty Committee. Guess what their symbol was?"

Yep, he's finally lost the plot.

"Not a clue."

"The Roman numerals XX. It's clever because it also means double cross."

"But what's that got to do with ...?" And then the realisation hit her and her heart rate quickened. Beamer was right. Chromosomes.

Morven covered the mouthpiece of the phone and in a low voice, said, "Of course, twenty written in Roman numerals is also a symbol for female. Two X chromosomes."

"Yes, which means your theory's spot on. The killer's making the point that biology is real and he's targeting those who believe otherwise."

She could hear the excitement in Beamer's tone. He almost sounded like he was back to his old self. She paused for a few moments, then said, "Do you think that'll be enough to convince Dougie?"

"Well it's hardly a smoking gun but it's an important piece in the jigsaw." His tone became gravely serious, "Morven, can I offer you a piece of advice?"

"Of course, sir."

"Be very careful how you proceed and who you trust. Cases like this can make and break careers."

She thanked him and hung up. His words did little to allay her worries. She drained her coffee and headed back to the office. On the way, she spotted Dave walking Mugly on the opposite side of the street and she crossed over to join him. Lines of exhaustion were etched across Dave's face and his usual vibrancy had faded. He looked as tired as she felt.

She stooped and petted the dog who licked her hand. "I thought you were taking him for rehoming."

Dave shook his head and sighed. "I cannae bear to. He's already had a crap life and several owners."

She met his gaze. "You keeping him?"

"Just until I can find him a good home. It's the least I can do." He looked at her for several long moments as if deciding whether to say more. "I split up with my girlfriend and I've moved to a new place where I'm not supposed to have pets. That's why I've brought him to work."

Surprised at his candour, she said, "I'm sorry to hear that." An awkward silence followed which she broke. "You'll just have to hope Dougie doesn't spot him."

As they strolled back towards the station, she told him about her phone call with Beamer.

Dave stopped and gawped at her. "Jesus," he said. "Beamer's right. You're right. That's the killer's message."

"Do we tell Dougie?" she asked.

He shook his head. "It's only a theory, not evidence so I doubt he'll change his mind." After a pause, he added, "In fact it might be best to keep this to ourselves until we've done some more digging." Then, hesitantly, "But only if you're okay with that."

Morven recalled Beamer's words about being careful how you proceed and who you trust. But Dave was right — this was speculation, not proof — and she agreed to keep quiet.

"I'll take responsibility," he said, "if it comes out later that we knew." He gave a deep sigh. "Quite frankly, they can hand me my arse on a platter for all I care."

As she watched him traipse to his car with the dog, she worried about the effect the investigation was having on her partner, made worse by the breakup of his relationship. Was the pressure of it all affecting Dave's judgment? Was it affecting hers?

Chapter 24

Morven's phone was ringing when she arrived in the office, and she answered it. Without any greeting or introduction, Dr Hellberg, the pathologist, informed her that she'd read the reports on Pat Duncan's case.

Hellberg said, "It's called the 'silent killer'. We see about forty deaths each year from carbon monoxide poisoning. CO is an odourless, colourless, tasteless and poisonous gas, and poorly maintained central heating boilers are the most common culprits."

She went on to explain how CO poisoning can occur when even small amounts of the gas get into the blood stream and prevent red blood cells from carrying oxygen. Without oxygen, body tissues and cells die. Low levels can cause serious harm when breathed in over a long period of time, including paralysis and brain damage.

"People often mistake the symptoms for food poisoning or flu," said Hellberg.

"Humour me for a moment doctor," said Morven, conscious she was beginning to sound like Dave. "If I wanted to kill someone, could I just block up the ventilation system on their boiler?"

Hellberg took a few moments to reply. "There are lots of other factors to consider."

"But even so, stuffing newspapers into the vent would do the job, yes?"

"Possibly, but I can't say for certain."

Morven suppressed a groan. Trying to get a definite answer out of a pathologist was like grasping a shadow. "How long would it take to poison them?"

"If there's a high enough concentration of CO, loss of consciousness can occur within two hours."

Morven thanked Hellberg and ended the call. Her headache throbbed and she ached all over. Stretching, she gazed out of the window at the town below. She couldn't help but wonder how many other deaths might be linked to this investigation.

She thought about the various means employed and the increasing levels of violence, as if the murderer had been starting tentatively and testing his resolve before gaining in confidence. Or did his methods have some bearing on the reasons the victim had been selected? The youth worker's murder had, as Hellberg put it, all the hallmarks of a ritualistic killing so perhaps the poisonings were significant. But, if that were the case, what possible justification existed in the killer's twisted mind for the brutality involved in Claire's slaughter. A flashback of the crime scene made Morven shudder.

This was deeply personal for the killer; of that she was certain.

Ross's appearance ended her wool-gathering. He stood beside her at the window and flashed her one of his secret smiles, the type she was sure was reserved only for her. She resisted the urge to reach out and touch him although every sinew yearned to. He seemed to feel it too and let his hand brush against hers.

"Penny for your thoughts?" he said.

She explained about Pat Duncan and how she thought this case may be linked to theirs.

His brow furrowed. "But no number twenty was found at the scene?"

"It could have been missed. I'll ask Bill; he was assigned to the case."

"I'll trawl Pat's client list," said Ross, "just in case there's a connection."

A ping on her computer alerted Morven to an email. Her heart sank as she read it. It was from the Professional Standards Department, known colloquially as 'The Complaints', informing her of a hearing to discuss the allegations made against her by Haydon Murphy. Wondering if this heralded the end of her career, she let out a pained sigh. Another ping, this time a meeting reminder. Morven groaned aloud.

Right now, I'd welcome instant dismissal.

She stomped up the stairs to the fourth floor, furious at being compelled to attend a training session in the middle of a murder investigation. All attempts to excuse herself had been met with refusal.

The classroom was packed and she recognised several faces amongst the uniforms and plainclothes officers seated in rows. A young WPC of south Asian descent stood at the front with a clipboard. Morven took a seat between DI Bill Arnold, and Tricia Barnton from the Woman & Child unit.

In her mid-forties, Tricia had short blonde hair and piercing green eyes. She and Morven exchanged a greeting. She'd worked with Tricia on many occasions, most recently after a particularly vicious domestic which Morven and Rob had responded to after neighbours reported screaming. Morven would never forget the victim's howls of agony and the bloody pulp between the woman's legs where her partner had repeatedly kicked her. And, as if the attack wasn't bad enough, it had been witnessed by their two-year-old child. Morven later discovered the woman had been so badly injured that she'd required reconstructive surgery. She still felt sick just thinking about it.

The instructor closed the classroom door and flicked on the overhead projector which displayed a slide entitled 'Policing Hate Crime'.

"I'm Radia Banerjee," she said, "and I'm attached to a specialist unit dedicated to policing the Hate Crime and Public Order Scotland Act."

Bill folded his meaty arms and muttered in a low voice, "Otherwise known as the Pronoun Police."

Radia explained the Act was aimed at protecting vulnerable groups from prejudice on the basis of age, disability, race, religion, sexual orientation, transgender identity or variations in sex characteristics.

She gazed at her audience and said, "Today's session has been developed in close consultation with community groups and diversity associations to prepare for when you have to respond to hate crimes and incidents." She smiled, adding, "We want everyone targeted by hate crime to have the confidence to come forward, assured they'll be treated with respect and dignity, and any reported incident fully investigated." She spoke as if reading from an autocue.

"God, this is all we fuckin' need," grumbled Bill.

Radia displayed a definition of a hate incident on the screen which she explained is, "Any incident which is perceived by the victim or any other person, to be motivated, wholly or partly, by malice and ill-will towards a social group but which does not constitute a criminal offence."

Bill said, "So, we're expected to police insults?"

"It's called a hate incident," said Radia.

But Bill wasn't for letting it go. "What if the insult isn't meant as one? Like if I'm in the pub with my mates and Irish Brian arrives and we greet him with 'Awright Paddy'. It's a term of endearment but he or someone else could report it, and on paper it'd sound like we were racially abusing him."

"Irish is not a race," said Radia, as if talking to a four-year-old.

Undeterred, Bill continued. "Okay, so if we said 'Awright auld yin' then we could be accused of being ageist. Is that what you're telling me?"

Radia gave him a patronising smile. "In theory, yes, if someone thought it was malicious."

Morven thought Bill had a point but remained silent. He'd many years of service under his belt and was close to retirement, which probably explained why he'd the courage to speak out.

"How can we know if it's motivated by malice?" he asked.

Radia said, "It's the perception that's important. But evidence of malice or ill-will is not required for a hate crime or incident to be recorded and investigated."

"So thought crime is actually a thing," exclaimed Bill.

Radia tutted, "Now you're being ridiculous."

"What's ridiculous," said Bill in increasing volume, "is this bloody law. I mean how the hell are we supposed to police insults unless we know what's in a person's heart when they utter them?"

Radia had no answer. Flustered, she continued to her next slide which showed that in 2020-21, there were almost 7,000 reported hate crimes in Scotland.

Tricia piped up, "In the same year, there were more than 15,000 sexual crimes, almost all perpetrated by males."

There were rumblings of support for Tricia's point.

Hands on hips, Radia said, "No one's suggesting that we shouldn't prosecute other crimes. It's not a case of one or the other."

Bill said, "It is if you've staff cuts, a budget squeeze and lack the basic kit to do your job." He raised his hands, palms upward, to represent scales and in a voice dripping with sarcasm said, "Ooh, sexual assault or hurtful words... hmm... that's a toughie."

There was more murmured agreement. Radia glared at Bill with undisguised loathing and then continued to assail her audience with statistics, flowcharts and phrases such as 'holistic assessment of wellbeing concerns.' To Morven's ears, it sounded like white noise.

At the end of the presentation, Radia appeared to have gathered her composure enough to ask if there were any questions. When Bill's hand shot up, she ignored him and pointed to Anne, one of Tricia's colleagues in the front row.

Anne asked, "I notice biological sex is not mentioned in the Act. Does that mean women and girls are not protected from hate speech?"

Radia confirmed this was the case but that a separate law against misogyny was being brought in.

Bill interjected with, "Which, by the way, includes men who identify as women."

Morven couldn't believe what she was hearing. How were they supposed to implement this?

Anne then asked what the Act meant for women's rights campaigners and whether they could be reported for hate crime simply for stating that trans women are male.

Radia replied, "If, for example, someone identifies as female and a person refuses to respect that, yes, they could be breaking the law."

Exasperated, Anne said, "What? For saying that a man is not a woman?"

Imitating the voice of DCI Jim Taggart in the popular TV series, Bill boomed, "There's been a MISGENDERING".

There were peals of laughter and Morven sniggered behind her hand. But it was far from funny and she wondered when it was that Scotland had become a totalitarian state. The government had surreptitiously pushed this legislation through during the pandemic, and she questioned the cynical timing.

Radia, her mouth puckered like a drawstring purse, shot a furious glare at Bill and bit out, "Quit being an eejit."

Bill waved a finger at her. "Careful officer, you might hurt my feelings and I'll have to go lie down in the soft toy therapy room."

When the laughter died down, Anne said, "But don't gender-critical campaigners have the same right to freedom of speech and assembly as other groups? These are the foundations of our democracy."

Radia snapped, "Not if their purpose is to stir up hatred against transgender people."

She flicked to the next slide which showed a photograph taken outside the Scottish Parliament when Gender Recognition Reform was being debated. It showed a group of women's rights activists holding placards that read "Women's rights are not hateful" and "Protect women & children - scrap GRR".

Morven gasped. There, front and centre, was a face she recognised. It was Natalie.

***

When Morven returned to the office, she was still seething about the Hate Crime training session, and she wondered how her colleagues in Community Policing were ever going to carry out their duties based on this flawed legislation. As she passed Bill Arnold's desk, she heard him ranting to Dougie about 'wrong think'.

Dave appeared at her desk. "Enjoy the training?"

She rolled her eyes. "Don't. Even. Ask." Morven knew he'd been to an earlier session.

He chuckled and then in a low voice, "Carpark in five? I've something to show you."

Fifteen minutes later, they were sat opposite one another in the local café with cups of coffee and Mugly at their feet. The dog scratched behind its ear with a hind foot, eyes squinting with pleasure, and then settled with his head on his paws. Dave confessed he was keeping him in his car during the day and walking him regularly with the help of a couple of DCs in Mugly's fan club.

"It's not ideal," he said. "I can't leave him all day in the flat. I'm negotiating with my landlord and if it comes to it, I'll find another place."

Morven petted the dog. "I can always take him for a bit if you're stuck. Ollie's been on at me for years to get a pet."

He smiled. "Thanks Morv, I'll keep it in mind." Dave fished his mobile out of his pocket and scrolled to an email. He passed it to her saying, "I thought we could have a gander."

Morven scanned the message which was about a speaking event due to take place in Glasgow hosted by *Real Women Scotland*. Dave explained RWS was a feminist group who opposed gender ideology and the erosion of women's sex-based rights.

He said, "It might be the sort of thing our killer will show up at."

"Won't it be full of women though?"

"Probably, but we won't know until we go. And who's to say our murderer isn't female?"

Unconvinced, Morven said, "Well, you can't go."

"Why not?"

"Because you look like a copper, that's why."

Taken aback, he said, "Do I?"

"Yes Dave. If Hellberg cut you open, 'police' would be written through you like a stick of rock."

He laughed and she spent the next few minutes convincing him that she should go alone. He only agreed to her plan on condition she wore an audio-visual device so he could keep an eye on her and those around her.

"You're taking all this fluffy safeguarding training too literally," she teased.

Dave laughed. "Not where you're concerned."

Not quite knowing what to make of his words, she changed the subject. "So, what do you think about all this gender business?"

He shrugged. "If that's how people want to live their lives, then fair enough as long as they're not harming anyone. But men shouldn't be in women's spaces, no matter how they dress or identify. Having a lack of respect for a woman's boundaries is the worst quality a man can possess."

Dave Newton continued to surprise her. "I'm pleased to hear you say that," she said. "A lot of guys don't seem to care because they don't think it affects them."

"Then they're fools because we've got mothers, sisters, wives and daughters."

"Turns out, it affects sons too," she said.

He gave her a curious look and it was as if a floodgate had opened and all her worries came spilling out. She told him about how Ollie was caught in the vice-like grip of a trans identity, and how concerned she was about him.

Dave rubbed the bristles on his chin. "I'm sorry Morv, I'd no idea you were dealing with this. I've been so wrapped up in my own issues. Listen, forget this event, you've enough on your plate."

"No, I'm going, I want this bastard caught as much as you do." She glanced at the time, "Hey, we'd better go or we'll miss the morning meeting."

As they left the café, Morven said, "And bring Mugly, we'll tell Dougie he's our therapy dog.

Dave guffawed.

Chapter 25

Kerry spotted a message in her 'Terven' Signal chat and opened it. It was from Natalie.

> Hey Kerry, want 2 meet me and Amruta on Sat for quick drink before the RWS event? Better 2 arrive together as its gonna b jumpin! Nat x

Kerry replied asking where and when. She could already feel her heart rate rising.

***

Morven approached the venue with trepidation, aware that counterprotests around *Real Women Scotland* events could get lairy. A tiny device that resembled a brooch was attached to her jacket which allowed Dave to monitor the event remotely. He'd called in a few favours to get a hold of it, and he was parked a few streets away at a discreet distance listening and watching. With Mugly.

She heard the commotion before she saw it. A large group of trans rights activists had gathered outside the theatre and were yelling abuse and waving placards. She wondered what it was about women wanting to exercise their right to free speech that triggered such hostility.

The noise became deafening as she drew closer. A line of police observed the protesters, with officers pushing back any foam-flecked nutters who ventured too close. Morven kept her head down and made her way to the end of the queue, hoping not to be recognised.

A man in a shock-frock who resembled a bricklayer grabbed his crotch and screamed at her, "Suck on my girl dick." The police pushed him back but he continued to yell as other women filed in behind her.

Morven shuffled forwards in the line, anxious the militants might at any moment overwhelm the officers and break through. She'd policed numerous protests and marches in her time but rarely had she witnessed such vitriol. Hatred and fury rolled off these activists like a boiling wave.

The women around her appeared terrified and some cowered in fear. Stood in front of her were a mother and teenage daughter escorted by a man, an ordinary looking bloke in his fifties. Watching the activists warily, he kept asking if the women were sure about attending.

A scuffle broke out nearby when an enormous trans 'woman' in a wig and pink dress launched himself at a group of middle-aged women, shouting "Death to all terfs!". He was quickly and forcibly removed, and Morven wondered what the local custody sergeant would make of him.

It was a relief when she finally reached the entrance to the theatre. Morven overheard the man in front promise to collect his family later and, when he turned to leave, she saw fear in his eyes.

Inside, security was tight with numerous burly doormen clad in black. Morven handed her ticket to a security guard who checked her over, glanced inside her handbag, and directed her into the main hall. Although it was busy, the auditorium felt serene compared to the melee outside. Morven slipped into a seat at the back and removed her outer coat, ensuring her brooch was pointing forwards.

The crowd comprised mainly of middle-aged females but among them were girls in their teens and women old enough to be grandmothers. A few men, many wearing pride colours without the black trans symbol, peppered the hall.

Morven gasped when she spotted Natalie sitting near the front. She wasn't surprised to see her friend at this event, only that she hadn't mentioned going.

Once everyone was seated, the security personnel closed the doors and stood along the edges of the hall with their hands behind their backs. Morven could still hear the protesters outside shouting. A young woman with long dark hair bounded onto the stage and introduced herself as one of the organisers. She thanked everyone for braving the activists outside and announced the main speaker.

The hall erupted in cheers and applause as Imogen James walked up to the podium. She was smaller than Morven had imagined, with platinum hair and a dazzling lipstick smile, but she'd a presence that belied her stature. It was several minutes before she could be heard above the cheering.

Speaking in a soft English accent, she said, "You're probably wondering what all the gentlemen outside have their knickers in a twist about."

This was met with howls of laughter which soon died down when the screen behind her flickered into life. The footage showed an angry bunch of trans rights activists mobbing her at a speaking event abroad. Morven had read how the police had failed in their duty to protect her and, had it not been for her security detail, she might have been badly injured or killed.

"When people ask me what I do, I say I'm a campaigner for women's rights. Despite what the media report and what's on my 'Mikipedia' page, I'm not a Nazi, a transphobe or a bigot. My sole aim is to defend women's spaces, our language, and our sports."

Clapping ensued and she paused to let it subside. "What we mustn't forget is that these were hard-fought rights, and they must be defended from the type of men who would do us harm."

A picture of Adam Graham appeared, the convicted double rapist who went by the name Isla Bryson. Graham had made headline news when, after declaring himself transgender, he demanded to serve his time in a woman's prison and have his crime recorded as that of a female. His picture was met with shouts of anger from the audience.

Imogen leaned closer to the microphone. "Female-only spaces exist for a reason, and we must never cede them, and certainly not because a group of deluded, narcissistic men demand it." The noise from the rabble outside punctuated her words.

She went on to describe how language was under attack from the trans lobby. She said, "I'm not a bleeder with a bonus hole, nor am I a womb-haver or an egg-carrier. I'm a woman — an adult human female. And the irony is that this so-called inclusive language reduces women to nothing more than our biology ... and from the very people who deny that biology is real. It's catsuit crazy!"

This was met with whoops and applause. Imogen then explained why she refused to use preferred pronouns or have people tell her what to say, which she termed 'compelled' speech. A list of pronouns appeared on-screen including Ze and Zir, and an even longer list of genders. To the audience's amusement, Imogen highlighted a few of these including alien-gender and clown-gender. She read out the definition of astro-gender as "a fluid gender identity that transitions from male to female to non-binary depending on the current configuration of the night sky."

Morven could barely believe what she was hearing.

"They will not control our tongues," said Imogen. "If you're asked your pronouns or your gender identity, politely decline to answer."

That received ear-splitting applause. When the theatre quietened, she talked about the 'gender-goofy' newspapers that accepted large donations to peddle trans propaganda. She displayed an article from a broadsheet about a 'woman' who'd murdered her boyfriend and brother, before explaining that these violent crimes had actually been committed by a trans woman — a male.

"Language," she said, "is being twisted to the point that it's non-sensical, and we can no longer trust journalists to accurately report the sex of violent men."

There then followed a discussion about trans athletes competing in women's sports, and a picture of the 6'4" trans swimmer Lia Thomas filled the screen. It showed him towering over the females he'd triumphed over in a women's university competition.

Imogen said, "Not only were these women forced to race against this man, but they'd to suffer the indignity of changing in the same locker room as him, a fully intact male. When the women complained, they were told that they needed to be re-educated."

A rumble of fury rippled through the audience.

Indicating the screen behind her, she said, "The university was gaslighting these women. Their feelings clearly didn't matter and they were told to put up and shut up."

Footage then showed a rugby game in which an Australian female player was poleaxed by a trans-identified male. The lady beside Morven remarked it was a miracle the woman had walked from the pitch unharmed.

She said, "Rugby finally stood up to this madness by refusing to let males play against females because they realised that, were they to do so, women would be badly injured or killed."

"Biological sex is real," said Imogen. "Humans, like all other mammals, come in two reproductive varieties: male or female. Almost every cell in our bodies is sex stamped. Typically, women have two X chromosomes, while men have an X and a Y."

Thinking about the killer's signature, Morven shuddered. She cast her eye over the audience and wondered if the murderer was here. She hoped Dave could see and hear what she saw.

Imogen continued, her voice growing in volume. "Sex is not a feeling or a spectrum, it's an immutable biological fact."

A photograph of a protest outside of the Scottish Parliament appeared which showed a woman holding a banner declaring, 'Women are born, not worn.'

"We cannot change our sex. Men cannot be women, and women cannot be men." She gave a dark chuckle. "Yet, simply stating that fact in Scotland is enough to have me charged with hate speech."

The hisses of anger from the crowd were drowned out by the racket outside as activists banged on the doors and windows. The security guards glanced nervously at one another and one spoke into a walkie talkie. Morven hoped Dave was aware of what was happening.

Despite the disturbance, Imogen went on. "But the real issue is how this insidious ideology affects our children. Thousands of kids have been sold the idea that they're born in the wrong body, and this has led to them undergoing experimental treatment with hormones that will likely shorten their lives and render them sterile."

A photograph of a young woman suffering from early-onset osteoporosis appeared. Her spine was so weakened that she'd developed a Dowager's hump.

"We know these drugs do harm," said Imogen. "They don't just pause puberty; they cause irreversible damage to children's physical and mental development. We're talking weak bones, cancer, heart disease, and changes in brain development."

She said in a low voice, "And that's before they've had the surgeries."

A collage of photographs featuring girls with double mastectomy scars appeared, and a deathly silence fell. Morven felt nauseous looking at the mutilation inflicted on these young women.

Imogen ploughed on. "Same-sex-attracted, autistic and troubled girls are being fooled into believing that if they cut off their breasts, they'll be happy."

A shocking picture appeared of a boy whose genitals had been removed, and it caused howls of anger and disgust.

Imogen said, "I apologise if you find these pictures upsetting, but what I find more disturbing is that the head of the Clownfish charity took her son to Thailand on his sixteenth birthday to be castrated. And this is the same charity the Scottish government fund to spread this ideology in schools."

Thinking of Ollie at the mercy of the gender abattoir made Morven well up. The crowd's wrath was almost palpable, matching the fury levelled at them from outside.

Imogen's voice rose to the challenge. "Our children are being medicated, sterilised and mutilated in the name of gender ideology."

Her words were cut short by a cacophony of aggressive pounding on the windows and doors. The sound reverberated through the room, creating a ripple of unease. Attendees exchanged worried glances as the reality of the threat sank in. The thuds intensified and the security team flocked to block the doors. The atmosphere inside the theatre turned to fear.

The main entrance doors became the target of the protesters' kicks and blows, and the noise of splintering wood pierced the air. Several people from the audience rushed to help the doormen form a barricade.

Morven jumped in fright as a brick shattered a window and landed nearby. Panic ensued as other missiles followed and the audience were showered with glass. Morven dived for cover beneath the seating and dialled Dave's number on her phone, realising she'd missed several calls from him. He answered on the first ring.

"Get the troops in here NOW," she yelled. "They're about to break through."

Dave sounded as frantic as she felt. "On their way, just get yourself to safety."

Morven watched in horror as one of the rear fire exits gave way and an angry mob of activists stormed into the hall. Chaos followed as they set about the women, punching, kicking and pushing them. Morven darted towards the main entrance, almost losing her footing in the stampede. Her phone was knocked from her hand and trampled underfoot.

Some of the security guards began funnelling the women towards a side exit. As Morven joined the throng trying to escape, she saw one lady hit in the face, pushed to the ground and stamped upon. Without thinking, Morven ran full pelt at her assailant and sent him flying into the chairs. The man, dressed in a red tutu and bra, scrambled to his feet roaring in fury. Morven tried to tug the dazed woman to her feet but tutu man sprang at her. Morven sidestepped and kicked him hard in the groin and, with a grunt, he folded like a deckchair. She dragged the terrified woman to her feet just as police swarmed into the hall.

Pulling the woman out of their path, she fled to the side entrance and they spilled out onto the pavement. Blue lights flashed and uniformed police in high viz were everywhere. She'd never been so happy to see her colleagues.

"Thank you," sobbed the woman, "you probably saved my life."

Morven got a proper look at the lady for the first time. Only five foot tall, she looked to be in her sixties. Blood poured from a deep gash above her eye which was already painfully swollen. Morven slid a protective arm around her and supported her towards a waiting ambulance where a couple of paramedics helped her inside.

Morven heard her name being called and she turned to see Dave sprinting towards her. He enveloped her in his arms for several long moments. And then, seemingly embarrassed, he pulled away and scrutinised her.

Raking his hand through his hair, he said, "Thank God you're okay. I couldn't see or hear a damn thing on your camera."

She found his unexpected concern quite touching and she smiled. "I'm fine, just a bit shaken."

He glanced around and shook his head. "I'm sorry you were caught up in that. If I'd known what it was going to be like..." His words trailed off.

"What took the cavalry so long?"

He rolled his eyes. "Cavendish."

Enough said.

Morven described the assault on the woman that she'd witnessed, and said she'd lost her phone.

"Stay here," said Dave. "And that's an order. I'll find your phone and deal with the twat in the tutu."

She watched as he disappeared back inside the theatre where officers were still hauling activists out in handcuffs. She rejoined the woman in the ambulance where the paramedics were tending her eye. Morven perched beside her and asked how she was.

"I need to go to hospital," she said, "they think my eye socket might be broken." She squeezed Morven's hand and added, "But if it wasn't for you, it could've been a lot worse."

Morven sat with her a while until Dave re-emerged from the theatre rubbing his knuckles. He was followed by two uniforms manhandling the out-and-out psycho in the tutu. The thug had obviously resisted arrest and bore the marks. The bra was nowhere to be seen and his outfit was shredded, revealing silk panties that did little to hide his tackle. The officers covered the brute in a blanket and bundled him into a van.

A WPC passed and Morven asked her to accompany the injured woman to hospital and take her statement. Afterwards, she went to join Dave.

Indicating tutu man, Dave said, "I'll ensure our colleagues in Glasgow make our friend extra comfortable."

Morven hoped their hospitality was every bit as painful as a broken eye socket.

Chapter 26

A frown furrowed Ross's brow and he groaned. "Oh Christ, there's something you need to see," he said.

It was several days after the protest and he was sat at Morven's kitchen table on a laptop while she prepared a meal. They'd both worked late and then returned to hers and gone straight to bed. An hour later, exhausted, naked and sweaty, Ross had asked her about Ollie.

She explained how her son still refused to take her calls and had blocked her on social media. He was currently staying with Natalie but her friend had no idea what he was up to either. When not in school, he kept to his room and chatted to his online mates. Ross asked if she wanted him to take another peek at Ollie's computer.

After discovering that Ollie had been trying to source hormones without a prescription, Ross had installed monitoring software on his machine so she could keep an eye on his communications. Guilt pricked at her conscience, but she pushed it aside since she regarded her snooping actions as safeguarding.

With a feeling of dread, Morven dried her hands on a dishtowel and peered over Ross's shoulder. An email from Mark to Ollie was onscreen and she swore loudly when she saw it. In disbelief, she read it again to make sure. Mark's message confirmed he'd made an appointment for their son at a paediatric gender clinic in Glasgow, without Morven's knowledge or consent. The realisation hit her like a blow to the stomach.

"What the actual..." Morven collapsed into a seat beside Ross.

"I'm sorry," said Ross, "but it's better you know."

Morven continued to stare at the message in disbelief. "I can't believe Mark's done this. He has no right." She looked at Ross, tears pricking her eyes. "I'm scared I'll lose my son. If I stand in Ollie's way, it'll make him more determined. If I acquiesce, I'm worried what it could lead to."

Ross took her hands in his and fixed her with a penetrating gaze. He said, "You can't let this happen. If Ollie goes down this path, it's one way ticket to pharmaceuticals and surgery."

Fearing he was right, Morven surged to her feet and went in search of her phone. It was time to tear her ex-husband a new one.

***

Kerry spotted a direct message in the Signal app from Natalie asking if the RWS event had put her off.

Kerry had become separated from Natalie and Amruta after fleeing the theatre, but they'd messaged one another afterwards to confirm they were okay. Kerry had returned home, shaken but unharmed. She'd played down what she'd witnessed to her husband for fear he wouldn't want her attending another event.

The 'Terven' chat on Signal was full of outrage at the violence the women had experienced, and the police's apparent reticence to act. Several members of the wider group had been caught up in the fray, including a lady who'd suffered a broken eye socket. But, despite the brutality, there had been little mainstream media coverage, only bland reports of 'Trans rights protesters demonstrate outside feminist conference'.

There was further fury from the RWS members when they learned that an attendee had been arrested after she was overheard calling an activist a 'cock in a frock'. Accused of using words and behaviour intended to stir up hatred on the grounds of sexual orientation, the charges were later dropped.

After her own experience and having listened to Imogen's speech, Kerry was even more determined to fight on. She replied to Natalie's message to say she was ready to take action, and Natalie called her straight back.

"Can you talk?" asked Natalie.

Kerry said she was home alone since the kids were in bed and Andrew was away. Natalie explained that the Scottish National Party — or, as she called it, the Scottish Nasty Party — were holding a conference in Edinburgh. She suggested they target the arrival of the SNP leader in such a way as to get broad media coverage.

"What did you have in mind?" asked Kerry.

"I have a cunning plan," chuckled Natalie.

When she explained what it was, Kerry burst out laughing.

***

Morven hammered on her ex-husband's front door. It was dark and the rain had turned to sleet but she was too fuelled with anger to notice. She thumped again.

After a few minutes, the curtains twitched in the window above and she heard muffled voices. Behind the frosted glass of the door, a shape appeared and there was a rattle of keys.

Mark opened the door, tying the soft belt of his dressing gown. He scowled at her, "Do you know what time it is?" He cast a glance up and down the quiet suburban street.

"We need to talk. Now." She indicated her car parked opposite.

Muttering under his breath, Mark slipped on shoes and followed her out to the car. She sat in the driver's seat and as soon as he'd shut the passenger door, Morven rounded on him.

"What the hell are you playing at taking our son to a gender clinic without telling me?"

"Keep your voice down." He glanced at his neighbourhood nervously.

Morven thumped the steering wheel and yelled louder. "Don't you dare try to silence me. This is our son we're talking about. Have you any idea what could happen if you take him to that place? They'll affirm his new identity without question and before you know it, he'll be on hormones and having his body parts cut off."

"Have you any idea what Ollie might do if we don't take him? He threatened to kill himself for Chrissakes."

She gawped at him. "What? When?"

"He asked me whether I'd prefer a dead son or a trans daughter."

Shaking her head, she let out a pained groan. "That's exactly what they're told to say. It's straight out of the gender fairy run book — threaten suicide and you'll get hormones and surgery. But the truth of it is Ollie will be at far more risk of suicide a few years after transitioning when he realises what he's done and is still unhappy."

Mark stabbed his fingers through his hair. "What if he's not faking? Are you willing to take that risk?"

She put her head in her hands and swore. "You should have told me."

"He pleaded with me not to."

The silence that followed hummed with hurt and anger.

Glaring at him, she said, "You're putting me in a terrible position with our son."

Mark looked utterly defeated and a shard of sympathy pierced through her anger. "Sorry," he said, "I didn't know what else to do."

"You could at least have bloody told me."

He exhaled a long breath, and then looked back at the house where the bedroom light was still on. "Jesus, this is so fucked up."

Another heavy silence descended which she eventually broke. "Delay the appointment." When Mark began to protest, she cut him off. "I don't care how you do it but we need to buy him time. And when he does go, I want to be there to make sure he's not seeing some quack on the Gender Affirmation Station."

"He doesn't want you coming along."

She fixed him with a look. "It's not a request." Then, in a more moderate tone, "Ollie's not well. He needs therapy and support, not to be drugged and mutilated. He's vulnerable and we need to protect him from himself. That's our job as parents."

"Fine." He looked at her and huffed out, "Are we done?"

"Oh, we're done alright."

She started the engine and watched as Mark shuffled up the path to the house. Only when she'd driven out of sight did Morven let loose her tears.

***

Kerry sat opposite Amruta sipping coffee in a café close to the Scottish Exhibition Centre. It was the first day of the SNP's annual conference in Edinburgh, and Kerry's first taste of non-violent direct action. The cup shook in her hand and its contents curdled in her stomach.

Petite and in her early thirties, Amruta Singh had lustrous black hair tied in a plait that reached the base of her spine, and warm brown eyes. While they awaited Natalie's arrival, Kerry asked Amruta why she'd decided to become involved with RWS. In a soft Scottish accent, she explained that she'd been concerned about the risk to women in female-only spaces for some time.

"As a Muslim," she said, "I need access to sex-segregated fitting rooms. I can no longer try on clothes in many of the high street chains such as Marks & Spencer because they allow men in them. Most women aren't aware these areas are mixed sex, but the predatory males are."

Amruta then described the incident that had finally 'peaked' her into rejecting transgender ideology. A few months ago, she had collected her four-year-old daughter from nursery. Her child was distraught and when Amruta asked what was wrong, her daughter said there was a new 'man-woman' teacher who'd told her off for calling them 'mister'. Her daughter was upset because she knew the staff member was male but she'd been instructed to call him 'Miss Tiffany, and this didn't make sense to her.

At drop-off the following morning, Amruta ascertained that Tiffany was indeed a trans-identified male. When she spoke to the nursery manager about her daughter's confusion, she was informed that Tiffany was a woman, and Amruta was advised to have a word with her child to 'help her adjust'. When Amruta pointed out she'd raised her child to tell the truth and never lie, she was curtly told 'be kind'.

Amruta said, "Later, when other parents whose English isn't as good as mine voiced their concerns to her, the manager asked to speak to me. She told me I'd been reported to the police for organising a campaign of harassment against the staff member."

Amruta ferreted in her handbag for a tissue and blew her nose. In a wavery voice, she said, "I was asked to remove my daughter from nursery although she'd done nothing wrong." She looked at Kerry and added, "How is my daughter ever to trust what adults say again?"

She explained the incident had left her without childcare for several weeks which caused problems for her at work. Kerry asked about her job and Amruta explained she was a software developer at a bank in Glasgow.

"Work were really supportive but another employer might not have been so understanding."

Kerry said, "And what did the police do?"

"I was invited to a voluntary interview." She made air quotes around 'voluntary'. "If I didn't go, I would have been arrested. It was horrible. Fortunately, my cousin's a lawyer so I gave a 'no comment' interview and no charges were brought."

She looked at Kerry with large glassy eyes. "That's why I agreed to do this … and to hell with the consequences."

Impressed by her courage, Kerry reached over and gently squeezed her hand. Just then Natalie appeared, the jangling bell above the door announcing her arrival. Wearing a billowing summer dress despite the freezing weather and carrying a large shopper, she slid into the booth beside them. She was grinning from ear to ear.

"All set?" asked Amruta.

"Yes, I've been a busy beaver," said Natalie on a laugh.

Natalie cast a furtive glance around to make sure they couldn't be seen and opened the top of her bag. Kerry and Amruta peered inside and screamed with laughter.

***

As the First Minister's car pulled up outside the Scottish Exhibition Centre, Kerry reminded herself of all the reasons she was doing this.

She was acutely aware that all her friends, family and ex-colleagues would learn of it, and she fully expected to make the headlines on BBC's *Reporting Scotland*. Guilt pricked at her conscience for not warning her husband. What would Andrew think when he got the call or spotted his wife on the evening news? But she couldn't back out now; someone had to make a stand. Her gut writhed at the prospect of the stunt they were about to pull.

The three women had jostled their way to the front of the crowd which had gathered outside the entrance to the conference centre. The police had erected a flimsy cordon and several officers in high viz lined the street. A number of wheelchair users positioned close to the entrance waved yellow and black party flags and cheered for the benefit of the cameras.

As the doors of the black Mercedes opened, Kerry's stomach flipped. On Natalie's signal, the women darted forwards into the path of the minister. Standing shoulder to shoulder and in unison, they lifted their skirts high to reveal what the press would later describe as 'fulsome furry pubic wigs'. To the onlookers, it looked like the real deal and there were gasps of outrage and screams of delight. The First Minister halted in his tracks in front of Kerry and gawped at her crotch.

The women chanted, "If you don't treat women with decency, we will be indecent."

Their protest was cut short by several uniformed officers who manhandled them away, but not before the media had captured the spectacle. The women continued to shout as they were half dragged, half lifted towards a waiting police vehicle. As Kerry was bundled inside, she caught a glimpse of the red-faced minister and his entourage being ushered away by security into the building.

The doors of the police van slammed shut with a clang of finality. Only then did the enormity of what Kerry had done really hit her.

Chapter 27

Morven sat at her desk scrutinising photographs of androgenous adolescents with green hair and face piercings from Claire's youth group which Eddie Stewart had emailed to her. One boy looked familiar but she couldn't place him. Something was nagging at her but whatever it was kept floating away like Scotch mist before she could grasp it.

Her mobile phone rang and she answered it. The voice on the other end sounded panicked.

"You've done what?" gasped Morven.

She listened as Natalie described her stunt outside the party conference and where she was being held.

"Good God Natalie, what were you even thinking?"

Her friend sounded frightened but Morven was too busy to drop everything and drive to Edinburgh. The brass had just left Dougie's office after shouting at him because of the team's lack of progress, so there was no way she could desert her post.

Morven sighed. "I'm not sure there's much I can do except offer advice. Have you got a lawyer?"

Natalie confirmed she'd engaged the duty solicitor. Morven recognised the woman's name and reassured her that she was in safe hands.

"I can't believe I'm actually saying this," said Morven, "but don't say a word unless your lawyer's present. Understood?"

Morven offered to collect her after she was released and she ended the call. Although it was breaking the rules, she immediately searched the system for Natalie's charge sheet.

Ross sidled up to her desk, coffee mug in hand and smiled, "Everything okay?"

Shaking her head, she told him what Natalie had done. Ross chuckled and returned to his computer and looked for reports of the incident. He let out a belly laugh and turned his screen around for Morven to see. There, smack bang in front of the First Minister for Scotland stood Natalie hoisting up her skirt to reveal an enormous ginger muff.

Morven's jaw dropped at the sight of it and she rushed round to get a better look. The other women in the photograph sported similar kitty carpets in different colours.

Ross snorted, "Please tell me that's not real." He zoomed in on Natalie's furry triangle.

Morven stared at the monitor. "Nooo, it's a wig." She stared harder. "Surely to God it's a wig."

Their laughter drew interest from passing colleagues until several were gathered around the monitor sniggering. Dougie appeared from his office looking as though he bore the weight of the world on his shoulders. There was a sheen of sweat on his brow and dark circles ringed his eyes.

"What's up?" he asked. When the bodies parted to let him see, Dougie gawked at the photo. "Jesus wept. I tell you, if that was mine, I wouldn't show it to anyone."

"I believe it's a wig, sir," said Morven trying not to laugh.

The exchange caused further amusement. Hearing the commotion, Dave wandered over and voiced a similar reaction on seeing the image.

Dougie said to Morven, "And she's a friend of yours?"

"My best friend actually."

"I hope she realises the seriousness of what she's done," said Dougie. "They'll come down hard on her, with it being the First Minister and all." He seemed incapable of tearing his eyes from the photograph.

"Assuming it's a wig," said Morven, "at least they can't charge her with indecent exposure."

"But why do it in the first place?" he muttered.

With a hot flash of irritation, Morven felt the need to defend Natalie. She snapped, "Because she feels strongly about the government's callous disregard for women's rights."

Dougie glared at her. "Sounds like you do too."

Morven bit back the words she wanted to say.

Ross enlarged the image to show their faces. "Aren't they the same women who were at the RWS speaker event?"

Morven confirmed they were among the crowd.

"So they hate transgender people?" said Dougie.

Morven battled to control her temper. "They don't hate anyone. They're protesting against government policies on self-id and hate speech that harm women."

"Sounds like you share your friend's beliefs," said Dougie. He shot her a challenging stare.

Her face burned with anger and embarrassment. "After twenty years in this job, it's hard not to be concerned about what'll happen if they let the fox run free in the hen house."

The gaffer huffed out his annoyance and then, pointing to the photograph, he addressed Ross. "Dig around on those three, see what you can find."

"Oh, don't be ridiculous," yelled Morven, "they're harmless women exercising their right to protest."

"Who clearly hate the transgender movement," interjected Dougie. "The question is, do they hate it enough to murder people associated with it?" He pointed a finger at her. "You said it yourself, this could be about gender, so why not a bunch of militant feminists?"

Hands on hips, she stood to face him. "I know you're under pressure but if you truly think a group of middle-aged women are the ones eviscerating people, then you're clutching at straws."

Dougie's lips curled at the edges. "And your friendship with this woman is colouring your judgement. I suggest you stay clear of this part of the investigation." He turned to Ross and added, "I want no stone left unturned."

He spun on his heel and marched back to his office and slammed shut the door. Morven cursed beneath her breath.

***

Dave sat opposite Morven in the staff canteen and observed her over his coffee cup.

She asked, "Do you think our murderer is a woman?"

Dave shrugged. "I've little experience of serial killers but I do know that most murders, especially ones involving this level of violence, are almost always perpetrated by males." After a pause, he ventured, "But nothing about these killings is typical so that's not to say our killer isn't a woman ... or women." After a pause, he added, "You're probably right though and Dougie's clutching at straws but we will have to eliminate your friend."

Morven let go a deep sigh, knowing he was right, however, she refused to accept Natalie could commit murder. Of course her friend was worried about Ollie — they all were — but that didn't mean she was running round killing doctors and the like. And, in any case, some of the victims had been attacked way before Ollie ever announced he was trans.

As if reading her mind, Dave asked, "How well do you know your friend?"

"We've been mates for years and we've been through some tough times together; me with the divorce and Natalie with the death of her mother."

"How did she die?" asked Dave.

Morven explained Natalie's mother had suffered a stroke and had spent many months in hospital afterwards. Although she was eventually well enough to leave, she never fully recovered and later died at home. Natalie had taken it badly and had suffered depression for several years. Remembering it, she realised Natalie had never quite been the same afterwards.

"And the other women?"

"I recognise one of them from school. She's got a son the same age as mine, but I don't know the other woman." Morven shook her head in disbelief, "But Natalie? There's no way ... I mean she's Ollie's godmother and he's currently living with her."

Dave appeared to want to know why but didn't ask. Instead, he gazed at Morven for several long moments and said, "How well do we ever really know another person?"

***

The following morning, Dougie emerged from his office where he'd been ensconced with Bill, Ross and Dave for almost an hour, and called for the team to huddle round.

Morven shuffled into the meeting room with the others and stood at the back feeling like an interloper. The photograph of Natalie's stunt outside the conference was now pinned to the murder wall. Dougie began by asking Ross to outline what he'd discovered. Although Morven and Ross had spent the night together, he'd said nothing to her about his investigation of what Bill Arnold had termed the 'Pussy Riot'.

Ross pointed to Kerry's picture and explained that she was an academic who'd recently lost her job at Lothian University because of her gender critical beliefs. He showed them a local newspaper article in which she'd been defamed along with examples of online vitriol calling for her to be sacked. He said their colleagues had recently spoken to her about death threats she'd received.

Dougie said, "So, Kerry has a motive. She's anti-trans and she lost her job as the result of her views."

Morven stifled the urge to contradict her boss's assumption that Kerry was anti-anything, and the inconvenient fact that some of the murders had occurred before she had been hounded from her post.

Ross turned his attention to the other woman. "Amruta Singh is a software developer who was accused of stirring up hatred against trans people after the nursery her daughter attended hired a trans woman."

Dougie interjected. "For those of you who're as bamboozled as me, a trans woman is a male who identifies as a female."

Bill called out, "Otherwise known as a cock-frocker."

Dougie shot him a withering glare but said nothing. There were mutterings at the realisation they'd another protester with a possible motive. Ross displayed an article about the nursery incident which had been published in one of the tabloids.

"So Amruta also has a motive," crowed Dougie, casting Morven a pointed look.

Dougie's attitude was beginning to grate on her nerves. As Ross continued his exposé, anger began to gnaw away at his failure to share any of this with her. He was happy to share her bed so why not trust her with this information?

Ross then outlined what he'd found out about Natalie, leaving Morven wondering why he hadn't simply asked her. She could have told him and saved him a lot of time.

Avoiding Morven's eye, Ross said, "Natalie Wilson is a senior midwife at the Lothian and Borders hospital.

Again, Dougie butted in with, "Remember our killer has both medical knowledge and computer skills."

Panic began to set in as Morven could see where this was going. The thought that they would try to pin this on Natalie was so ridiculous that it made her seethe. And then Ross said something that astonished her.

"Natalie's mother was raped by a transgender hospital patient on the stroke ward."

Morven thought she'd misheard and she burst out with, "WHAT?"

Ross extended his palms and sent her a contrite look. "I'm sorry," he said, "I thought you knew."

With everyone's gaze upon her, Morven felt heat spread across her face and neck. Surely, Ross was mistaken; after all, Natalie would have told her about this. Wouldn't she? Morven remembered visiting Natalie's mother in hospital and being upset that Elisabeth was only able to lie there unmoving and unable to speak. But her mother had been a fighter and she'd defied the doctors and regained her speech and movement.

Running her hands through her hair, Morven recalled Dave's musings about how well you can ever know another person. Maybe he was right but that didn't make Natalie a murderer. But why had she concealed this awful event from her? Unless she intended to ... no, she couldn't go there.

Just as she was about to ask Ross how he'd discovered this, he displayed a report from the inquest into Elisabeth's death onto the screen.

"After Elisabeth, who was known as Betty, suffered a stroke," said Ross, "she was admitted to the Strathclyde hospital in Glasgow and placed on a female-only ward. However, unbeknownst to her and her family, there was a trans-identified male in the next bed. He raped Elisabeth."

Ross paused to allow the team to process the full horror of this appalling attack. Pondering on how helpless and vulnerable Elisabeth had been, Morven felt sick to her stomach.

"It was several months before Elisabeth could communicate what had happened to her," said Ross. "Worse still, when she did finally report it, she wasn't believed. The hospital denied there was a male present on the ward and argued the rape could not have happened".

Rubbing her arms, Morven felt lightheaded.

"How can you be certain she was raped?" asked Bill.

"CCTV," said Ross. "The investigating officers found footage of her attacker wandering around the hospital on the night it happened, and the nursing staff confirmed there was a trans patient on the ward. He got seven years."

Dougie said, "Why the hell was he in a female ward in the first place?"

Ross shook his head. "The NHS allows patients to be allocated to wards depending on their gender identity, not their sex."

"Jesus," muttered Bill, "what fucking idiot thought that was a good idea?"

Apparently fearing this debate would escalate, Dougie interrupted. "Policy decisions aside, the fact is Natalie Wilson has a strong motive for carrying out these murders."

"Then why would she target people promoting gender reassignment?" asked Morven. "Why not just bump off trans sex offenders instead?"

Dougie fixed her with his gaze. "Those are questions we intend to find the answers to." Then, indicating the photograph of the women, he said, "But this explains why we've struggled with this investigation. We've been working on the assumption that a male committed these murders, not a group of females."

He cast a triumphant eye over the team. "And make no mistake, together these women are capable of carrying out these killings. We've a whip smart academic, a midwife, and a software engineer. All three have a motive and combined, they have the skills."

Unable to believe her ears, Morven could only gawp with incredulity at the prospect of her dearest friend being charged with murder.

Chapter 28

Kerry sat alone in the cell on a blue mattress with a scratchy blanket draped over her knees. A harsh fluorescent strip light flickered above, casting a harsh glow over the stained walls. It stank of cleaning fluid, urine and stale alcohol. The metallic clang of a cell door closing reverberated through the air and Kerry clutched the edge of the hard cot, feeling the cold seep through her trembling fingers.

The adrenaline rush she'd experienced during the protest had subsided leaving fear and exhaustion in its wake. She rubbed her knuckles into her eye sockets, not caring what it did to her mascara. No way could she sleep. Not here. It was going to be a long night.

Following her arrest, she'd been formally charged with breach of the peace for 'conducting herself in a disorderly manner', and tomorrow would appear in front of the Sheriff. The duty solicitor, a kindly woman in her thirties, reassured her that since she'd no previous convictions, she'd likely be released on bail afterwards.

Listening to the unfamiliar sounds of the custody suite and occasional distant voices, Kerry felt as if she'd been cut off from the life she'd once known. Thinking of her beautiful home and family, she wrapped her arms around herself and wept.

***

Morven kept her head down and tried not to get in the way while the team dug into every aspect of the three women's lives. Dougie had made it clear he didn't want her involved as they built a case against Natalie and her friends. A message popped up on her monitor from Ross.

> Sorry!

Ignoring the message and him, she continued with the task of cross-referencing De Garcia's transgender patients with those of Dr McNab's, and the names of the young people in Claire's youth group, although she was certain Ross had already done this.

After twenty minutes, Ross sidled up to her desk. "Fancy a coffee?"

She shook her head without looking at him. Couldn't look at him.

He whispered, "Morven... I'm sorry, I don't know what else to say."

"There's nothing to say." She got up and walked away conscious of her colleagues' stares.

She went to the ladies and slunged her face with water until her pulse rate had slowed. Although she knew he'd only been doing his job, she felt hurt and betrayed by Ross for not sharing what he knew. And she couldn't understand why Natalie hadn't confided what had happened to her mother. Why had she withheld this?

After a few deep breaths, Morven returned to her desk to discover Dougie had called an impromptu meeting. She lingered at the back of the conference room and listened to the latest developments. On-screen Ross displayed what appeared to be a list of records from a telephone service provider. Several entries were highlighted.

Dougie pointed to them, saying, "Ross has obtained location data from Amruta Singh's mobile phone which places her in Brighton around the time Barry Mills was murdered."

Murmurs of excitement rippled around the room. Ross refreshed the display to show another set of phone records. Dozens were highlighted but he focused on one item in particular.

"These records are from Natalie Wilson's provider," said Dougie. "We believe Natalie may have been present at the protest outside the library where Mike

Carrigan was found dead. However, using this data, we can also place her in the area of the GP's surgery on the evening that Dr McNab was killed."

The burble of excitement increased in volume. Morven knew location data was circumstantial and proved nothing, and any good defence barrister would have a jury disregard it. In any case, as a midwife, Natalie might have had cause to be at the surgery. However, to her dismay, he had not finished.

"Records also show Natalie was in the vicinity of both De Garcia's and Claire Angus's homes when they were murdered." He turned to the team and grinned. There were cheers and whoops from several officers. For Morven, it felt like a lead weight was pressing down on her chest.

Victorious, Dougie continued. "As a midwife, she possesses the medical skills and knowledge needed to carry out these killings."

Morven could barely breathe and felt dizzy. Someone asked what they'd dug up on Kerry.

Dougie said, "Oh, she's a sly one for sure. There's nothing in her phone records but you'll never guess what Ross found."

Feeling the need to vomit, Morven fled to the bathroom before she could learn what it was.

***

Despite her rumbling stomach, Kerry had no appetite and she ignored the unappetising tray of food the custody sergeant had brought her. She sipped the tea. At least she thought the brown oily liquid was tea; it might have been coffee. Either way, it did little to settle her tummy.

Hearing a distant conversation and footsteps in the corridor outside only heightened her anxiety. The sounds drew nearer, and the hatch on the door slid open to reveal the sergeant's face. Kerry jumped.

"Some people wish to speak to you," he said before closing the hatch.

The door swung open with a low groan. Kerry's mind raced and her heart pounded in her chest.

"What's going on?" she asked. Her voice sounded tiny even to herself.

"Follow me please."

With her stomach in knots, she trotted down the corridor after him. He led her up a flight of stairs into another long corridor lined with doors leading to interview rooms. He paused outside one and indicated for her to enter. Inside were two plain-clothed officers; a man with a scar across his neck and an older heavyset guy. The room was sparse and equipped only with a table, chairs and digital voice recorder.

The younger guy said, "I'm Detective Sergeant Newton and this is my colleague Detective Inspector Arnold."

Newton indicated for Kerry to sit opposite and she flopped into the chair before her knees gave way. Newton sat opposite and despite Kerry's panic, she clocked his handsome features. He offered her coffee which Kerry declined, afraid she'd spew it up. She sat on her hands to stop them from trembling and asked for water. When the WPC stationed inside the door went to fetch some, Kerry asked what this was about.

"Just a few questions," said Newton, switching on the recorder.

He stated the date and time and who was present, including his colleague who'd returned with a plastic cup. He explained to Kerry that she was being interviewed under caution and asked if she wanted her solicitor to be present.

Kerry shook her head. Maybe if she cooperated, they'd let her home sooner. After all, her only wrongdoing was a cheeky flash of a pubic wig. Hardly the crime of the century.

"Please state yes or no for the tape," said Newton.

"No, I do not want my solicitor," she said.

Newton produced a plastic bag from his pocket, inside of which was what appeared to be her smartwatch. The custody sergeant had taken it from her earlier when she was booked in.

"For the purposes of the tape," said Newton, "I'm showing Mrs Connelly a Fitbit activity tracker." He looked at Kerry. "Is this yours?"

"Yes," she whispered. "And it's Dr Connelly."

"Louder please," he said, hitching his chin at the recorder.

"Yes, it's mine. Why do you ask?"

"We'll come to that." He placed the bag on the table out of her reach. Then he fixed her with an icy blue gaze. "Where were you on the evening of Monday 4th of December?"

Taken aback at the question, Kerry spluttered. "I've no idea, it was weeks ago. I'd need to consult my diary." Alarmed, she said, "Hey, what's this about?"

"We'll ask the questions, Dr Connelly," said Arnold.

Newton opened a thick manilla folder and slid a photograph towards her. Kerry peered at it. It was a picture of a protest outside what looked like her local library. She remembered reading about it in the local rag.

"Ring any bells?" said Newton, pointing to a blurry face in the crowd that vaguely resembled her own.

Alarm bells were now ringing in her head. She rasped, "I wasn't there and that isn't me."

Newton pursed his lips and stared at her. "Okay, what about on Monday 8th of January?" He showed her a photograph of the local doctor's surgery.

The realisation of where this was heading hit Kerry like a physical blow and she gasped. These were crime scenes. The Strathmurray Slasher stories were all over the media.

She gawped at him in disbelief and in a shaky voice said, "You don't honestly think I had anything to do with this? I was nowhere near these places."

Arnold leaned towards her and in a voice filled with venom, snarled, "Really, because the data on your Fitbit says otherwise."

Holy fuck!

In a shaky voice, Kerry said, "I'd like my lawyer now please."

***

Kerry hadn't stopped trembling from the moment the police had begun their questioning until her arrival at the courthouse next morning. The interview had seemed endless and then she'd spent a sleepless night in the cells, unable to face the breakfast provided, and she'd shaken with fear on the journey in the Serco sweatbox. Inside the court building, there was no sign of Natalie or Amruta and she wondered what had happened to her friends.

She was taken to a holding cell which was full of young males, many with tattoos and face piercings, and older guys who looked like rough sleepers. The place stank of stale sweat and despair. Kerry shuffled to a seat in the corner and kept her head down until she was called.

At the sound of her name, her stomach flipped and she stumbled on wobbly legs along the corridor after the clerk. A sturdy oak door led into the courtroom which blended traditional oak panelling with state-of-the-art technology. In front of the raised bench where a small balding man with glasses sat, were rows of plush seating occupied by a smattering of people in suits. Kerry spotted the friendly face of her lawyer amongst them. To the side were desks where a couple of clerks in black robes shuffled folders and typed into computers.

Kerry's heart raced as she faced the sheriff. A clerk announced the case, naming Kerry as the accused, and read the 'Breach of the Peace' charges aloud. The sheriff asked her to enter a plea but her mouth was so dry that she could barely speak. She pleaded guilty and then held her breath, hoping and praying she'd be released. Long moments passed while the sheriff perused the paperwork in front of him.

Regarding her over the top of his halfmoon glasses, he said, "Given you're of good character Dr Connelly, I'll grant bail pending background reports and expect you back here in a month's time for sentencing. In the meantime, you are required not to approach the First Minister or to participate in further protests or demonstrations." With a stern glare, he added, "Is that understood?"

Relief flooded through her as she squeaked out a "Yes sir".

The clerk led her from the court and back along the corridor where her husband Andrew waited. Kerry fell into his arms and he held her tight as she released the tears she'd been holding in.

Thank God that's over.

As Kerry and Andrew emerged from the courthouse, DI Arnold appeared accompanied by a young, uniformed WPC. Kerry's heart thudded and she gawped at him in horror.

In a stentorious voice, he said, "Kerry Connelly, under the authority of Scottish law, I am arresting you on suspicion of murder. You do not have to say anything, but it may harm your defence if you do not mention when questioned something which you later rely on in court —"

Kerry never heard the rest. A wave of dizziness washed over, her knees buckled, and she fainted.

Chapter 29

Back in the incident room, the atmosphere was triumphant as the team revelled in their victory. News of the arrests had been announced by the brass at a televised press conference to the media. Along with several others, Morven huddled around a screen watching a reporter broadcast the fact that three women had been charged with the 'Strathmurray Slasher' murders. The Chief Constable appeared, expressed sympathy for the families of the victims and shoe-horned in the annual drop in crime figures. Dougie was present in front of the cameras but Dave had dodged the limelight.

Morven's limbs felt heavy and she sloped back to her desk. Amidst the cheering, all she could think about was Natalie. All of it felt wrong. And Ollie still hadn't responded to her messages. She'd need to ask for Ross's help in pinpointing her son's location using his phone.

She glanced around but there was no sign of Ross and she wondered where he was. Things had been strained between them since Natalie's arrest and they'd hardly spoken. She pondered on what would happen after the team was disbanded and whether she and Ross would continue with … she hesitated to even think the word 'relationship'. They'd been lovers, nothing more, and she realised how shallow their affair was and how little she really knew him. Ross remained an enigma although she was familiar with every line and contour of his body.

Dougie entered and the detectives erupted into applause. All except Morven. Grinning, their boss raised his coffee mug in a mock salute.

Dave appeared at her shoulder. "Looks like someone could do with a drink."

She exhaled. "Tempting but I really ought to get home. I can't get hold of my son and it's really beginning to worry me. He doesn't know about Natalie yet and it's better he hears it from me and not the media." She checked her phone again but there were no messages.

Dave frowned. "Want some help?"

"Thanks but it's okay, he's probably at his dad's but Mark's not picking up his phone either. I'll just have to brace myself and talk to his wife." She pulled a face.

"Harridan?" inquired Dave.

She pulled a face. "It's not the word I'd use."

Dave gazed at her. "You okay? This must be really hard, what with it being your friend and all."

Feeling tears well up, she turned her head away. "I'm still trying to process it."

He gave her forearm a gentle squeeze. "Phone me if you need me ... even if you just want to talk."

She nodded a tearful thanks. Dave gave a small smile and wandered off. Morven watched him go, aware of how much their working relationship had developed over the weeks. Her first day in CID felt like a hundred years ago. No longer did she despise him; in fact, she'd grown rather fond of Dave Newton and the realisation surprised her. She wondered what he'd do after all this was over and if they'd continue to work together. She hoped so.

Morven tried Ollie's mobile again and then Mark's but without success. Nagging worry was replaced by a feeling of dread as her imagination conjured a series of worst-case scenarios, each one more terrifying than the last.

With a heavy sigh, she grabbed her coat and car keys and set off to face the harridan.

***

Morven parked outside Mark's home and dialled his number one more time.

Pick up, pick up, pick up.

The phone rang out. Why wasn't he answering? And where the hell was Ollie? She tried his number again only to receive the same familiar voice message.

She'd rung round all her son's mates but no one had seen him for a couple of days. Surely, he must be here. Morven gazed up at the house and puffed out a breath. Dealing with her ex-husband's wife was the last thing she wanted to do right now. Since Mark had left, Morven had managed to avoid meeting Brittney, 'the other woman'. She'd seen plenty of photos of her and had stalked her on social media for a time, but they'd never actually spoken.

Swearing beneath her breath, Kerry checked her reflection in the rear-view mirror and wiped her smudged eye makeup. In the images she'd seen, Brittney was young, pretty and polished, like the models who grace the covers of magazines. With a despairing sigh, Morven got out the car, trudged to the door and rang the bell. With any luck, Brittney wouldn't be in.

A small dog barked and there was the sound of young children. Several figures appeared behind the frosted glass, one of them a woman. Morven forced her lips into a smile.

The woman who answered the door was anything but polished. Wearing oversized joggies and a stained t-shirt, Brittney's long blonde hair looked like it hadn't been washed for weeks, and she wore no makeup. She had one child on her hip and another wrapped around her leg. A baby's cry came from the rear of the house. At the sight of Morven, Brittney's mouth fell open and she stiffened.

Morven put on her best police officer voice. "I'm sorry to bother you Brittney but I'm trying to find Ollie, and Mark's not answering his phone. Are either of them here?"

Brittney's eyes were red and she looked even more exhausted than Morven felt. Shaking her head, she said, "Mark's in bed with flu. He's been sleeping for hours." Then she frowned. "Isn't Ollie at Natalie's?"

Morven's panic surged. "No, he's not there and ... well, she's not seen him for several days either."

The children clamoured for attention. Brittney shushed them and hoisted the toddler higher. "Sorry, I'd normally invite you in but you probably don't want to catch this bug." After a pause, she said, "If you don't mind waiting, I'll wake Mark."

"No need, just ask him to call me when he's awake. Have you any idea where Ollie might be?"

Brittney listed the names of Ollie's mates who Morven had already contacted, and she couldn't think of any others. The baby howled.

"I'll let you get back to it," said Morven. "Thanks for your time."

Over the baby's squawking, Brittney called, "I'll call you if I think of anyone else. And Morven ... I hope he's okay."

Morven smiled, unforced this time, although fear was putting down deep roots in her chest. She'd have to report her son as missing unless they could trace him. She called Ross again but there was still no answer.

**

The buzzing of Morven' phone wrenched her from a nightmare.

After visiting Brittney, she'd returned to the station to find Ross absent, and then driven to his apartment. When her knocks went unanswered, she'd called Rob and asked for his help in locating Ollie. Rob's assurances that her son would be found safe and well did little to allay her fear. She'd gone back home and spent a sleepless night by the phone worrying herself sick about Ollie. Stress and exhaustion finally took their toll and she finally drifted off to sleep as dawn broke.

Morven peered at her mobile to see Dave's name and she answered with a sleepy hello.

"There's been another one," he said. Morven needed a few moments to pull herself from sleep inertia and ask what he meant. "A murder," he said, "and it's one of ours."

The shock of this news was tinged with relief at what it might mean for Natalie. But still there was no communication from either Ollie or Ross, and no update from Rob. She told Dave that her son was missing.

"I'll call Bill Arnold," said Dave. "His team will track Ollie down. Just get yourself over here."

An hour later, Morven drew up in front of the address Dave had texted her, a haughty Victorian mansion nestled in the heart of Edinburgh. Dressed in a paper over suit, her ashen-faced partner loitered next to a wrought-iron gate which opened onto a sweeping driveway lined with mature trees.

Swarms of SOCOs were already on-site and she spotted Dr Hellberg's car further up the street. Dave appeared like a ghost at her window bearing a grim expression and a plastic bag containing a forensic suit. He tried to reassure her Arnold's team were doing everything they could to find Ollie. Then, as Morven pulled on the Tyvek overall, he told her what he knew about their victim. The property belonged to a surgeon who ran a small clinic from his home. A member of his staff had come into work early and discovered him.

"It's bad," said Dave, "really bad. I hope you've not had breakfast."

Morven felt a tightening in her chest. Once she was attired, he led her up the gravel path to a door at the right-hand side. Painted a rich glossy black, it bore a brass plate engraved with 'The Merchiston Clinic'. This part of the building lacked the ornate architectural details and stone carvings on the façade, and she guessed it had probably been the servants' quarters in times gone by.

Inside, a plush reception area lined with tub chairs and coffee tables led to a spacious consulting suite at the rear. The first thing she noticed was the blood, its acid-copper stench assailing her nostrils. Black pools of it had seeped into the deep pile carpet leaving an inky silhouette around the body. Or what remained of it.

The butchered corpse of Lawrie Mathieson lay in the centre of the consulting room, naked and facing upwards. The surgeon's genitals had been hacked off and stuffed into his mouth leaving a gory mass of pulp around the groin area. The arms were splayed out but only bloody stumps remained where his hands ought to have been.

Morven slapped a hand over her mouth and gagged.

Dave tugged her back by the sleeve and said, "You don't need to see anymore, I can take it from here." Concern was etched deeply in the lines around his eyes.

She found his chivalry both endearing and irritating and she stood her ground. "No," she said, "I really must."

It took every ounce of willpower to force herself to take in the gruesome scene: the blood spatter pattern over the white walls and ceiling, the discarded heap of clothes, and the acrid nauseating smell filling her nostrils. She glanced at the smouldering fireplace, realising the stench was burnt flesh and bone. She swallowed the bile rising in her throat and covered her nose and mouth with her hand.

She noted there was something absent from the grisly tableau: there were no bloody footprints leading away from the body. Whoever had done this was forensically aware and she suspected that again they'd find little trace of the killer.

Dave had turned an unhealthy shade of white. In a low voice, he said, "It all fits with your theory about the motive — butchering a surgeon who does genital reassignment." He gazed at Morven with something akin to respect.

One of the SOCOs popped his head round the door and told them there was something else they ought to see. They followed him to a small office at the rear equipped with oak furniture and shelving. There daubed in large red numerals behind the desk was the number twenty. Blood had run in rivulets down the wall to the carpet giving it the appearance of a horror movie title.

"This looks very recent," said Dave peering at the blood.

Morven nodded. "If Dougie needs any more proof he's got the wrong people banged up, then here it is in large red numbers."

They heard Dr Hellberg talking to one of the uniformed officers and Dave went off to find her, leaving Morven to poke around. Wearing nitrile gloves, she searched the desk and drawers which were empty except for stationery. The filing cabinets contained neatly ordered financial statements and medical files. She scanned the titles on the bookshelves, an eclectic mixture of medical textbooks, historical fiction and Shakespeare's complete works.

On the lowest shelf were several leather-bound albums. Morven pulled one out and flicked through its leaves. Each page contained photographs of what she presumed were Mathieson's patients. Most were teenage girls and all had undergone gender reassignment surgery. Each page of the album featured a head and shoulders shot together with before and after images.

Most pictures showed 'top surgery' to remove healthy breast tissue leaving a scarred chest with repositioned nipples; nothing that resembled a male torso. However, on some pages were a series of images showing the various stages of phalloplasty. Morven flicked through the photographs with a mixture of revulsion and fascination. The album was a collage of self-destruction.

And then she spotted a face she recognised and her blood turned to ice. She shouted Dave's name at the top of her voice and he came rushing through accompanied by Hellberg.

Almost hyperventilating, Morven stabbed a finger at a photograph. "I've seen this girl before. It's Ross's sister."

"Ross?" exclaimed Dave.

They scrutinised the photographs of her extensive surgeries. The first was of a vaginectomy to remove the female sex organs, followed by phalloplasty to construct a penis from skin grafts. Some pictures had been taken just weeks after the operations and showed significant bruising and swelling.

One particularly gruesome corrective surgery had been undertaken to prevent urine leaking from the patient's anus. A later image showed her holding the healed phallus against a heavily scarred thigh. Her delicate fingers looked small against the enormous appendage.

"Good grief!" cried Hellberg. It was the first time Morven had witnessed the pathologist display any emotion.

Morven said, "I'm pretty sure this is the same person in the photograph Eddie sent of Claire Angus's trans group except, in that one, she looks like a boy. That's why I didn't make the connection before."

"Where else have you seen her?" said Dave frowning.

She felt her face flush. "At Ross's flat, in family photos."

Have I been sleeping with a serial killer?

Morven felt sick to the pit of her stomach.

Dave's shoulders slumped and he made a strangled noise in his throat. In a low voice, he said, "Ah, okay." He looked away and twisted his mouth into a bitter smile. "I'd better call Dougie."

His reaction surprised Morven but, amidst her maelstrom of emotions, she had no time to ponder on it. They needed answers fast. She tried phoning Ross again. And then Ollie.

Neither answered.

***

Morven and Dave took his car and journeyed to Ross's apartment back in Strathmurray. Mugly was asleep in the back seat. It was late afternoon, darkness had begun to fall, and an icy wind had mustered a legion of black clouds. Dave drove in brooding silence for the entire journey and Morven sensed there was an anger simmering inside of him, but her own mind was in too much of a swirl to quiz him.

She hoped … prayed … that she was mistaken about Ross's sister. Maybe her likeness to the photograph in the album was a coincidence. Ross had told her his sister had died but he hadn't revealed how and she hadn't pushed him. And why wasn't Ross answering his phone? Perhaps there was a perfectly reasonable explanation for his absence. Maybe he also had flu and they'd find him at home, snotty and feverish. Because the alternative was too horrific to contemplate.

Dave parked outside the sandstone tenement and they bolted up the stairs to the second floor. Yelling Ross's name, he thumped on the front door of his flat. There was no answer. Across the landing, a curious neighbour popped her head out. She was an elderly lady and Morven suspected she watched everything and everyone in the apartment block.

"Police," said Morven, showing her badge.

"Mr Forsyth isn't in," said the woman, "I saw him leave yesterday evening."

"Any idea where he's gone?" said Morven.

She shook her head.

"Was he with anyone?"

"A young lad. They left together in his car."

She asked for a description of the passenger but all she got was a vague 'young, medium height with dark hair' response. But whoever had accompanied Ross appeared to have gone willingly and had carried a holdall. She thanked the woman who disappeared back inside.

Morven's sense of panic grew as she watched Dave run a palm up and down the wooden door and its frame.

"We'll need a warrant," she said.

Ignoring her, Dave took a step back and, with an explosive kick, struck the door so hard it almost came off on its hinges. He strode through the apartment calling out Ross's name. Morven followed, her heartbeat pounding in her ears.

The flat was as quiet as the grave. The fridge was switched off and lay open to reveal bare shelves. The bin had been emptied and the bed stripped. Some of Ross's personal items were missing and his laptop was nowhere to be seen. Morven's stomach knotted at the stark realisation of what this meant. The sense of betrayal hit her like a blow and she wrapped her arms around herself.

Dave began ransacking the place. He searched cupboards and drawers, pulled out clothes, rifled through paperwork. He moved furniture, overturned the sofa, and flipped the mattress. Morven looked on in stunned silence. It felt like an out of body experience.

"Find the photograph of the sister," said Dave, his tone wrenching her from her torpor.

Morven carefully examined the girl in each picture on the wall and compared her to the photograph she'd taken on her phone of Mr Mathieson's transgender patient. There was no doubt, it was the same person. Taking a step back, she cast her eye over the collage of holiday snaps. Many had been taken along Dunbar's picturesque coastline with its distinctive reddish-brown cliffs and views of the North Sea.

In the background of several, appeared a small stone-built cottage that bordered the coastal path. Morven removed one of the photographs from its frame. It showed Ross and his sister stood in the foreground, and the house behind.

Calling out her name, Dave appeared holding a sheaf of documents. He handed Morven a birth certificate saying, "His sister's called Maxine." Then he passed her another sheet. "Or at least she was."

Morven peered at the death certificate. It was for a Max Forsyth with the same date of birth but the sex was recorded as male. The cause of death showed that Max had died from a drug overdose which was 'deemed to be suicide'.

Dave said, "It's got to be the same person. She had a sex change."

Morven showed Dave the family photograph. "Mathieson's patient was definitely Ross's sister."

Feeling the room spin, she slumped into a chair before her legs gave way as the full horror of what this signified hit her.

"We need to find him," said Dave taking out his mobile.

Before he could dial, they heard a phone ping. It sounded as though it had come from a kitchen cupboard. They exchanged a look and began searching. Morven raked through tins and packets, opening storage jars and Tupperware boxes while Dave emptied cabinets and drawers. He leapt onto the worksurface and ran his hand along the top of the units. In the corner, he found a clear plastic bag, inside of which were two mobile phones.

"Here," he said, jumping down and opening the bag.

Recognising her son's Apple phone, Morven made a primitive sound in the back of her throat. "Oh God," she wailed. "He's got Ollie."

Trying to quell her growing panic, she snatched up the device, unlocked it and began scrolling through his messages. Dave peered over her shoulder as she read the communications between her son and Ross. The most recent message was Ross arranging to collect him from Natalie's house.

Suddenly, the other phone pinged and a message flashed up onscreen. It was from Ross.

> I'm sorry Morven. Sorry for it all.

Dave and Morven gawped at one another and then, in unison, gazed up at a corner of the kitchen ceiling. There, buried within the plaster coving was a tiny camera. Swearing, Dave clambered onto the counter, prised it out and stamped on it.

Morven began to sob uncontrollably and Dave enveloped her in his arms and rocked her.

Chapter 30

Dave ended his call to Dougie and crouched in front of Morven who was sat gazing at her hands, breathing deeply, willing her heart to keep beating. Gently holding her shoulders, he said, "We'll find him, I promise."

"Why would he take Ollie?" she cried. "He's not part of this."

He fixed her with his gaze. "Has Ross any family or friends he might go to?"

She shook her head. "His mother's dead and his father's remarried, lives in England somewhere."

"The team are already in touch with the local police so if he goes there, he won't get far. But can you think of anywhere else?"

She battled to remain calm as thoughts of what Ross might do to Ollie threatened to overwhelm her.

Think damn it!

She picked up the family photograph and pointed to the cottage. "This place appears in several pictures. It's in Dunbar."

Dave peered at it, and then turned the picture over. Printed on the back of it was 'Gaugers End' and a date. Using her phone, Morven googled the name and an image of a house appeared. It was the same cottage as the one in the family photographs.

"Let's go," said Dave. "I'll drive, you call it in."

***

The journey to Dunbar was a blur, the urgency of the situation hanging heavy inside the vehicle. Wet snow slapped against the windscreen as they sped along country roads and through rural towns and villages. As the landscape flashed by, Morven's mind raced with possibilities about why Ross had taken Ollie. The only option that made sense was that Ross was insane. Picturing the earlier murder scene, Morven began to cry.

Dave stretched over and squeezed her hand. "We'll get him," he said.

She wasn't sure if he meant Ollie or Ross.

Dave stopped for fuel at a garage and returned with a takeaway coffee and a chocolate bar for her. The hot liquid swirled in her stomach but she was grateful for the sugar. As the car fishtailed out of the forecourt, Morven's mobile rang and she answered. It was the gaffer informing them that a tactical support team was on its way to the cottage.

"Under no circumstances", bellowed Dougie so loud she pulled the phone from her ear, "do either of you enter that property without backup. Understood?"

Morven hung up. Dave glanced at her; his jaw clenched as he accelerated out of a turn.

"What did Dougie want?"

Certain Dave had heard every word, she said, "I couldn't quite hear, the signal's very poor."

Gripping the steering wheel, Dave put his foot down and the car hurtled towards Dunbar. As they approached the outskirts, Morven directed him along a road that led to the clifftop trail. She knew the area well having spent many summers here with her parents; fond memories that would be forever tainted.

It had stopped raining when they pulled into a carpark close to the start of the walk. Spotting Ross's car, Morven gasped. They drove past slowly but it was empty, the moon casting an eerie glow over the interior.

The cottage lay a few hundred yards away, close to the cliff edge. The house was accessible via a footpath which was too narrow for a vehicle. Only a metal handrail separated walkers from the sheer drop to the rocks below. Spotting a light on inside the property, Morven's heart thumped in her chest.

Dave doused the headlights and parked at the far end of the lot, out of sight of the cottage. Morven made to leave but Dave grabbed her arm.

"We should wait for backup," he said.

Shrugging free of his grip, she said, "Screw that, my son's in there with a madman."

He tugged her back. "But you cannae just storm in there. For starters, we don't know if Ollie's in there and who's with him. Ross might be armed for all we know."

Pointing to the other car, she said, "He's here alright, and he can do what he likes to me, but if he as much as harms a hair on Ollie's head—"

Dave took her hand and, in a voice choked with emotion, said, "And if he harms a hair on yours, I swear I'll kill him."

Morven blinked at him in surprise. This ... whatever the hell this was ... would have to wait.

"I'm going to try and talk to him," she said. "Ollie had no part in what happened to his sister, so he has no reason to harm him. I just want my son back."

"Jesus Morven, he has every reason to hurt you. He knows you're aware of what he's done."

She pulled her hand free and got out the car. "I'm not here to make an arrest. I'm here to take my son home."

"Ollie is his bargaining chip," called Dave, "he'll not give him up willingly." Trotting after her, he muttered, "I don't like this one bit."

"Then don't come," she muttered.

He ignored her and together they tiptoed towards the cottage. The sky was still spitting snowflakes as they circled the front of the building and peered into the mullioned windows. Every room was in darkness except for one downstairs where the curtains were drawn. It was preternaturally quiet with barely a rustle of leaves or a creak from the weathered structure. The moon cast elongated shadows across the small garden giving the place an otherworldly feel. They exchanged a glance that communicated the gravity of the situation before Morven rapped on the door.

She called out, "Ross, it's Morven. I've come for Ollie."

Dave hid at the side of the house with his back against the wall.

When there was no answer, she called again, "I'm unarmed and no one else knows you're here. I just want my son."

Still no answer.

Dave darted to the rear of the cottage. As she reached for the doorknob, a chill ran down her spine. It was unlocked and the door swung open with a slow, ominous groan. The stale scent of damp wood and neglect greeted her and she stepped inside.

Using her phone torch, Morven moved cautiously along a small hallway towards a dim glow which cast distorted patterns on the worn carpet. The place was silent except for the sound of a distant dripping tap. Holding her breath, she pushed open a door where a light glowed beyond.

A gunshot echoed through the cottage and cliffs beyond.

***

Kerry battled to retain her composure as Bill Arnold's relentless barrage of questions continued. As the hours stretched on, with each passing minute feeling like an eternity, a migraine pounded behind her eyes. The flickering strip light overhead in the interrogation room only added to her torture.

The detective kept returning to the evening when Dr McNab was murdered, and the fact her Fitbit placed her in the locale. With her hands trembling in her lap, she repeated her argument that she was nowhere near the surgery, nor any of the other crime scenes. But under the relentless pressure, Kerry was beginning to doubt her own memories and sanity.

Bill's eyes bored into her with an intensity that made her squirm in her chair. Each question he fired felt like a verbal assault, leaving her feeling defenceless and exposed.

"Why were you at the surgery that evening?" he demanded, his voice sharp and accusatory.

"I already told you, I was nowhere near it," she replied, her voice quivering with frustration and disbelief. "I had nothing to do with it."

Her arguments were futile and his questions only grew more pointed and invasive, despite her solicitor's objections. He dissected her every word, searching for inconsistencies or signs of guilt, refusing to accept her protestations of innocence.

As the interrogation dragged on, exhaustion set in, both physically and emotionally. Tears welled in Kerry's eyes as her protests fell on deaf ears. She felt like a pawn in a cruel game, trapped in a nightmare from which she could not awaken. Then, just as she was about to surrender to the despair, there was a knock at the door and another man entered. His face was unreadable.

"A word please, Bill," said the man. From Bill's deference, it was clear the other guy was a more senior rank.

Arnold left, leaving Kerry wondering what was going on. When her tormentor returned, his expression stony, she prepared herself for the worst.

"Dr Connelly," he said, "You're free to go."

Chapter 31

Morven screamed. She dived back into the hallway and pressed herself against the wall. Nearby, someone groaned in pain and it took her a moment to realise it wasn't her making the sound and she was unharmed.

Pulse racing, she risked a glimpse around the door. The sight beyond curdled her blood. Ollie lay pale and motionless on a couch. In the kitchen beyond, Dave was slumped in a pool of blood. And sat in the shadows of the living room was a figure she barely recognised, his eyes reflecting a mixture of defiance and desperation. Ross held a pistol aimed directly at her head.

Ducking behind the door again, she cried, "Ollie. Ollie, are you okay?"

There was no reply.

"He can't hear you," said Ross in a tone suffused with steel.

Panic soaring, she called out Dave's name. Her partner responded with a grunt.

Fearing it was a suicide mission, Morven stepped onto the threshold saying, "Don't shoot. Please don't shoot." Palms raised in front, she placed a tentative foot inside the room, half-expecting to be gunned down. Ross sat motionless staring menacingly at her. An age seemed to pass in which he appeared to weigh his options. Finally, he lowered the weapon.

Morven rushed to Ollie's side and put her hand on his brow. He felt warm. "Oh God," she wailed, "what have you done to him?"

"He's fine, he's had a couple of roofies. He'll be out of it for hours."

She glared at Ross. "You gave him Rohypnol?"

Dave moaned in agony. She crept towards him, conscious Ross might kill her at any moment. Her partner had been shot in the stomach and was bleeding out, but he was conscious. She crouched beside him and examined the wound. It was bad, really bad, and she knew that without medical help, he'd bleed to death.

"You'll live," she lied.

She removed her jacket and jumper and peeled off the top beneath to reveal a white lacy bra. She pressed the t-shirt firmly against Dave's abdomen to stem the blood flow. He tore his eyes from her and winced in pain.

"Sorry," she whispered, guiding his hand to maintain pressure on the wound.

He tried to speak but she shushed him and pulled her sweater back on, aware of his eyes tracking her every movement. After popping a cushion behind his head, she draped her jacket over him to keep him warm. She settled beside him and pressed on the wound. Blood oozed between her fingers and onto her clothing. Dave gripped her wrist and they locked eyes.

"He needs a doctor," she said to Ross.

Ross gave a dark chuckle. "Why did you come here? Did you think I'd let myself be captured?"

Feeling her anger rise, she bit out, "To fetch my son. Why did you come here? Ollie's done you no harm."

Stay calm, don't antagonise him.

"You disappoint me," said Ross. "I thought that was obvious."

"Is he your hostage? Is that your game?"

Dave squeezed her hand as if in warning. Morven took a steadying breath and squeezed back.

"I don't bargain." Ross's tone was ice cold. "I'm stopping Ollie before he destroys himself. Something I wish I'd done for my sister."

She glared at their captor. Did he mean to save Ollie or kill him? She was too afraid to ask. Ross seemed too mercurial, too unstable, too disturbed. But the warm dampness seeping into her hand reminded her of the urgency.

"Please let me call an ambulance," she said, taking out her mobile.

Ross aimed the pistol straight at her. "Put the phone down or I'll put another bullet in Newton. Pass it to me. And his."

Morven did as asked and slid both devices towards him. "Please Ross, no one needs to die."

He approached, gun at his side, and cast a contemptuous eye over Dave. Addressing Morven, he said, "You should have come alone."

"Please let me get him help."

"SHUT UP! SHUT UP! SHUT UP!" Ross put his hands on his head and began to pace like a caged lion, the pistol waving about dangerously.

Dave's eyes reflected her own panic and she attempted to cover his body with her own. For the next few minutes, Ross seemed to swing between rage and serenity. One minute he was yelling; the next muttering calmly to himself. He was clearly psychotic.

Keep him calm. Dave doesn't have long.

"Tell me about your sister." She held her breath, hoping her question didn't trigger another outburst.

Her voice seemed to return him to the moment and he stared at her. "Maxine killed herself," he said in a small voice.

"I'm so sorry. What happened?"

"She was captured, same as your son."

Morven asked what he meant and he told her the whole sorry story, all the while patrolling back and forth waving the gun around.

Ross explained that as a child, Maxine had been a tomboy who enjoyed running wild and climbing trees. She'd never shown any interest in dolls and all attempts to corset her into a dress were a battle. By age thirteen, it was apparent she was same sex attracted, something their parents struggled to accept. When his sister finally 'came out' as a lesbian aged fourteen, her pronouncement earned her a vicious beating from their father.

Dave shifted with a groan and Morven adjusted her pressure on the wound.

Don't die, please don't die.

Ross recounted how Maxine went from being a confident, outward-going teen to an anxious wreck who spent most of her time on Tumblr. There, in that world, she became immersed in the fiction that she could change her sex and find love and happiness. For Maxine, the idea of being someone else was enchanting. The chance to opt out of womanhood and become a man meant freedom from the restrictions femininity placed upon her. It gave her the social acceptance she craved and the liberties that Ross enjoyed.

"She was so young and naïve," said Ross, gazing down at Ollie's sleeping form.

Outside of the family home, Maxine began identifying as a boy. She'd always worn masculine clothes and cut her hair short, but she began binding her breasts. Friends already called her Max, but at school she insisted on male pronouns and using the boys' toilets. The teachers didn't inform their parents and instead, without their knowledge, put her in touch with a social worker who made her an appointment with the family's GP and referred her to an LGBTQ+ group.

"Is that why you murdered Pat Duncan and Claire Angus?" asked Morven.

Ross stopped pacing and regarded her as if he'd forgotten she was there. His face twisted in fury and he yelled, "Those bitches should've helped her accept who she was, not push her into being trans. But as soon as Maxine met them, her fate was sealed."

Battling to keep her voice steady, Morven said, "But why kill Claire so brutally?"

He looked at her in disgust. "Really Morven, I thought you would've worked it out." When she said nothing, he added, "It was poetic. You know ... bleedin' heart liberal."

Morven gawped at him. "You need help Ross, you're sick in the head."

Dave grunted a warning. Ross threw her a thunderous look and loomed over her. Shielding Dave, Morven braced herself for a blow.

Ross snarled, "I'm sick? No, the zealots who did that to my sister are the ones who're sick, not me."

She asked, "Why kill the librarian? He didn't harm your sister."

Ross screamed so loud in her ear that she flinched. "Where the hell do you think she got some of her ideas? Maxine was never out of that bloody place."

He began to pace manically back and forth as he recalled the leaflets and books his sister had brought home about queer theory and gender ideology. He described how the library's shelves were stuffed full of trans propaganda, some aimed at children as young as three.

"That's tantamount to grooming!" he shouted. "There was not a single gender-critical book on the shelves. I even tried ordering one but I was told it was out of stock." With a murderous grimace, he snarled, "Turns out there were plenty of copies in the storeroom." He paced some more adding, "I didn't think I could do it at the start ... you know ... kill. Didn't think I had it in me."

Keep him talking.

"Turns out I was wrong." Ross swivelled his eyes to her. "And then they invited that toxic sack of shit to entertain kids."

"Barry the drag queen?"

"Filthy perverted bastard! He was a regular at the youth group run by that leftie cunt."

Morven asked what had happened to Maxine after she'd met Claire. Ross recalled the influence the 'alphabet soup people', as he called them, had on his sister, and how suddenly they were all her new besties. Maxine worshipped Claire who, along with Barry, schooled her about exactly what to say to the family doctor to ensure she got a referral to a gender clinic. Without their parents' knowledge, the GP diagnosed gender dysphoria and referred Maxine to a paediatric clinic.

Risking his wrath, Morven asked, "Was McNab really a paedophile?"

Ross turned to her. "Doubt it, but I needed you lot looking the other way. Making him out to be a kiddie fiddler gave me enough time to finish the job."

His words sent icicles down her spine because if wokery hadn't thwarted the investigation by sending them off in the wrong direction, maybe they could have prevented another murder.

"McNab later told my mother that if he didn't refer Maxine to the clinic, she'd likely commit suicide." He fixed his eyes on Morven, "What kind of doctor says that to a parent in front of their child? And what kind of social worker tells a mother to plan a funeral for her daughter so she can adopt a son?" Ross's pain was almost palpable.

Morven asked, "And the evidence against Natalie and her friends?"

With a smug look, he said, "I'm the tech guy remember. It's easy to forge records, fake photos and disable CCTV."

Dave's breathing was becoming shallower and his hand felt cold.

Where's the support team? They should be here by now.

Fearing Ross's sanity was hanging by a thread, Morven asked about the gender clinic. Ross told how his sister had made the journey alone and then, after just two appointments lasting just sixty minutes, she was prescribed testosterone. He then described the rapid changes in Maxine over the next few months: her voice deepened, she grew facial hair, and her shape altered. Her personality also changed, and she became short-tempered and aggressive.

"Did she consult De Garcia?" asked Morven. "Is that why you killed him?"

"That bastard poisoned her and robbed me of the sister I loved. He deserved to die the way he did."

When he began muttering to himself, Morven steered him back to the story and asked what had happened after Maxine had been on hormones for a while.

Ross sounded close to tears. "Once she was on that bus, it was a one-way ticket to surgery. She liked the physical changes but hated her breasts. The chest binder caused her backache and she'd this horrible rash." He shook his head, "She'd not been well since starting the T but instead of coming off it, she opted for surgery."

Ross described how Maxine had undergone 'top surgery' which left her with infected, painful scars where her breasts had been.

He sobbed, "She was too young to buy a lottery ticket, yet they let her remove body parts."

When Ross calmed a little, he explained how, following the double mastectomy, she'd then had phalloplasty. He broke down in tears as he recalled the surgeries to remove her vagina, uterus and ovaries, and the painful skin grafts to create a penis using donor tissue from her thigh. She'd later undergone further operations to place erectile and testicular implants beneath the skin, as well as a host of other corrective procedures.

Weeping, he said, "The surgery was brutal and she suffered so much. She endured one infection after another."

Morven shuddered, remembering the photographs. "Was the end result not a success?"

Ross wiped his tears with the back of his hand. "It took a while for her to fully realise what she'd done but, when she did, it hit her hard. She knew she could never truly become a man and she couldn't switch back easily to being a woman either." In a shaky voice, he added, "She was consumed with regret and, when it dawned on her she could never have a baby, she spiralled into a deep depression."

"Did she get help or support?" asked Morven.

Ross exhaled loudly. "Of course not. The clinic cut her loose, and her new buddies treated her like a heretic." He gazed at Morven and, in a voice steeped in sadness, said, "She'd damaged her body beyond repair to the extent she would have needed medical care for the rest of her life."

"I'm so sorry," whispered Morven. She didn't know what else to say.

Then a switch seemed to flick inside of him and he snarled, "I butchered that Mathieson fucker the way he butchered my sister, and what's more I enjoyed it. I made him suffer until he begged for death."

She said nothing, trying to contain her panic now that he'd reached the end of the story. Ross knelt next to Ollie and stroked his hair back from his forehead with the pistol. Morven's heart skipped a beat.

"My mother came home from work and found Maxine dead from an overdose. She was nineteen years old." Fixing Morven with a watery gaze, he said, "I won't let that happen to your son."

His expression and his words sent an icy chill through her veins.

"Let Morven and the boy go," rasped Dave. He coughed up blood and flinched in agony.

"SHUT UP NEWTON!" Ross pointed the gun at Dave.

Morven placed herself between the two men and pleaded. "I only want Ollie. Let me take him and then we'll be gone. That's all I want. I'm not here for you."

"Not going to happen," said Ross, pacing again. He fixed her with a manic stare. "I had my exit all worked out but you screwed up my plans."

She gave him a quizzical look. "Did you really think you'd walk away from this?"

He shook his head. "I didn't expect to get this far." He produced a bottle of pills from his pocket and shook it. "You were supposed to find me dead from an overdose too. But how can I go when your boy's about to do the same thing as my sister? He's got to be stopped."

Morven gawped at him as though he was mad. He was mad. "You can't keep him drugged and locked up here."

Ross sat down. "I'm taking him somewhere safe, somewhere he can't make the wrong choices." He glanced at Ollie who was still unconscious. "The boy is gay and he needs to accept that, and not let anyone convince him to trans it away."

"You won't get far," she said, "every officer will be hunting for you."

Ross glanced at his watch. "One of Kennedy's boats will pick us up soon. We'll disappear."

She gaped at him. "You're trusting your fate to gangsters?"

"Drugs. Guns. People. They don't care what the cargo is as long as they get paid. We'll be half way across Europe before anyone knows we've gone." He paused and looked at her. "I'm only telling you this because Newton's dying and I want you to come with us."

Morven gripped Dave's hand and gawped at Ross in disbelief. "You're crazy."

"I'm serious." He approached her. "We can make a new life together. You, me and Ollie. We'll keep him safe, make sure no one hurts him."

Wide-eyed, she said, "You're actually serious?"

Ross outlined his plan to cross the North Sea in the smuggler's boat and then travel to a commune in France where they could hide. He looked at her with pleading eyes. "Come with us."

When she shook her head in bewilderment, he pointed to Ollie. "Look at him Morven. If he stays here, the doctors will poison him with hormones and castrate him. Sure, he might be okay for a few years but one day he's going to wake up and realise he made the wrong decision. And he'll hate you for letting him, and then he'll hate himself. Is that what you want? Your son to take his own life after he faces the horror of what he's done?"

Tears formed behind Morven's eyes as Ross voiced her darkest fears. She gazed at her beautiful son and sobbed, "Of course not."

"You and me," he said. "We're good together. We can make this work."

Somewhere off in the distance, she heard the whir of a boat engine. Ross got up, went to the window and pulled back the curtains. Dave stirred and made a groaning sound. He was pallid and clammy.

Ross held up a lamp and switched it off and on in rapid succession. A light out at sea flashed in response. "It's time," he said.

Ross stuffed the pistol into his waistband and put on his jacket. He produced a cable tie from the pocket and told Morven to sit down. Her heart thumped against her ribcage fearing he might put a bullet in her skull. He bound her wrists behind her back so tight the plastic bit into her skin and she yelped.

He grabbed two large holdalls and looked at Morven, "I'll be back for you and Ollie in a few minutes. Don't do anything stupid or I'll shoot the three of you."

She didn't doubt it.

After he left, Morven struggled to her feet and went to the window to see Ross disappear down the steps to the cliff walk. She cursed, realising there was still no sign of the tactical support team and she'd no way of summoning them.

In a raspy voice, Dave said, "Let me untie you."

She knelt at his side with her back to him and offered him her wrists. Dave fumbled with the cable tie but his fingers were slippy with blood and he couldn't get a grip. With a grunt of pain, he leaned over and used his teeth.

"Think you can walk?" asked Morven, aware the seconds were ticking by.

"Get Ollie out, then get help."

"I can't leave you," she cried, "he'll kill you."

Tugging at the cable tie with his mouth, he mumbled, "It's over for me either way."

Her eyes filled with tears. "Don't say that. Help is coming."

Dave continued to wrestle with her binding until finally it snapped. Morven rubbed her wrists and scooted round to face him.

"Don't you dare leave me," she cried, realising Dave's life was ebbing away in front of her eyes.

He gripped her hands and in a barely audible voice, said, "Tell my daughter I love her."

Tears streamed down Morven's cheeks. He whispered something barely audible and she leaned closer to listen.

"You're a brilliant detective and if I ever made you feel otherwise ..." She tried to shush him but he placed a bloodied finger on her lips. "I need you to know how I feel about you ... before it's too late." Struggling for breath, he gasped out, "Maybe in another life, you and I ..."

Ross burst through the door. Confronted with this scene, his nostrils flared. He raised the gun and aimed at Dave. Morven leapt on top of her partner as two blasts of gunfire cracked through the air.

***

Morven lay completely still. Was she still alive? Had she been hit? She didn't feel any pain but perhaps she was dead and this is how it felt when you made the transition from this world to the next.

At the sound of approaching boots and a blast from a radio, she eased herself into a sitting position as the tactical team stormed into the cottage. Ross's body lay face down in the doorway. He'd been shot twice, once in the head, once in the back. Ollie hadn't stirred and Dave appeared to be unconscious.

With one hand pressed to Dave's wound and the other raised above her head, she shrieked, "Get an ambulance."

An officer approached. He was dressed from head to foot in black and carried an automatic weapon. "Are you hurt, ma'am?"

She felt Dave's neck for a pulse. It was faint, dangerously faint. "Just get my partner a doctor."

Once the team had checked the cottage, paramedics swarmed in and Morven watched in horror as one medic worked on Dave and another on Ollie. She refused to leave their side when both were taken to a waiting ambulance, and the crew let her ride in the back with them.

On the interminable journey to the hospital, she witnessed Dave's heart give out and the paramedics' frantic efforts to save him. As they wheeled her son and dying partner into the emergency room, a nurse stopped her.

Shivering and drenched in blood, Morven paced outside in the corridor like a mad woman. And, not for the first time in her life, she prayed to God to save the ones she loved.

Chapter 32

3 months later, Strathmurray

Kerry's mouth was dry and she took a sip of water. Adjusting her headphones, she swapped a glance with Amruta and Natalie who sat next to her in the studio looking every bit as nervous as she felt. By contrast, Kuzi appeared as though she gave radio interviews every week and the psychologist sent Kerry a reassuring smile. Although Kerry was accustomed to giving lectures and speaking in public, she'd never addressed millions of listeners before. She rubbed her sweaty palms on her trouser legs and pressed a hand on her knee to stop her foot from bouncing.

Even at her first meeting as a newly elected local councillor, Kerry hadn't felt as tense. Encouraged by *RWS*, she'd stood as an independent candidate to give women and children a voice. Although she'd always been left leaning, particularly in her youth, she could no longer support Labour after the leader stated that 99.9% of women 'haven't got a penis', or his Liberal Democrat counterpart who believes "some women 'clearly' have a penis". Kerry wondered how these fools could be trusted to run the country when they 'clearly' didn't know the difference between a man and a woman.

On cue, Jenny Deacon, the *Female Matters* presenter gave a nod and spoke into the microphone. She announced that she was joined on the programme by the three women who had been wrongfully arrested for the 'Strathmurray Slasher' murders. The case had gripped the nation for months and required only a brief introduction, but she reminded the audience of how the real killer had later been shot dead by police. Jenny also introduced Kuzi as the psychologist who was now working with the women.

Jenny turned to Kerry. "Perhaps you'd like to begin by telling our listeners how you first met one another."

Leaning closer to the microphone, Kerry described how she'd been hounded out of her position at Lothian University for supporting Kuzi's research into detransitioners and how, after losing her job, she'd contacted the RWS group. Then, one by one, the women talked about the protests they'd taken part in, the stunt they'd pulled in front of the First Minister, and their wrongful arrest.

Addressing Kuzi, Jenny said, "However, is it fair to say that something positive has emerged from this dreadful experience?"

Kuzi began by explaining that she, like many other psychologists, believed that gender dysphoria was a mental health condition known as an identity disorder. She attributed the 8,000-fold increase in females identifying as 'trans' to a psychic contagion fuelled by social media, and talked about how teenage girls are more susceptible than boys to psychogenic epidemics such as anorexia and self-harm. She then spoke at length about the stress of puberty and the fact women are more likely to experience negative emotions than men. It was no surprise, therefore, that adolescents confused normal pubescent feelings with gender dysphoria.

"Puberty is hard at the best of times," she said, "and it's especially difficult for young people who are on the autistic spectrum, who are same sex attracted, or who've experienced a troubled home life or abuse. Sometimes they turn these feelings onto their bodies."

These problems, she explained, are exacerbated by the amount of misinformation on the internet about transitioning. To combat the online bunkum, Kuzi described how she and the women were banding together to develop a radical new therapist chat bot which took the form of a fictional character called *PsychologistNow*.

Using AI technology, their online 'psychologist' would provide information and advice to young people who reported feelings of gender dysphoria. The AI was trained on evidence-based knowledge and underpinned by a sound 'therapy first' framework. With Amruta's technical knowhow, Kerry's research skills, Natalie's medical knowledge, and Kuzi's clinical expertise, the chatbot would deliver therapeutic advice which would be exploratory in nature.

"I believe your beta version is already causing quite a stir," said Jenny.

Kuzi replied, "We've been overwhelmed by the response and the glowing reviews on social media."

Jenny read out several of these describing *PsychologistNow* as a lifesaver, and how it had helped a young woman realise that the source of her inner turmoil would not be fixed by cutting off her breasts.

The presenter paused to let that sink in, then added, "It must be humbling to read reviews like that."

In a voice catching with emotion, Kerry said, "It makes what happened worth it, knowing the difference this project will make."

"But surely," said Jenny, "a virtual therapist is no substitute for a real one. It makes me sad to think of distressed youngsters turning to their smart phones for advice, rather than friends and family. Aren't you in danger of commercialising therapy?"

"I'm the first to agree," said Kuzi, "about the importance of the personal connection between therapist and client. However, given online misinformation and long NHS waiting lists, we want to ensure gender-questioning people receive prompt and holistic advice that explores all the reasons behind their dysphoria and which does not automatically affirm a trans identity. It's a free service whose sole purpose is to offer evidence-based information and support."

Jenny then asked Amruta to outline her role in the software development aspects. Amruta explained that the company for whom she worked had allowed her to take a sabbatical to focus on the project.

Jenny said, "I want to turn now to Natalie because you've had a very different experience."

Natalie revealed how her employer had taken disciplinary action against her after her part in the protest outside the party conference. She also explained the appalling way she'd been treated by her colleagues for expressing gender critical views. She described the toxic atmosphere at work and how this had culminated in her being unable to continue in her employment.

Shaking her head, Natalie said, "I'm a midwife who is being told to deny that biology is real although I spend my working life helping women give birth and breastfeed babies."

The presenter interjected, "I understand you're taking your case to an employment tribunal but since that's ongoing, we'll simply say that the right to hold gender critical beliefs is enshrined in law."

Jenny reminded listeners about Maya Forstater who was dismissed from the Centre for Global Development after tweeting that people could not change their biological sex. Despite losing her first tribunal when the judge stated her views were "not worthy of respect in a democratic society", Maya won her appeal in the High Court which ruled that her belief was protected by the Equality Act 2010.

"Ms Forstater," said Jenny, "believes biological sex is immutable and not to be conflated with gender identity."

"We all share that view," said Natalie. "Biological sex is real. Gender identity is a belief which has no place in law or in public institutions."

Natalie then discussed how she'd teamed up with Kerry after receiving funding for a study into the use of accurate language in healthcare, and she talked about the importance of using plain and simple English with patients.

As Jenny brought the interview to a close, Kerry flopped back in her chair with a sense of relief. Despite her nerves, it had gone well and they'd gotten their main points across. She also hoped their story would give others the courage to stand up to the mob and speak up for what they knew to be true.

***

With a smile, Morven switched off the car radio. She was sat in the lot at the rear of the station with a takeaway coffee and the door open. She'd wanted peace and quiet to listen to Natalie's interview which had been recorded a few days ago, and to prepare for her meeting with Dougie. In any case, it was a beautiful summer day and far too nice to be stuck in the office.

She took out her mobile and sent Natalie a text.

> [Morven] You were brilliant, all of you. Well done! So proud of you x

Natalie responded with a love heart which made Morven smile. She knew how much this opportunity to work with Kerry meant to Natalie after losing her job. Although her friend still had a tough road in front of her, Morven was certain she'd triumph in court and this project would occupy her in the meantime.

Kuzi was helping Natalie work through her issues and come to terms with the grief of losing her mother. The horrific circumstances surrounding Betty's rape and subsequent death had come as a terrible shock to Morven, and she knew it would take time before her friend was ready to open up about it.

But Natalie wasn't the only person that Kuzi was helping. Traumatised by his kidnap and what had happened to his mother and her partner, Ollie had also agreed to therapy and had been attending regular sessions with Kuzi. After waking from his drug-induced coma, he had demanded to know every detail about the killings and Ross's motives. When Morven showed him pictures of Maxine's operations her son had broken down in tears. A few days later, Ollie had reverted to his given name and there had been no more talk of being trans. Morven was quietly hopeful.

Ollie had also latched onto Dave's dog after Morven took pity on the creature and gave it a home. Her son had formed a close bond with Mugly and her resolve to keep the animal off her new furniture had all but vanished.

Morven glanced at her watch and sighed. It was time to face Dougie and tell him that she'd decided to go back to Community Policing. With Beamer's imminent return, Cavendish was being transferred to bigger and better things for her to wreck. Rob and his girlfriend, Usha Patel, were throwing a house party to celebrate and had sent Morven an invitation. Morven missed her old colleagues and her beat and now, without Dave as her partner, CID would never be the same.

The role, which was supposed to have been a shelter in a storm, had turned out to be the storm and, consequently, continuing in her current job was unthinkable.

Morven made her way up to the CID office for what she supposed would be the last time. Come Monday, she'd be back to dealing with anti-social behaviour, drunks, domestics and break-ins. It was probably for the best.

After making herself and Dougie a strong brew, she perched in front of his desk ready to give her notice. Dougie thanked her for the tea and closed the door.

"I can't believe it's been six months," he chuffed "it seems like just yesterday you arrived." He sat opposite and regarded her, "I worried you and Dave might murder one another."

She gave a rueful smile. "That was a real possibility at the start."

Dougie shook his head slowly. "I've a small confession." When she looked at him quizzically, he said, "Err ... Dave actually asked to work with you." When she gawped at him, he said, "He pushed hard for your secondment, even suggested I paired the two of you up."

Morven gaped in disbelief. "He never said a word."

Dougie gave a heavy sigh and gazed pensively out of the window. "He didn't want you to know." Turning to her, he said, "But goodness, what a start you had. Most officers spend their career without ever encountering a serial killer, while you end up dealing with one on your first day." He met her eye and with a look akin to respect, said, "And by heck, did you deal with it."

Morven swallowed hard. "Ross had us all duped, me especially."

"Don't be so hard on yourself. He was a sleekit bastard." Indicating the thick manilla files piled up on his desk, he said, "He'd been planning this meticulously for years, even got himself a job with the investigating team. You don't get more cunning than that."

Morven agreed, although the humiliation of her involvement with Ross still burned. She was still working through her self-loathing and questioning whether she could ever trust another man or her judgement again. Perhaps she too would talk to Kuzi.

Dougie continued. "But the more I learn, the more I realise the vital part you played in catching him. If you hadn't been so damn stubborn, Ross may have succeeded in getting away with it." Pointing to where his desk had been, he said, "Without you, he might still be sitting there laughing at us."

Morven's eyes filled with tears. "Ross and I were ..." Unable to voice the word 'lovers', she whispered, "what a bloody fool I was."

Dougie shook his head. "We were all fools, and me the biggest one of all. I should never have shied away from examining every angle of this case, however politically unpalatable." He fixed her with his gaze and smiled, "You taught me that."

She wiped her eyes with a tissue and thanked him.

"And you'll be relieved to know," he said, "that Professional Standards have dropped the case against you and Rob. The investigator deemed Murphy's complaint malicious so there'll be no further action."

Morven let go a breath. It felt like a weight had lifted.

Dougie searched through the detritus of paperwork on his desk and slid an application form towards her. "I'd like you to join us on a permanent basis. You belong here in CID Morven."

She couldn't believe her ears because, despite everything, he was offering her a job.

Dougie continued his sales pitch. "I know things won't be the same without Dave ..."

Suddenly a cheer went up outside his door and Dougie glanced over, exclaiming, "Talk of the devil ...."

Morven spun round to see Dave limp into the office to be greeted by his colleagues. He was walking with a stick but grinning from ear to ear. Her heart skipped a beat at the sight of him, although she'd visited him every day while he was in hospital and then at home. Dave had almost died on the operating table but he'd fought like a lion for his life.

During his recovery, they'd pored over every detail of the case and what had happened at Dunbar, and she'd kept him appraised of developments since. The team had laid bare the whole sorry tragedy and Morven had learned more about Ross after his death than she'd ever known about him when he was alive. A few months after Maxine's suicide, Ross's mother had also taken her own life. Faced with this cataclysm, Ross had dropped out of veterinary school where he'd been a second-year student. Hellberg's suggestion that the killer had medical knowledge had been spot on, although it was not in human anatomy.

At the rear of 'Gaugers End' cottage, the police discovered an outhouse full of tools which the pathologist reckoned had been used on the victims, together with large quantities of Rohypnol. They also found a laptop that Ross had used to tamper with phone records, Kerry's fitness tracker, and CCTV. And, chillingly, this computer contained communications between Ross and his victims which showed how he'd lured them to their deaths. Some of the worst messages were between Ross and Ollie revealing how he'd cultivated a relationship with the boy.

Morven and Dave had discussed everything ... well, everything except his last words to her in the cottage before he'd passed out. Had he been delirious in the face of death? Had he simply forgotten what he'd said, or was he choosing to forget? She was too afraid to ask.

Dougie opened his door and strode towards Dave, smiling, "What are you doing here Newton? You're supposed to be recuperating."

Dave said, "Daytime telly. Enough said."

The two shook hands but Dave's eyes were locked on Morven. She approached, hands thrust deep into her trouser pockets, conscious of her colleagues' stares. Most of the team had been disbanded but a core remained who knew about her relationship with Ross. She'd also been honest about it with Dave and the shame of it still blazed.

With a shy smile, she said, "Welcome back ... but shouldn't you be at home?"

He flashed her a dazzling smile, seemingly unable to tear his gaze from her, and she felt her face flush pink.

Laughing, he said, "Chrissakes, I'm hardly through the door and Morv's already giving me a hard time."

She rolled her eyes and their colleagues laughed.

"This truly is a cause for celebration," said Dougie. Indicating Morven, he added, "Not only do we have a new DC but we've also got a new DI'."

This earned them a round of applause. Morven had known about Dave's promotion to Detective Inspector but, until now, there had been no official announcement. It meant that, if she chose to remain in CID — as she probably would — she'd likely have a new partner. As sad as she was about this, she understood it was inevitable.

Dougie suggested a round of drinks in the local pub. "I'll even pay," he added, which raised another cheer.

As the detectives filed out, Dave and Morven hung back until they were alone.

Leaning on his stick, Dave gazed at her and smiled. "Congratulations, Detective Constable MacLeod."

She laughed. "I haven't said yes, Detective Inspector Newton."

"Why the hell not?" he said, raising an eyebrow. "I know I was a bit of a bastard at the start but—"

"— you were a complete twunt," she giggled.

Grinning, he conceded, "I was, wasn't I?"

Their eyes locked and in that moment, she knew he hadn't forgotten his words in the cottage. But did he regret them? She swallowed, unsure of whether to say something.

"I'm sorry," he said, "I should have treated you better. But don't pass up this opportunity because of me. I'll be stuck behind a desk somewhere so you won't even have to see me."

Agh, so he did regret it and now he's letting me down gently.

She clipped out, "It's fine Dave, I'll be out of your hair soon enough."

Turning away, she made for the door but he grabbed her sleeve and tugged her back. "Morv, there's stuff I need to say, things I want to tell you ..." He cast his eyes around, "but not here."

She swallowed the lump in her throat and searched his face for clues. His blue shirt set off his eyes.

"What are you doing tomorrow?" he asked, "I know you've the day off."

She explained that she was taking Ollie back to the cottage at Dunbar after Kuzi suggested it might help him come to terms with what had happened. She said, "I doubt you'll want to put a foot near that place again."

"Actually, if Ollie's alright with it, I'd like to join you. Maybe I can also help him understand what Ross did. In fact, it might help me too." He looked at her uncertainly, "Then after, maybe you and I can have a chat...?"

She nodded. "Okay, tomorrow we talk."

Morven's heart skipped another beat.

Chapter 33

'Gaugers End' cottage was boarded up and still covered in police tape which fluttered in the gentle sea breeze. Gulls soared overhead in an unbroken blue sky as Morven and Dave circled the perimeter on foot with Ollie firing questions at them. Mugly, sporting a new collar, trotted at Ollie's heels. As Dave recounted his memories of that fateful night, the young lad hung on his every word.

Ollie stopped, turned to Dave and, with something resembling admiration, stuttered, "Thanks ... you know ... for stopping him."

Dave glanced at Morven. "You've your mum to thank for that, she saved us both. If not for her, I'd be deid and you'd be living in a hippy commune."

Amongst Ross's possessions, the police had found newspaper clippings about an off-grid collective based in the Pyrenees mountains where they believed he intended to hide out with Ollie.

Still smiling at Morven, Dave added, "It's actually the second time your mum's saved my life. Has she told you that story?"

When Ollie shook his head, Dave explained how he'd gotten the scar on his neck after he and Morven were attacked during the Blackford operation. Ollie gazed at both of them in awe, and then, with a shy smile, he put his arms around Morven's waist. She hugged him tight and as they wept, she reminded her son of how much she loved him. During this display of affection, Dave shoved his hands in his pockets and shuffled his feet, and the dog whimpered.

They broke apart and Morven wiped her eyes, saying, "How about we take Mugly for a walk on the beach?"

Ollie grinned and patted the dog, "Aww, he'll love that."

Morven drove them to a café overlooking Belhaven beach, a picturesque stretch of coastline near Dunbar. While Ollie sprinted along the golden sands throwing a ball for the dog, Morven fetched coffee and doughnuts. She returned to the car to find Dave getting out without the aid of his stick.

"I thought you'd want to rest up," she said.

"Nope, I need fresh air and exercise, I've been cooped up for too long."

They strolled down towards the water munching doughnuts and enjoying the stunning view of the North Sea. Mugly and Ollie were far off in the distance but the wind carried the sound of his laughter. Dave and Morven stood in companionable silence and watched as Ollie launched the ball and the dog raced after it. Mugly then bounced like a spring at Ollie's heels until he threw it again.

Morven said, "It's the first time I've seen Ollie happy in months."

Dave drained his coffee cup and stuffed it into his jacket pocket. She thought he looked worn out.

"Do you want to go back to the car?" she asked.

He took her empty cup and put it in his other pocket, and then turned to face her. Her breath hitched as she gazed into his eyes.

"Morv," he said, "I said some things to you ... you know ... when I didn't think I was going to make it."

Swallowing hard, she finally voiced her fears. "Forget about it, it won't affect our working relationship."

Tentatively, he reached for her hand, sending pulses of electricity up her arm. "I meant what I said and, now I've been gifted another life thanks to you, I'd like you to be part of it." Then, hesitantly, "Or am I completely crazy to hope for that?"

Morven couldn't quite believe what she'd just heard. She smiled and squeezed his fingers. "No Dave, you're not completely crazy."

Epilogue

4 months later

Natalie watched the house from the shadows opposite, as she'd done many times before. Waiting.

She was certain he was in there, having trailed him to his home. By now, she knew his Thursday evening routine well: an hour spent creeping out women and girls in the ladies-only swimming session at the leisure centre. Not that he ever swam. Wearing a blonde wig and a tucked 'no-op transwoman' swimsuit, he merely ogled his prey from the shallows and then, afterwards, spent an inordinate amount of time in the gender-neutral changing area. Earlier this evening, concealed beneath a baseball cap and a hoodie, Natalie had observed his salacious behaviour from the café overlooking the pool.

He always followed his dip with a visit to the chip shop for a takeaway, and the off-licence for four cans of special brew. Back home, he'd spend the rest of the night in the front room with the curtains open masturbating. His bedsit was located at the end of a cul-de-sac, so there were few passersby, but neighbours kept their heads down and eyes averted. Women tugged their children quickly past his door with muttered warnings.

Voyeurism, exhibitionism and perversion.

Natalie doubted the local community knew he was also a convicted double rapist. Amruta had identified him as the man who'd attacked Natalie's mother while she lay helpless in a hospital bed. She had also discovered that, after his release from jail, while dressed as a woman, he'd lured a schoolgirl into his car before subjecting her to a horrific sexual assault. Although he'd served two back-to-back prison sentences, he was now free to prey on others and Natalie was sure it was only a matter of time until he struck again.

Unless someone stopped him.

She had little faith in the authorities. Lax parole conditions and an entry in the sex offenders register wouldn't stop a monster like him. Over the months she'd been observing him, she'd become increasingly concerned about his apparent, growing desperation. The single mum who lived in the flat above him had a young child and Natalie could see the longing in his face every time the girl appeared.

Amruta had suggested outing him as a paedophile in the community social media pages or giving his details to a group of online vigilantes. However, Natalie suspected this would simply drive him underground. Better to know where vermin like him were and deal with them properly.

Which was the reason she was currently skulking in the alleyway opposite. Catching sight of him peering out of the grubby window with his panties around his ankles, her heart pounded in her chest at the thought of what she must do. She had little fear of getting caught — Amruta would ensure there was no CCTV footage and provide her with an alibi. And the other women need never know. Let Kerry and Morven believe the therapy was working wonders. It was … but just not in the way that Kuzi had anticipated. The counselling had made Natalie realise that she must act. For closure. For justice. For the safety of other women and girls.

Tanya Hellberg had inadvertently given Natalie the idea. After Morven had introduced the two of them, they'd begun seeing one another and things were going well. Very well, even if Tanya's pillow talk needed some work. Natalie found Tanya's job as a forensic pathologist fascinating and she often asked about her cases. When Tanya told her about a death caused by carbon monoxide poisoning, Natalie had insisted on knowing every detail.

But, finally faced with the monster, could she go through with it? It was one thing to fantasise about killing someone, quite another to actually carry it out. Then she thought about the horrific attack on her mother, the sickening assault on the schoolgirl, and what he might do to the neighbour's child. He was a devil who belonged in hell.

Pulling her hood over her face, Natalie strode towards the lane that led to the rear of his home. In the cool night, plumes of steam vented into the air from the boiler flue. Natalie put on latex gloves, removed a canister of expanding foam, and sealed the outlet closed.

"Mum," she whispered, "this is for you."

THE END

Author's Note

Dear Reader,

I hope you enjoyed reading The Twenty Murders. I welcome feedback from my readers, and I read each and every one of your reviews so, if it's not too much trouble, please leave me a review on Amazon.

Although this is a work of fiction, sadly much of the backdrop is true including the rape of a woman on a female-only hospital ward by a trans-identified male, the hounding of academics from their jobs, and the medicalisation and mutilation of vulnerable children. All of this is being done in the name of gender ideology.

If you'd like to find out more about me and my reasons for writing this story, the issues it raises, and/or to sign up for my newsletter, please visit: https://drewaugustine.com/

With warm wishes,

Drew

P.S. I'm not on Twitter/X so if you spot someone of this name swimming in its sewers, it's not me.

Acknowledgements

I would like to thank my friends, family and my incredible band of beta readers for their help and support in developing this story.

I'd also like to thank sheroes such as Kathleen Stock, Helen Joyce, Maya Forstater, JK Rowling, Kellie-Jay Keen, Jo Phoenix and the scores of other courageous women (too numerous to mention all of you!) for holding the line, often at great personal cost. And, of course, the men who support this, including Graham Linehan, Barry the EDI Jester, Jordan Peterson and Andrew Doyle (again too many to list), because trans ideology is not just a women's issue — it affects entire families and divides generations.

This will only end when people speak up.